I0779003

PAYBACK BROTHER

Jack Dillon Dublin Tale 13
Second Edition

PAYBACK BROTHER

Jack Dillon Dublin Tale 13
Second Edition

Mike Faricy

Published by

MJF Publishing
https://www.mikefaricybooks.com

ACKNOWLEDGMENTS

I would like to thank the following people for their help & support: Special thanks to Nick, Roy, Julie, Mittie, and Toui for their hard work, cheerful patience and positive feedback. I would like to thank family and friends for their encouragement and unqualified support. Special thanks to Maggie, Jed, Schatz, Pat, Av, Emily and Pat, for not rolling their eyes, at least when I was there. Most of all, to my wife, Teresa, whose belief, support and inspiration has, from day one, never waned.

To Teresa
"She's an absolute slapper…"

PROLOGUE

Dillon opened his eyes on the second ring and looked into the deep brown eyes staring back at him. Unfortunately, the deep brown eyes belonged to Lucifer, his dog. Lucifer gave him a look suggesting something along the lines of *'Are you going to answer the damn thing?'*

Dillon rolled over in the opposite direction and pulled his cellphone from the bedside table. Special Branch calling. It wasn't quite 6:00 AM on Saturday. This couldn't be good. "Marshal Dillon," he said.

"DI Bennet, Marshal Dillon, sorry to wake you."

"Not to worry. I've been up for a bit," Dillon lied. "It can't be good news if you're calling at this hour on a Saturday."

"A shooting, sir, in Finglas. Your presence was requested."

"Is it an American?"

"I've no idea, sir, just that your presence was requested." Dillon's phone suddenly indicated an email coming through. "I sent you what little information we had just a moment ago."

"Has DI Suel been notified?"

"No, sir. You're the only one from Special Branch, at least at this time."

"And you said you sent me the information?"

"Yes, sir. What little we have, basically the name of the officer in charge and an address of the scene. One victim shot."

Dillon exhaled. "I'm on it. Appreciate the call," he said, meaning anything but. He disconnected and rolled out of bed. Lucifer was already back asleep and breathing heavily. So much for a leisurely Saturday. He went down to the kitchen, turned on the coffee, and took a dog biscuit from the cookie jar, clanging the lid as he did so. He eventually heard Lucifer hop off the bed. A moment later, a nose poked around the upstairs newel post.

"Come on. Biscuit, outside," Dillon called and waved the biscuit. Lucifer bounded down the stairs, and Dillon opened the front door. He tossed the biscuit out onto the drive, and Lucifer leaped off the front stoop. Dillon closed the door and headed upstairs to shower.

Showered, shaved, and dressed in clean jeans and a black sweater, he checked the address on his email and the victim's name, Patrick O'Shea. It didn't ring a bell. He filled his travel mug with coffee, slipped on a black leather jacket, and opened the front door. Lucifer hurried inside, headed to the kitchen, and started in on his bowl of food. Dillon locked the door behind him and drove over to the address in Finglas, a mere ten minutes from his home and a completely different world.

He turned onto Deanstown Avenue and could see the scene from two blocks away. Three squad cars, an EMT van, and white tape with blue letters blowing in the wind, warning people in English and Irish not to cross the line. He pulled to the curb and climbed out of his car.

He flashed his warrant card before one of the two officers at the gate had the opportunity to tell him to stop. "Who's the officer in charge?" Dillon asked, although he'd read the name Ronan Mullen in the email.

"DI Mullen," one of the officers said. Both men sat on the three-foot wall running across the thirty-five-foot property. Their arms were crossed, and they didn't make the slightest effort to stand, nod, or smile. Dillon figured they'd probably been there for hours and were now working overtime.

"Thanks, lads. Enjoy the day," Dillon said. He pulled a pair of latex gloves from his jacket and slipped them on as he headed for the front door.

ONE

The houses, there were actually six of them, were attached, two-story units with slate roofs, all exactly the same. Dillon had lost count of the number of times he'd been in similar layouts. The first floor would feature a sitting room with a coal-burning fireplace that had originally been the source of heat for the room. The kitchen and dining area would be just behind the sitting room with another fireplace. The entryway was actually a small hall leading back to the dining area. The staircase to the second floor would be approximately six feet beyond the front door. There would be a landing twelve steps up where you'd make a ninety-degree turn and take two more steps to the second floor hallway. Two or possibly three bedrooms and the bathroom would be on the second-floor.

Dillon walked up the driveway, past the dark blue Mercedes Benz E300. According to the Irish license plate, which listed the year, it was a 2021 model. He peeked inside through the driver's window and studied the comfortable-looking blue leather interior for a moment. He stepped on the stoop, glanced once more at the Mercedes, opened the door, and stepped inside.

Voices were coming from the back of the house. He listened for a moment before heading into the sitting room. A couch was positioned opposite the fireplace, with a coffee table in front of the couch. A wine bottle and two wine glasses were sitting on the coffee table, each inside an evidence bag. One of the wine glasses had lipstick on the rim. Dillon headed toward the conversational noise coming from the kitchen.

As he stepped into the room, the conversation stopped, and all three individuals, one wearing white protective gear and a face mask, looked at Dillon. There was a sliding glass door leading out to a back garden. The glass was mostly shattered, with three bullet holes in the remaining upper portion. Outside, a gurney with a black body bag was positioned on the edge of a brick patio. Two men, probably medical examiners, were outside in white protective gear. One was photographing a pool of blood and splatters on the steps leading into the house. The other was filling out a form on a clipboard. Behind them was a patio dining set, a glass-topped table with six wicker chairs. The table was empty, and the chairs were all pushed in against the table, suggesting it hadn't been used recently.

"I'm looking for DI Mullen," Dillon said.

"You got him," a man with thinning brown hair and a mustache replied with a nod.

Dillon guessed he might be forty, maybe forty-five. He wore jeans, a blue flannel shirt, and a wrinkled navy-blue sport coat. He was about six feet tall. His chest and squared chin suggested a muscular build. Possibly an athlete as a younger man.

"I'm Marshal Jack Dillon, Special Branch. I got a call about forty-five minutes ago directing me here."

Mullen extended his hand in a latex glove, and they shook. "Appreciate you making the time, Marshal. We've got a victim shot multiple times. Appears to be an American. We've found a passport." Mullen turned and sorted through a half-dozen evidence bags on the kitchen table. "Yeah, here we go," he said, handing Dillon the bag. The passport in the bag was opened to the page with the photograph and basic information. Dillon looked at the image, a younger red-headed man named Patrick Joseph O'Shea. The date of birth was April third, 1997.

"I don't recognize him," Dillon said, looking at the photo. He turned the bag over to check the cover just to make sure it was an American passport. It was. "Was he living here, visiting, going to school?"

"Apparently, he owns the house. It was purchased by a Boston Company, Bridge Street Capital, although Patrick O'Shea is also listed on the title. He moved in two years ago. Thus far, no sign of employment that we've been able to determine. We'll be making calls later in the day."

"Any idea of the time of death?" Dillon asked.

"Sometime after 3:00 this morning. A next-door neighbor phoned in a report of gunshots maybe ten minutes after 3:00. We've got a recording. Didn't say anything about your man being shot, but then at that hour, well….”

“Is he, or rather, was he the owner of that Mercedes parked out in the driveway?”

“Again, it’s registered to Bridge Street Capital at this address, with O’Shea also listed. We’ll double-check just to be sure, but as of this moment, yeah, he’s the owner.”

“Nice set of wheels for anyone, let alone someone in their mid-twenties.”

“Like I said, no word yet on employment, although we’re just getting started. Who knows, maybe he was living on one of your American trust funds.”

“Or maybe self-employed, is there an office? Could be he was a computer guy or someone working from home.”

Mullen gave a slight shrug. “Possibly. We’re really just getting started on going through things. Nothing to suggest an office upstairs, but you’re welcome to have a look. I should mention I got your name from a friend of mine, Paddy Suel. We went through the same training class together when we first signed on.”

Dillon smiled. “Paddy and I are partners, although he’d seldom admit to that.”

“Well, he said he’d be joining us, but knowing Paddy, he probably rolled over and went back to sleep.”

“Sounds like you know him well,” Dillon said, and they both laughed.

"Paddy mentioned you've got a contact at the American Embassy."

"Yeah, Eric Bergman. If you'd like, I'll give him a call. It would probably be best to wait another hour or two. I'll call him sometime after 9:00 if that works."

"Works for me," Mullen said.

"I noticed on the wine glasses out in the sitting room one of them had lipstick on the rim. Any idea who that might be?"

Mullen shook his head. "I only wish. No idea if she was here when your man was murdered. Did she run out the door, hide upstairs, or behind the sitting room couch?"

"Or, was she the shooter?" Dillon said.

"Yeah, that too," Mullen replied and shrugged.

"Have you been upstairs?" Dillon asked.

"Only for a quick look around. Didn't see anyone. Feel free to take a look. Just don't touch anything. We'll be up there soon enough, taking pictures."

"If it's all right, then I'll take a peek."

"You find your woman hiding under the bed, let us know," Mullen said and set the bag with O'Shea's passport back on the table.

Dillon walked into the sitting room again and looked around. He made a mental note that there wasn't a TV anywhere in the room. He glanced in the fireplace. It was swept clean, with no ashes. There wasn't any wood stacked in the room to burn. It seemed unlikely someone would have cleaned out the fireplace last evening. The wine bottle in the evidence bag was half-full. Two glasses on the coffee table suggested both parties each had at least one glass of wine. He wondered if they may have been interrupted.

He made his way up the staircase, being careful not to touch the stair rail on the way up. There were two bedrooms and a bathroom on the second floor. The first bedroom, the larger of the two, had a double bed, a dresser, and a white wardrobe. A flat-screen rested on the dresser. A lamp and a TV remote were on the bedside table next to the bed.

Although the duvet on the bed was pulled up, both pillows appeared to have been used and flung haphazardly. It didn't suggest anyone was trying to hide something. He thought of it more as someone climbed out of bed, tossed the pillows against the wooden headboard, and maybe wandered into the bathroom.

He opened the double doors on the wardrobe. Hanging shirts and jerseys, all men's, filled the upper area. Four drawers and a rack holding eight pairs of men's shoes and boots were arranged along the bottom. He closed the doors, gave another quick look around the room, and headed into the second bedroom.

Almost immediately, he mentally labeled the second bedroom as a guest room. There was a small antique chest of drawers and, next to that, a wooden folding luggage rack. The single bed had a flower-patterned bedspread and one pillow. He pulled open the three drawers on the antique chest of drawers. They were all empty.

He stepped into the bathroom. There was a toilet, sink, and shower. The glass on the shower was spotted, and Dillon guessed it hadn't been cleaned or squeegeed in quite some time. The small shelf in the shower had two white plastic containers, one labeled Body Wash and the other labeled Shampoo. A gray towel hung haphazardly on the towel rack. The mirror above the bathroom sink was bolted to the wall. The lower righthand corner of the mirror was cracked. The white bathroom sink could do with some cleaning. A tube of toothpaste, a toothbrush, a shaving razor, and a can of shaving cream rested next to the sink. Three drawers, one on top of the other, were on the right side of the bathroom cabinet. The two bottom drawers were empty. The top drawer held a box of cotton swabs and three wrapped condoms.

Nothing in the bathroom or the bedrooms, including the almost empty roll of toilet tissue, suggested any long-term presence of a woman.

"Dillon, you up here?" Mullen called as he came up the stairs.

"In the bathroom," Dillon replied.

Mullen appeared in the doorway a moment later. "Come up with any ideas?"

"Yeah, just looking around. I don't think there was a woman living here. He might have had the occasional overnight guest, but I'm sure they would have fled the scene come morning."

Mullen chuckled at that.

"Hello, anyone home?" a voice called from downstairs.

"That would be Suel," Dillon said.

TWO

Dillon followed DI Mullen down the stairs. Suel was standing in the entryway carrying a white bag and a tray holding six paper cups with plastic lids.

"Hi, Paddy. Just on the way home from last night?" Mullen asked.

"I only wish," Suel said. "I've some scones and teas for you lot and a coffee for my crabby partner."

Mullen laughed and said, "Come on back to the kitchen."

"You get your beauty sleep?" Dillon asked.

"Are you kidding? I waited in a bleeding line for the teas and coffee for almost a half-hour. Now be nice, or there'll be no scone for the likes of you." Dillon placed a thumb and forefinger on his lips and pinched them. "Much better," Suel said and headed for the kitchen.

He set the tray of cups and the bag of scones on the table and stepped over to what remained of the sliding door. The gurney with the body bag was gone, along with the medical examiners. "God bless, this looks like a number of rounds fired. How many times was your man hit?" Suel asked.

Mike Faricy • 18

"Four that we know of," Mullen said. "All in the chest. Initial examination suggests death was immediate and sometime between 3:00 and 3:30 this morning. Close range shots, I'm guessing at maybe a distance of five or six feet."

"So he's outside at that hour? Was someone in the back garden trying to get in?"

"Obviously, someone was in the back garden," Dillon said. "The time suggests that maybe Mr. O'Shea heard someone. Maybe they caused the motion detectors to turn on the lights. How was he dressed?" he asked Mullen.

"Jeans, a short sleeve Six Nations jersey, and barefoot. No wallet on his person. We haven't found one in the house yet. From what we can determine, he was unarmed."

Dillon shook his head. "The bed upstairs appears to have been more or less made. If you were jumping out of bed because someone was prowling in your back garden, I don't think you'd adjust the pillows and straighten the duvet."

Mullen pulled a paper cup from the tray and opened the lid. Steam rose from the cup. "Any Milk?"

"In the bag with the scones," Suel said. Mullen pulled out a small container holding no more than a tablespoon of milk. Suel bent down and called through the broken glass to the two men taking pictures on the patio. "Tea and scones, lads." He stepped over to the table and handed a cup to Dillon. "Your coffee, sir, just as you requested, black and paid for."

"Well done, Paddy. I take back some of the things the others have been saying about you."

Everyone laughed. Suel took a tea from the tray and pulled a scone from the bag. They chatted for fifteen minutes, discussing who may have been responsible and why. Nothing was known of the victim, Patrick O'Shea, except that, apparently, he was an American. No one had knowledge of a prior arrest. Other than the wine glass with lipstick, there was nothing that indicated interaction with anyone; no mail, no bills, no personal photos, nothing, and thus far, no phone.

Once they'd finished their tea and scones, Dillon, Suel, and Mullen went through the bedrooms and bathroom. Absolutely nothing unique was found other than the three wrapped condoms in the bathroom drawer.

"Why wouldn't he keep these in the drawer of that bedside table?" Dillon asked.

"Maybe he didn't have women here. Maybe he only participated in the event at their place," Mullen said.

"Yeah, maybe. Although based on the wine glass in the sitting room, he served wine to a woman."

"Yeah, and you saw how well that worked out," Suel said, and they all smiled.

Dillon and Suel left forty-five minutes later. They were in the Special Branch office in Phoenix Park before 10:00 and none the wiser on the death of Patrick O'Shea.

The first thing Dillon did was phone Eric Bergman at the American Embassy.

He was placed on hold for a half minute before his call was sent through. "Hi, Jack, how are things?" was how Bergman answered.

"Morning, Eric, the usual, unfortunately."

"Oh, what do you have?"

"A shooting last night in Finglas. An American named Patrick O'Shea. Shot on the back steps of his home sometime between 3:00 and 3:30 last night. I've been in the house. There's just something funny about it. The place didn't seem lived in, although there were clothes in the wardrobe, food in the refrigerator, soap, and a toothbrush in the bathroom. Let me give you his passport details."

"Hang on for just a second. Okay, I'm ready. Go ahead."

Dillon read off the passport number, O'Shea's full name, date of birth, date of passport issue, and date of expiration.

"What do you know about him?" Bergman asked.

"Other than he was shot four times, not much. No idea of employment. No mail on the premises, no wallet, or any form of identification except for the passport. Nothing like a U.S. driver's license or credit card. Who can get by in today's world without a credit card?"

"I'm sure those will turn up. Let me see what I can find out."

"So this is the first you've heard of it? You haven't been officially notified yet?" Dillon asked.

"No official notification as of yet, but it's just before 10:00. I'm guessing we'll hear something around the noon hour or early afternoon."

"If you find anything out, let me know. I'd be interested in any travel information you can dig up on O'Shea. I neglected to page through his passport," Dillon said. They chatted for another minute or two, promised to get together soon, and hung up.

Suel looked over from his desk and shrugged. "Anything?"

Dillon shook his head as he headed over to Suel. "I'm going into McCabe's office and give him an update. You want to join me?"

Suel shook his head. "No, you go ahead and deal with it. Let me know how it goes. I'll be on the line to a friend at the Bureau." Suel meant the National Bureau of Criminal Investigation, a team most recently investigating various relationships between serving members of the Gardai and criminals.

"You expect to learn anything?"

"No, it's more a case of just checking the box and giving a friend a heads-up. I feel as if that house in Finglas was staged. The clothes there, the bathroom, food in the refrigerator. If your man wasn't living there, I'd say it's a safe bet he was just staying there from time to time. No washing machine, no dirty clothes, no wallet, not so much as a bill or letter. How many twenty-five-year-olds do you know without a computer? The whole thing is almost too perfect. We're lucky they found that passport," Suel said.

"You know, as you say that, I'm wondering if your man O'Shea was planning on traveling somewhere. Let me bring McCabe up to date, and I'll check that out. I'll check with Mullen, too. I want to know where they found that passport."

Dillon knocked on DCI McCabe's doorframe. McCabe looked up from his computer screen and waved Dillon in. "Have a seat, Dillon. You were on site over in Finglas this morning?"

Dillon settled into one of the chairs in front of McCabe's desk. "Yes, sir. I was, although not an awful lot to see. A victim by the name of Patrick Joseph O'Shea, an American, was shot four times on the steps of his back door. At least seven shots were fired, possibly more."

"I'm getting the impression you're thinking there might be something wrong with the investigation."

Dillon shook his head. "Nothing's wrong with the investigation, sir. It's more what we didn't find." He went on to describe the lack of any personal information, no mail, cellphone, computer, or wallet. Nothing that suggested a long-term residence. "It's as if someone cleaned the place out. But the initial response was just minutes after a 999 call reporting gunshots. The entire place just seemed to have a staged look to it."

"Did you contact the American Embassy?"

"I did, sir. Eric Bergman, we've dealt with him a number of times in the past. I trust him. If something isn't right, he'll let me know. He hadn't been informed yet and said that probably wouldn't come through until around noon. I was able to give him the victim's name, Patrick O'Shea. It may take a while, but if he finds anything, he'll let me know."

McCabe seemed to think about that for a long moment then said, "Keep me posted. If I'm reading between the lines, you may be suggesting some sort of what? Possibly a governmental intelligence situation?"

"Mmm-mmm, that could be one of a number of options, sir. It might be some criminal enterprise, or maybe Mr. O'Shea was living on a trust fund, and he didn't need a job. Maybe he just enjoyed life. Or, God forbid, the poor guy just has an office somewhere, and he confronted a prowler who shot him."

"Let me know what you find out. Anything else?"

"No, sir. I just wanted to keep you up to date. Anything changes, either Suel or I will let you know."

"Very well, don't let me hold you up on your investigation."

"Thank you, sir," Dillon said and hurried out of the office.

THREE

It was after the noon hour before Dillon phoned DI Mullen, expecting to leave a message. Instead, Mullen answered on the second ring. "Marshal Dillon, calling to tell me you've already solved our investigation?"

"I only wish. Actually, just checking in to see if you've come up with anything. I did phone Eric Bergman, my contact at the American Embassy. My call was the first he'd heard of the murder. O'Shea's name didn't ring a bell with him, which, on a certain level, is a good thing. He expected to receive official notification around the noon hour. I've not checked in to see if that happened. Anything new on your end?"

"Unfortunately not. Nothing that would suggest any personal information. I've one of our tech people searching the internet as we speak. We've come up empty-handed thus far in looking for any sort of a business. A google search brought up everything from a painting company to doctors, solicitors, schoolteachers, athletes, and restaurants. Suffice to say Patrick O'Shea is a rather common name."

"Did you search the US?"

"Ireland, the US, UK, and Australia, trust me, it's a common name in every English-speaking country."

"Where did you find that passport?"

"That was another strange thing. One of the medical examiners was going to warm up their tea in the microwave. They opened it, and there was the passport just sitting in the microwave."

"Did you have a chance to look at the passport? There might be pages stamped from different trips."

"No, not yet, and I don't know when I'll get to it. We're investigating an assault at the moment. All the evidence from the O'Shea scene has been sent to the station. You know where we're located, on Mellowes Road?"

"Yeah, I know it. I'd like to swing by and take a closer look at that passport."

"I'll make a call as soon as we're finished. When you get to the station, ask for Sergeant Micheál O'Mara. He's in charge of property. I'll tell him you'll be stopping by and want to view your man's passport. We only sent a handful of items over, so he should have no problem finding it, even if things haven't been logged in yet."

"If you'd make that call, I'll head over there in the next half-hour," Dillon said.

"I'm on it. Ask for Sergeant Micheál O'Mara," Mullen repeated and disconnected.

Dillon touched base with Suel and then walked out to his car. He gassed up on the way over before he drove to the Finglas Garda station. The station was a contemporary four-story red-brick and stucco building on Mellowes Road. Dillon wasn't wild about the appearance but figured it had probably won some architectural award somewhere. He showed his warrant card to the officer and pulled into the secured parking lot. A car was just pulling out, and he was able to park near the door.

The front desk was another contemporary affair, only in more of a spiral design. Two uniformed officers watched Dillon as he approached. "How can I help you?" the younger of the two asked.

Dillon presented his warrant card and said, "I'd like to see Sergeant Micheál O'Mara, in the property room."

The officer examined the card, turned it over to look at the back, and then handed it to the older man, a sergeant.

"You're an American?" the sergeant asked.

"Yes, Marshal Jack Dillon assigned to Dublin's Special Branch. I report to DCI McCabe."

The sergeant nodded, seemed to think for a moment, and then handed the card back to Dillon. "You were involved in that incident out at the airport, Terminal Two. What was that, four years ago?"

"Closer to six, but yeah, that was me."

"Nice work, lad," the sergeant said. "Let me make a call, and I'll get someone to escort you down. Take a seat. It might be a few minutes," he said.

Dillon walked over to an area filled with five rows of black plastic chairs. Only one other person was seated, a middle-aged man wearing a gray suit. Dillon took a seat at the end of the row and pulled out his phone to look busy in the event the man thought about striking up a conversation. He noticed a framed item on the wall. At no real surprise, it was an architectural award dated 2009.

Five minutes later, a voice called, "Dillon." Dillon stood and hurried over to the uniformed officer holding the door open.

"Hi, I'm Marshal Jack Dillon. You need to see a warrant card?"

"No, you're good. Follow me. We're downstairs." They walked down the hall to an elevator. The officer pushed the down button, and a half-second later, the door opened. They stepped into the elevator, and the officer pushed a button labeled -1. Apparently, it was the only level below the main floor. There was no conversation during the brief ride. Dillon followed the officer off the elevator and down a hallway. They entered the second door. "Here's that American, Sarge," the officer said and then stepped behind the counter and disappeared behind a rack of metal shelving.

As he disappeared, another man stepped in front of the counter. He wore sergeant stripes on his uniform, and Dillon said, "Sergeant O'Mara?"

"Yes, and you're Dillon from Special Branch. I got a call from Ronan Mullen not twenty minutes ago saying you'd be stopping by."

"Yes. I was with him this morning at the O'Shea house. Apparently, they sent over a few items. One of them was an American passport. I'd like to take a look at it, see if there's any travel information."

"I have it set aside. Amazing the few things they sent in."

"Yeah, unless I'm mistaken, the passport was the only identification item. No wallet, no paperwork or mail. Absolutely nothing."

O'Mara nodded and said, "They did manage to grab the vehicle license, a Mercedes if I recall."

Dillon nodded. "Yeah, a dark blue car. An E300, I think. Could I look at that license too, please?"

"Coming right up. Help yourself to some gloves," he said, nodding at a box of latex gloves at the end of the counter. "And if you'd fill this in. I'll be back in just a moment," he said and slid a form across the counter to Dillon. Dillon checked the three boxes on the form, wrote down the number on his warrant card, and signed the form at the bottom.

He slipped on the latex gloves just as Sergeant O'Mara reappeared, holding two evidence bags, one with O'Shea's passport and the other the vehicle registration document. The registration document had been in a holder attached to the bottom of the windshield on the passenger side of the vehicle. "You can grab one of those cubicles over along the wall," O'Mara said as he placed the evidence bags in front of Dillon.

"Thanks, this should take just a couple of minutes," Dillon said and walked over to the far wall. There were six white Formica countertops with a panel on either side, allowing for a degree of privacy. Dillon set the evidence bags on the countertop and turned on the light switch. A light in the ceiling came on, but it illuminated the chair rather than the countertop.

He settled onto the plastic chair, turned off the light, and glanced at the vehicle registration document. The car was a 2021 Mercedes E300 registered to Bridge Street Capital and Patrick Joseph O'Shea. Dillon pulled out his cell phone and took a picture.

He opened the evidence bag and pulled out the passport. He studied the main page with O'Shea's photograph for a moment and then paged through. All the pages were blank, with one exception. The first page allowing for stamps was stamped in green ink with the date 04 JAN 20. Dillon paged through the passport again to make sure he didn't miss anything. Apparently, at least based on this passport, O'Shea had arrived in Dublin on January 4, 2020, and never left the country. Dillon took a photo of the page, took another photo of the page with O'Shea's picture and information, and placed the passport back in the evidence bag.

"That was fast," O'Mara said as Dillon approached the counter. "Find what you were looking for?"

"Unfortunately not. The guy looks to have been even more boring than me."

O'Mara laughed and said, "Well, better luck next time. Nice to meet you. Give my best to Ronan Mullen when you see him."

"I will. Thanks for your help."

"You can find your way out?"

"Yeah, not a problem. Thanks," Dillon said and headed back down the hall to the elevator.

FOUR

D illon was at his desk the following morning when his phone rang. "Jack Dillon," was how he answered.

"Hi Jack, Eric Bergman, how's your morning going?"

"The way you say that, Eric, I'm thinking you've got either good or bad news. Which is it?"

Bergman laughed. "As far as I know, neither. I got the official call late yesterday morning on your man, Patrick O'Shea. Turns out he had dual citizenship, Irish and American. His parents were both born in Ireland and emigrated as a married couple in 1988. Father owned a bar and restaurant in Boston, Charlestown actually, at no surprise, a place called O'Shea's."

"Are the parents still alive?"

"No, they died back in 2019, supposedly a gas explosion in their home."

"You say supposedly. Is there some question about the explosion?"

"There was talk about the father, Emmett, owing money to some underworld types. Nothing ever really established. Anyway, Emmett and his wife, Aoife, died in the explosion along with two children."

"Doesn't sound good, and that happened in 2019?"

"Yeah, November fourth, actually."

"Interesting that the son Patrick arrives here two months later, and he has, or had, dual citizenship."

"Yeah, but that's a long process. His dual citizenship was granted in 2016, well before the parents died."

"Any other living family members?"

"An older brother, Sean, born in 1987. An army veteran, served as an officer in Iraq and Afghanistan, Special Forces. Left the army, and the last position on the information I read, he was a professor at Boston University."

"He sounds like the only one in the family who made it over the wall."

"Yeah, certainly looks that way. Maybe he was just the lucky one," Bergman said.

"I have the sense there's something that's not adding up with Patrick O'Shea. The dual citizenship adds some credibility to his basically unused US passport. By the way, they found it in the microwave in his kitchen."

"What?"

"Yeah, nothing providing any personal information in the house, no wallet, cellphone, mail, nothing, including the Irish passport you mentioned. Then someone opens the microwave to warm their tea, and there's O'Shea's US passport."

"Yeah, you're right, that is strange. Very strange."

"I was over at Finglas Garda station this morning looking at the US Passport. The only stamp in the entire passport was from his entry into Ireland back on January fourth of 2020."

"Well, after losing his parents and two younger siblings in an explosion that may have been questionable, maybe he came over with the idea of never going back. That doesn't sound too far-fetched."

"You're right, it doesn't, but then why was he murdered? Seven or eight shots fired doesn't strike me as some potential burglar attempting to break into the guy's house. Based on what you've told me, I think we have to look at the possibility of a mob hit. It sounds as though there were at least rumors to that effect with the father. Maybe O'Shea was over here getting protection from someone or some group. Coming out of Boston, it's possible he could have had those sorts of connections here. Any info on the parents? What were their names, Aoife, and what was the father's name?"

"Father's name was Emmett. Owned a bar and restaurant."

"Anything else?"

"No, that about does it for now. If I hear of anything else, I'll give you a call."

"Thanks, Eric. I owe you a beer."

"I'll be sure to take you up on that, Jack. You hear anything, please let me know."

"Will do," Dillon said, but Bergman had already disconnected.

Dillon glanced over at Suel's desk. He still wasn't in, so he decided to head back over to Patrick O'Shea's residence in Finglas. He drove over and parked on the street. There was no sign of the dark blue Mercedes, which made sense. DI Mullen would have had it towed to a Gardai lot and had the thing searched. He sat drumming his fingers on the steering wheel for a minute and then climbed out of the car, walked over to the unit next door, and rang the doorbell.

A heavyset woman opened the door a minute later. She wore a powder blue terrycloth robe and held a cigarette in her right hand. She clearly wasn't wearing makeup, not that it would have made much difference, and she was barefoot. He pegged her as maybe fifty or fifty-five.

"Hi, sorry to bother you. My name is Marshal Dillon. I'm with An Garda Síochána," he said, holding out his warrant card. "I'd like to ask you about the incident the other night at the O'Shea residence if you can spare a minute."

"Honey, for a man like you, I've got all the time in the world. What do you want to know?" She took a long drag from her cigarette, crossed her arms over her chest, and exhaled a cloud of blue smoke up toward the top of the doorframe.

"Well, did you hear anything or see anyone coming or going the other night?"

"No, I'd been out with the girls at the Jolly Topper, lost count of how many glasses of wine. Thank God I wasn't driving. I can't even remember coming home. All I know is there were four or five Garda cars out on the lane when I woke up the next morning, and that was just before noon."

"So you never heard any shots fired?"

"Even if I had, I wouldn't have known what it was. I was out of it, honey. Besides, little Paddy O'Shea pretty much kept to hisself. Believe me, we all would have enjoyed a piece of the lad, but he didn't seem that interested. Every so often, there was a young slapper coming around. You ask me, they probably enjoyed each other's company if you get what I'm saying."

"You know what he did for a living?"

She chuckled for a moment. "No idea. That was always the question. He had that fancy car, but he never seemed to leave for a job. He might be gone a day or two, but no idea where he went."

"Let me give you my card. If anything comes to mind, feel free to call me," Dillon said as he handed his card to her.

"If you have any more questions, you're always welcome here. Stop by, you never know what I might come up with," she raised her eyebrows flirtatiously.

"Thanks, I'll keep that in mind." Dillon headed back down toward the street. He knocked on the next two doors but got no answer. He walked up to the next place, four doors away from O'Shea's, and knocked.

An older man in his seventies answered. "Whatever it is, we're not interested. Good day," he said and started to close the door.

"An Garda Síochána," Dillon said quickly. "I'd like to ask you some questions if you have a moment."

"This about that dreadful event the other night? The O'Shea lad, was it?"

"Yes, sir, it is about the event the other night, and it was Patrick O'Shea."

He nodded and said, "Please come in. Sorry if I sounded rude. Hopefully, you can understand. We've all sorts of knackers pounding on the door day and night, one worse than the other, and half of them I can't decipher what in God's name they're saying. Please, please come in," he said, stepping to the side as he held the door open.

"Thank you, sir. My name is Marshal Dillon. It's a pleasure to meet you."

"Eoghan Walsh, can I talk you into a tea?"

"Yes, that would be nice," Dillon said and followed him into the kitchen. The layout was exactly the same as O'Shea's. Down the short hall, past the staircase, and through the door into the dining area. Instead of a sliding glass door leading outside, there was a wooden door with a yellow frosted glass window, no doubt original to the place. A gray-haired woman sat at the dining table reading the paper.

"Kiera, your man's with the Gardai, here to ask about the other night," Walsh said to the gray-haired woman reading the paper.

She nodded, smiled, and then folded the newspaper.

"Good morning, ma'am. Sorry to interrupt your morning. My name is Marshal Dillon. I'm with An Garda Síochána. Trying to see if you might have something to add to our investigation."

She smiled, and her blue eyes seemed to sparkle. "Well, we don't wear our hearing aids to bed, so we slept through the entire event. Didn't know anything was going on until Eoghan stepped out to get the newspaper, and there were all these Garda vehicles down the lane. That's the first we learned of the incident."

The kitchen was suddenly filled with the sound of water boiling in the kettle. The Walshes remained quiet for the better part of a minute as if a low flying plane was going over and conversation just had to stop. Once the kettle came to a boil and Eoghan began to fill the cups, Kiera said, "Now your young man's name was O'Shea?"

"Patrick O'Shea, nice neighbor, we never heard so much as a sound coming from the unit. Drove a nice car, a fancy-looking Mercedes," Eoghan said as he set a mug in front of Kiera and then Dillon.

Kiera added a drop of milk and two sugars, stirred the mug, and said, "Eoghan, don't forget the biscuits, dear, and serve them on a plate, please." She flashed a smile at Dillon, suggesting that wasn't it amazing she had to tell her husband about the biscuits.

Eoghan brought over a small plate piled with chocolate-covered wafers referred to as biscuits and sat down. "So, do you have someone in mind for this?" he asked and dipped a biscuit into his tea mug.

"We're still in the preliminary part of our investigation," Dillon said. "Trying to learn as much as we can about Mr. O'Shea and any contacts he may have had."

"Well, I think it's fair to say there never seemed to be any noise coming from the place. Nothing along the lines of a wild party or people coming and going," Kiera said.

"Oh, you'd think the lad was a hermit. In all the while he lived there, we only saw the same girl come and go, pretty young thing."

"Nothing inappropriate, maybe there for an hour or so. Never late at night that we were aware, but of course, we're in bed before ten almost every night."

"She was over quite a bit. But, as I say, it wasn't every day, maybe once or twice a week," Eoghan said and took another biscuit off the plate.

"She drove a red car," Kiera said.

"A Toyota Corolla," Eoghan said.

"Oh, of course, he'd know. Never misses a thing," Kiera said.

"Can you describe her? Was she tall or short, thin or heavy? Maybe her hair color."

"I'd place her around your man's age. Of course, I'm seventy-six, so anyone under forty-five looks like a child to me."

His wife smiled. "I'd say no older than twenty-five and probably closer to twenty, maybe even younger."

"She had that spotty hair," Eoghan said.

Kiera smiled again. "Dark hair, blonde highlights. Always nicely dressed, although, like all the young ones, the dresses were way too short. I'd say she paid attention to her figure."

"And she was there twice a week?" Dillon asked.

"At least that often, almost since the day he moved in," Kiera said, and they both nodded.

They talked for a few more minutes. Dillon gulped down his tea and hoped he didn't make a face because he was not a fan of the stuff. Finally, he smiled, stood, and thanked them for their time.

"Do you have a card? We may come up with something else, and we could call you," Eoghan said.

"Yes, of course," Dillon said, thinking for half a second that they could join him with the large woman in the blue bathrobe. He reached into his pocket and pulled out two business cards.

Eoghan read the card. "Special Branch, and you're an American. Are things that bad here?"

Dillon smiled and said, "No, just a long, ongoing, working relationship."

"Hmm-mmm, interesting," Eoghan said. He walked Dillon to the door. They shook hands, and Dillon walked back to the street. He knocked on the next two doors, but no one answered. As he walked back to the opposite end of the block, a squad car pulled up and parked behind

Dillon's car. A uniformed officer stepped out of the car, watched Dillon approach for a moment, and then stepped between the vehicles as Dillon grew closer

.

FIVE

illon asked the officer, "You going into the O'Shea house? I'm Marshal Jack Dillon with Special Branch. I was here the other day with DI Ronan Mullen. In fact, I was at Finglas Garda Station yesterday. Ronan put me in touch with Sergeant O'Mara down in the property room. I wanted to look at a couple of items they brought in from this scene."

At the mention of DI Mullen and Sergeant O'Mara, the officer seemed to relax. "Oh yeah, you're the American. I can hear it in your accent. I'm Devan McGuire. The lads were talking about you this morning at roll call. You partner with DI Paddy Suel, don't you?"

"I do, but I never mention it."

He laughed at that. "Aye, he's a crazy bugger. You're here?"

"I was knocking on doors trying to chat up the neighbors, but only two of them were home. I suppose everyone else is probably working. I was hoping someone might show up so I could get in and take another look around. We didn't find much the other day."

"Ah, so we heard. I did hear they thought your man had been shot four times, but during the autopsy, they found a fifth round, all in the chest. Tore him up something awful. Easy to see how they would have missed it," McGuire said.

"Five rounds? That explains all the blood on the back stoop. Your man must have been dead before he hit the ground. An awful event. Any chance you might be able to let me in?"

"Yeah, I can do that. I'm only supposed to check the front door. They sealed up the back entry. I'm to make sure no one has tampered with the front door or tried to break in. Follow me. I've got a key," he said and moved toward the front door.

Dillon followed him up the sidewalk and slipped on a pair of latex gloves as he went. The front door had two long pieces of crime scene tape crisscrossing the entrance. The tape was white with blue letters in English and Irish:

Crime Scene No Entry

CONFIDENTIAL TEL NO 1800 666 111

McGuire pulled off the top corners of the tape and attached them to the opposite corners of the doorframe, so the tapes were no longer blocking their entrance. He flashed a quick smile and then stepped in through the front door and closed it behind them.

Dillon stepped into the sitting room. Everything looked exactly the same, except that the wine bottle and glasses had been sent to the station property room. McGuire followed, settled onto the couch, and pulled out his cell phone.

Dillon noticed McGuire hadn't bothered putting on latex gloves and said, "I'm going to look through the bedrooms upstairs if that's okay."

"Help yourself," McGuire said without bothering to look up from his phone.

Dillon headed up the staircase and into the larger of the two bedrooms. He opened the doors of the wardrobe and then began checking out each athletic jersey and shirt hanging in the wardrobe. He pulled the hangers off the pole and checked the front and back of each item. He had no idea what he was looking for, and in the end, he came up empty-handed. He did the same with three pairs of jeans and then went through every drawer in the dresser coming up empty-handed once again. He checked behind the mirror and found nothing.

He attempted to lift the carpet around the walls in the room, thinking there might be a hiding place beneath the floor, but the carpet was completely attached. The bed appeared to be exactly the same. Dillon lifted the pillows, turned them over, and found nothing. He pulled back the duvet and then the sheet, and there it was, a thong. A red thong. He was pretty sure it didn't belong to Patrick O'Shea.

He went downstairs, and popped his head into the sitting room, where officer McGuire sat focused on his cell phone. "Just going out to my car to grab a couple of evidence bags," Dillon said.

McGuire nodded, still focused on his cellphone, and said, "Okay, no rush."

Dillon went back in the bedroom, placed the thong in an evidence bag, and went into the second, smaller bedroom. He didn't find anything else, and after less than five minutes, he moved to the bathroom. The razor, toothbrush, and even the condoms were gone, and he presumed they'd been sent to the property room, although the condoms may have been pocketed. He headed back downstairs and into the kitchen, not wasting time checking in with McGuire.

The sliding door leading out to the patio now had two wood panels covering it. Dillon proceeded to go through the kitchen drawers. He looked under the dining room table, checked the refrigerator and freezer, the oven, and last but not least, the microwave, and never found anything of interest.

He walked down the hallway and popped his head into the sitting room. "Hey, Devan, nice to meet you. I'm going to take off. Thanks for your help. Anyone I need to call and tell them I'm the reason you were delayed?"

McGuire seemed to think about that for a moment, then shook his head. "No, I should be okay." Dillon pulled a card from his coat pocket, placed his hand with the evidence bag containing the red thong behind his back, and handed the card to McGuire. "Anyone gives you a hard time, have them call me. Thanks again. Say hi to DI Mullen for me," Dillon said and then hurried out the door.

He debated heading back to the Finglas Garda station and filing the thong in the property room but then came up with a better idea.

He dialed the number for the Dublin Morgue and waited for three rings. A familiar female voice answered, "Dublin Morgue."

"Hi, is this Gráinne?"

"Yes?" she said, suddenly sounding cautious.

"Gráinne, this is Marshal Jack Dillon with Special Branch. How are you getting on?"

"Hi Marshal, Getting on just fine. How can I help you?"

"I'd like to talk with Noel Leonard if he's working today."

"He's here. Let me see if he's at his desk. Hold please," she said, and Dillon heard the phone click.

A moment later, a male voice came across, "Marshal Dillon, how are you?"

"Hi, Noel. I'm absolutely perfect," Dillon said and got a laugh from Leonard. "Say, I'm working a case and found an item I'd like to have you take a look at before I take it into Special Branch."

"A body part?"

"No, nothing like that. As a matter of fact, it's a thong. Part of the murder investigation into a Finglas murder. A man named Patrick O'Shea."

"Oh, sure, O'Shea. I assisted on his autopsy yesterday."

"Would you have time if I stopped over in, say, the next half-hour? I'd like to view the body if that would be okay."

"Come over anytime. We've got a reasonably slow day thus far, but you know how that can change."

"Thanks, Noel. I'll head over now, just leaving the Finglas site."

"See you when you get here, Marshal," Leonard said and disconnected.

Dillon placed a call to DI Mullen and ended up leaving a message. "Hi Ronan, Jack Dillon. Say, I went through the O'Shea house again. I found a red lace thong in the double bed in the larger bedroom. I've got it in an evidence bag. I'm thinking you should get a forensic team over there and have them grab the bedsheets. I didn't want to touch them, thinking I might screw something up." He disconnected and headed back into Dublin.

SIX

The Dublin Morgue is officially called the Dublin City Mortuary. It's located on the corner of Griffith Avenue and Drumcondra Road Upper. Dillon pulled to the curb on Griffith Avenue and parked in front of the last house. The postal delivery building was next to the house, and next to that was the Morgue on the corner. He slipped the evidence bag with the thong into a manila envelope and climbed out of the car. It happened to be a sunny day, and he took a moment to stretch once he was on the sidewalk. He closed his eyes and faced the sun, enjoying the warmth shining on his face.

He walked to the Morgue and entered through a side entrance. He stepped into the reception area, and there was Gráinne, the receptionist. She was a heavy-set woman, no older than thirty. She had short blonde hair, a diamond and a wedding ring on her left hand, and a tattoo on her right forearm that read "Daddy." He'd never asked her about the tattoo.

She was on the phone at the moment. She smiled and nodded at Dillon as he approached. Her desk was behind a counter with a thick section of bulletproof glass and a slot at the base to pass paperwork back and forth.

"Hi, Marshal, sorry about that," she said as she hung up the phone. "Here to see Noel Leonard?"

"Yes, I am. How have you been, Gráinne?"

"Just fine, thanks for asking. Let me alert Noel to your arrival," she said, picking up the phone and punching in a three-digit number. "Yes, Noel. I've Marshal Jack Dillon up here to see you. All right," she said and hung up. "He'll be out in just a moment," she said and flashed Dillon another smile.

"You're looking well, Gráinne. Any more trips planned? Last I heard, you'd been in Portugal, I think."

"Yes, it was lovely, warm weather, not a drop of rain, and the people were so nice. I wish I could say we have a return trip planned, but other than a wedding up in Cavan at the end of the month, I'm afraid we're here until after the first of the year."

"Back to Portugal then?"

"I'm not sure. The prices have skyrocketed in just the past few months. We'll just have to see."

The metal door marked private suddenly opened, and Noel Leonard appeared wearing blue hospital scrubs. He nodded at Dillon and said, "Hi, Marshal. Come on back."

"See you later, Gráinne," Dillon said and followed Leonard into the hallway. "How are things with you, Noel?"

"Going well. You said you were involved in the investigation on that shooting over in Finglas?" Leonard asked as he led the way down the hall.

"Yes, Patrick O'Shea. The body was bagged by the time I got on the scene. I believe I heard he was shot five times. They were thinking four when I was on scene, but apparently, you found a fifth round during the autopsy," Dillon said.

"Yeah, the rounds were LR 22, no doubt from an automatic. Were you able to find any shell casings on site?"

"I don't believe so, at least none that I'm aware of."

Leonard shook his head. "That's too bad. Given the concentration of the rounds, we've pretty much confirmed it was an automatic. That said, you know it could be anything from an Uzi to, well, just about anything. LR 22s are the most popular rounds literally across the world."

"You haven't released the body yet, have you?"

"No, it's still here, no point of contact we're aware of. You still want to take a look?"

"Yes, if it's not too much trouble. We're really scrambling for any evidence. No forms of identification initially. The Finglas team found an American passport in the microwave of all places, and then we learned this morning that he actually had dual citizenship, so theoretically, there should be an Irish passport around somewhere."

Leonard opened the door to the examination room. There were five metal tables lined up. Only one was occupied by a body bag at the moment. The bag happened to be closed." You searched the place in Finglas?" Leonard asked.

"The Finglas team went through it. I was there for a bit with my partner. I just came from there after going over everything again, which is where I found this," Dillon said and handed the manila envelope to Leonard.

Leonard stopped, opened the manila envelope, and looked inside. "Is that a thong?"

"Yeah, I found it in the bed. I placed a call to DI Mullen with Finglas and suggested he have the forensic team pick up the bedsheets and see what they find."

"Yeah, they should look at this thong, too. We start messing with it here, that's only going to piss them off. It would be better if you run it through your forensic team."

"You can't do a quick check and—"

"Not that we couldn't, but they're more equipped, would be faster, and won't be pissed off at us," Leonard said and handed the envelope back to Dillon.

"I don't know about faster. They're buried in a pile of work and, like everywhere else, short staffed."

Leonard nodded and said, "Let me show you Patrick O'Shea." They walked over to a series of doors for the refrigerated units mounted on the wall. Each unit theoretically contained a body. A small index card with a name and number was attached to the upper right corner of the door. Leonard stepped to a table and pulled a pair of latex gloves from a box and handed them to Dillon then slipped on a pair for himself. He quickly counted, pointing his finger at the doors. He counted five rows over and opened the second door from the top. He pulled out a shelf holding a black body bag. He unzipped the bag a third of the way down and pulled the opening apart, exposing the face of Patrick O'Shea.

O'Shea had close-cropped red hair and glassy-looking pale blue eyes. His mouth was partially open, revealing white teeth lined up perfectly. There was a large bruise on the left side of his forehead.

Dillon looked at him for a long moment. The face definitely matched what Dillon could recall of the passport photo. "That bruise on the forehead, was he clubbed?"

"No, we removed grains from it. When he was shot, death was instantaneous. He spun to the left and collapsed against the steps leading up into the rear entry of the house. He caught the edge of the steps with his forehead. Just a note, he had two teeth removed on his upper jaw for braces. Probably twelve or fourteen years ago, which accounts for the uniform positioning of his teeth. Care to see the wounds?"

"Yeah, show me," Dillon said.

Leonard unzipped the bag down to just below O'Shea's navel then reached over and opened the bag exposing O'Shea's chest and a shot pattern of four rounds about the size of a silver dollar.

"But he was shot five times," Dillon said, looking over at Leonard.

"Yeah, automatic weapon, from a distance of five maybe six feet, two of the rounds basically entered the same place."

Dillon shook his head, "It seems unlikely that this was the work of an upset lover, jealous husband, or someone looking to break into the kitchen."

"Anything is possible, but we're leaning toward the professional hit angle. The weapon alone would be very difficult to acquire."

"Okay, no information on next of kin?"

"Nothing, he'll be here for a while, and ultimately, if we can't locate next of kin, or if we do locate and they're not willing to bury, then the county will take over. The body will be buried rather than cremated just in case an exhumation might be necessary down the road. He'll certainly be in one of our drawers for at least a year. After a month or two, he'll be relocated to the storage area, but still, it could well be a good year he'll be here, somewhere. Anything else I can help you with?"

Dillon shook his head. "No, thanks for letting me see your man," he said as Leonard zipped up O'Shea's body bag, pushed the shelf back into the cooler, and closed the door.

"Wish I could tell you more, Marshal. If we should receive any contact from next of kin, I'll let you know. Are you aware of any family here in Ireland?"

"No, I believe there's an older sibling in the US. The American embassy will be pursuing that contact. I guess we'll just have to wait and see."

"If we can be of any help, let me know. Come on, I'll walk you out," Leonard said. They headed out of the lab and back down the hall. Leonard held the door open for Dillon.

Dillon lowered his voice and asked, "How much longer do you have to play the intern game here?"

"I have it on good authority that is currently a point of discussion. I'll take that as positive and be religious in following directions."

Dillon extended his hand, and they shook. "If a letter of recommendation from me would ever help, just let me know."

"Thank you," Leonard said and flashed a smile.

SEVEN

illon drove to Special Branch in Phoenix Park. He parked in the secured lot and input the code on the keypad to open the door. Rather than head up to Special Branch, he walked down the hallway to the Forensics lab and pressed the intercom next to the door.

"Yes?" a familiar voice responded a half-minute later.

"Hi, Rory, Jack Dillon. I've something I'd like you to take a look at."

The buzzer sounded, and Dillon pulled the door open. He walked over to a counter, and a moment later, Rory Phelan appeared. He was dressed in a white lab coat, wearing a hairnet and blue latex gloves. A mask was draped around his neck and pulled down below his chin. "Well, well, Marshal Dillon, to what do we owe the pleasure? Don't tell me, let me guess, something that needed an answer yesterday, and all we have to do is place it at the front of the line and let everyone else wait."

"How's it going, Rory?"

"I'll tell you in a minute, Dillon. What incredible find do you have for us today?"

Dillon set the manila envelope on the counter. "This is from the murder scene over in Finglas. A man named Patrick O'Shea was murdered. Any pieces of evidence have been few and far between."

"O'Shea? Is this your lad who was shot five times on the steps leading out to the back garden? Dean Swift Avenue?"

"Dean Swift is in Glasnevin. This was in Finglas, Deanstown Avenue. He was shot in the back garden and bounced off the steps, left a hell of a bruise on his forehead. Sounds like you've read the autopsy report."

"Just glanced at it. Anything happening?"

"Desperate for any information. I've been through the scene twice, little to nothing. Someone with Finglas found an American passport in the microwave. Other than that, no mail, no wallet, nothing, but the victim has supposedly been living there for two years."

"So, what did you find?" Phelan asked and nodded at the manila envelope.

Dillon picked up the bottom of the envelope and shook it once. The evidence bag with the red thong dropped onto the counter.

Phelan picked up the evidence bag and smoothed it out. "Your man O'Shea wore red thongs?" he asked, looking up at Dillon and smiling.

"I doubt it, but you never know," Dillon said. "I can't think of anyone better than you to find out."

"This isn't from someone who spent the night with you, and now you want to find out her name, is it?"

"No, I found it this morning in O'Shea's bed. Which reminds me, you might get a call from DI Ronan Mullen in Finglas to gather the sheets from the bed and search for DNA."

"Thanks for the heads-up. I have to be honest, Dillon, we're short-handed and jammed. It may be a while before we can get to this."

"Define awhile."

"If I put it on the fast track for you, we're still looking at almost a week, maybe even longer."

"You couldn't move it faster if there was a little incentive?"

"Don't even go there. That is moving it faster. We've got items that have been in line for over a month."

"Jesus, you need to add some staff, Rory."

"Tell that to Dublin County Council. We've been begging for the past year."

"Well, anything you can do will help, and thanks in advance."

Phelan reached beneath the counter and placed a form in front of Dillon. "Fill this out, and I'll see what I can do."

Dillon nodded and began to fill out the form. Phelan disappeared for a minute and then was back with a plastic tray. He placed the evidence bag with the thong onto the plastic tray and then waited until Dillon signed the form and pushed it across the counter.

"Appreciate the help, Rory."

"I'll call you when I've got an update," Phelan said, then picked up the tray and placed it over on a rack filled with plastic trays.

Dillon headed up to Special Branch and settled in at his desk. Suel was on his phone, and Dillon placed a call to DI Mullen in Finglas. He answered after three or four rings. "Ronan Mullen."

"Hi, Ronan, Jack Dillon. Did you get the message I left earlier?"

"The one where you told me you wanted your sheets washed?"

"Yeah, something like that. I literally just came from Forensics. They promised to put a rush on that thong, and we're looking at probably a week, at the earliest."

"A week? I knew they were shorthanded, but a week?"

"Yeah, and that's with a rush, maybe. They'll keep me posted. You learn anything else on O'Shea?"

"Not a thing. It's as if he arrived in Dublin and then sat in front of the telly for the last twenty-some months. Talk about staying under the radar. Your man didn't leave a mark anywhere. Nothing online, never on Facebook, Twitter, LinkedIn, and the lot, at least not using his name. That's pretty unique for someone that age. But then we never found a computer in the place either."

"Makes me think there's something here we're missing, something your man was involved in. I'm going to make some calls and have a few people check on it.

Give a yell to any contacts you have. Something has to be out there somewhere."

"Already on it. I'll let you know as soon as I hear something."

"Thanks, Ronan, and have Forensics get those sheets in Finglas."

"Yes sir," Mullen said and disconnected.

Dillon chatted with Suel for a few minutes. He suggested they head over to the Hole In The Wall pub for a pint, but Dillon begged off and headed home. He turned onto his lane and drove down to his place. A car he'd seen before was parked in front of his neighbor Tara's house. As he drove past, he glanced over and saw Tara and a guy in an animated conversation. At the moment, Tara appeared to be tearing the guy a new one. Dillon didn't envy him. He'd had a couple of interesting interactions with her over the years, always alcohol-fueled, and while most enjoyable, neither one of them had put in the effort to continue in that vein.

He pulled over the sidewalk and onto his drive, climbed out of the car, and closed the gates behind his car. He could actually hear Tara reading the poor guy the riot act. He thought about interrupting and offering the guy a beer, but that would just put both of them on the receiving end.

He unlocked the front door and stepped inside. Lucifer came bounding down the stairs a moment later. Dillon grabbed a biscuit from the cookie jar on the kitchen counter and tossed it out the door. Lucifer flew off the front stoop and caught it as it bounced off the front of the car. Dillon closed the door, picked up the mail on the floor, and headed into the kitchen.

Three envelopes, one was offering a discounted newspaper subscription, another offered a discount on baby supplies, and a third offered life insurance for six euros per month. All three went into the recycle bin. He pulled a pork steak from the refrigerator, sprinkled the top with lemon pepper, and set it off to the side. He cut up a red pepper, coated it with olive oil, and put the pan on low heat. He told the woman in his life, Alexa, to play Jimmy Buffett, and the music started with Buffett's classic "Come Monday." Once that song was finished, he headed upstairs to change.

As he got to the top of the stairs, he glanced out the window just in time to see Tara's latest victim climb into his car, slam the door, and barrel up the street. He'd been there before, not with Tara, but with more than just one woman.

He was back downstairs, put the pork steak on the burner, and let Lucifer back in the house. After dinner, the two of them watched a movie of no great value and headed up to bed around 11:00.

EIGHT

The following morning, Dillon hadn't been in the office fifteen minutes before he and Suel were called into DCI McCabe's office. "Have a seat, gentlemen," McCabe instructed as they entered. As they settled into the seats in front of his desk, he closed the file he'd been reading and handed it to Suel.

"Seems to be a bit of a problem in Tallaght. I'd like you to contact DCI O'Brien down there. He's expecting a call from you. You'll see by that file that the shooting and victim have all the elements of a gangland war about to begin if it hasn't already. I'd like the two of you to help out and make sure things are put back to rest. Any questions?"

"Can you give us an overview, sir?"

"Victim is a known dealer. An individual by the name of Dennis Bell. Maybe not so surprisingly, he's known as "Ding-Dong." He was found early yesterday morning parked in front of his house. He was seated behind the steering wheel of his car, shot between the eyes. His rather extensive record is included in the file. He was a middle-range player suspected of being a member of the Byrne Gang. The fear is a tit for tat response that will quickly escalate into a full-fledged war."

"Suspects?" Suel asked.

"You've heard the rumors of the Byrne Gang expanding their boundaries. Bell appears to have been active in that effort and may have had interactions with members of the Dodder Demons, two of whom were in hospital up until yesterday. It's all in the file. Questions?"

"Sounds like we should get in touch with DCI O'Brien," Dillon said.

"As I said, he's expecting your call, and he'll be able to bring you up to date faster and better than I can. I would like to be kept informed."

That last comment suggested the discussion was over. "Thank you, sir," they said in unison and headed out the door.

Dillon followed Suel to his desk. "Oh, shit," Suel said under his breath. "As if we don't have enough to do with that O'Shea mess. Okay, let me read through the file, I'll pass it on to you, and I'll call O'Brien while you're reading the file."

"You know him, O'Brien?"

"Can't say that I really know the man. Met him once or twice. He goes by the book, good reputation, and gives you some room to get the job done. Be interesting to see how happy he is having the two of us inserted into one of his investigations."

"You thinking this is a bit of overkill?" Dillon asked.

Suel shook his head. "No, McCabe was spot on with the concern this could escalate into an all-out war in no time at all. Hopefully, we can make it not worth the effort to ratchet things up."

"While you're going over that file, I'll give Mullen a call and tell him we're going to be splitting our time between Finglas and Tallaght," Dillon said.

Suel nodded, settled in behind his desk, and opened the file.

Dillon hurried back to his desk, phoned Mullen, and ended up leaving yet another message.

Suel stepped over and handed Dillon the file twenty minutes later, shaking his head.

"Things are that bad?" Dillon asked.

"Just more of the same. You'd think these knackers would cop on at some point, but that's not going to happen. Ding-Dong Bell was a real piece of work. I'd love to say the world will be a better place without him, but some damn fool just as bad if not worse is probably scrambling to take his place as I speak. Anyway, here you go. Let me call DCI O'Brien now, and hopefully, we'll get off on the right foot."

Dillon took the Dennis Bell file from Suel and started paging through it. There were three official black and white photos of Bell: one was facing the camera and left and right images of his face. All three photos had his name written at the bottom, along with the date and an

ID number. There were a series of arrest reports going all the way back to the tender age of fourteen, when he stole a neighbor's car and crashed it into a school bus just a block away. Fortunately, no one had been injured. He spent three years in a juvenile detention center from age fourteen to seventeen. Once released, he was promptly arrested twenty-four hours later for assault on an employee at the detention center.

His arrest record was broken up by periods of incarceration of anywhere from three months to, in two instances, a year. Murdered in Tallaght at the age of thirty-two, one had to conclude the world was a much better place without him.

Dillon was about to delve into the file in earnest when Suel walked over and said, "Come on, I'll drive, and you can read that in the car. O'Brien sounded only too happy to have us on board and wanted to meet up. The sooner, the better."

"Things are that bad in Tallaght?" Dillon said.

"Who knows? I just think it would be nice to be able to get along right from the beginning. You call Mullen in Finglas?"

"Yeah, and ended up leaving a message. He's probably up to his neck. The same thing as all of us, understaffed, juggling a number of cases. It's crazy."

With the traffic, it was close to a thirty-minute drive. Dillon read through the Dennis "Ding-Dong" Bell file while Suel drove to Tallaght. Dillon closed the file with about three minutes to spare. He shook his head and said, "This Ding-Dong Bell was a real class act."

"And that's just what we know. If he was arrested as often as it states, there have to be a few thousand crimes he managed to get away with," Suel said and pulled to a stop at the entrance to the Tallaght parking lot. They showed their warrant cards to the guard at the gate and were waved in.

The station was a two-story building with the first level painted blue and the second level white stucco. Above the entrance were two large circular windows with a small balcony positioned between the windows, barely large enough for two small people.

"I'm going to bring this file in with us," Dillon said as they climbed out of the car.

Suel nodded and said, "Good idea."

There was a keypad next to the door where you would enter a code, but neither Suel nor Dillon knew the code for the Tallaght station. Fortunately, a uniformed officer in a high visibility vest was just stepping out of the building. Dillon grabbed hold of the door as they both nodded at the officer and said, "Hi yas," as he headed into the parking lot.

Once they stepped inside, Dillon said, "Well, so much for tight security."

"Yeah, makes you think," Suel said.

The Homicide section was on the second floor, and they took the elevator. They stepped off, went down the hall to the door labeled HOMICIDE, and walked in. The office was similar to Special Branch, only smaller. Six desks were laid out, three on either side of a pathway leading to an office centered on the far wall. Two of the desks were occupied. Both individuals were on the phone and gave a quick glance at Dillon and Suel, who simply nodded back as they made their way to the office.

The door to the office was open. Suel knocked on the doorframe and said, "DCI O'Brien?"

"Suel? It's been a while. I specifically requested you from DCI McCabe," O'Brien replied as he stepped out from behind his desk. He was not quite six feet tall, with neatly trimmed gray hair, a square chin, and blue eyes.

"Nice to see you again, sir. We met a few years back," Suel said and extended his hand.

O'Brien shook his hand and said, "Nice to see you. You must be the American, Marshal Dillon?" O'Brien said and extended his hand. Dillon shook hands. O'Brien had a firm, solid grip and said, "Please have a seat, lads. Thank you for coming down on such short notice. Did you have a chance to read through the file on your man Ding-Dong Bell?"

Dillon and Suel nodded as they settled into the two chairs in front of O'Brien's desk.

"Bell was a member of the Byrne Gang. Despite that dismal arrest record, he produced and had a number of fans on the street. His murder was, on the one hand, a surprise, but on the other, not really. By that, I mean he was a, how should I put it? He was at the middle man-agement level, theoretically with a future if he could stop getting arrested. That said, the Byrne Gang has been pushing the Dodder Demons out of the district they controlled up until recently. We've since learned that Ding-Dong Bell was instrumental in accomplishing that task. The end result is a number of frustrated, unhappy members of the Dodder Demons, and who better to take out your frustration on than Ding-Dong Bell."

"Any suspects?" Dillon asked.

O'Brien shook his head. "Officially? Nothing we could hold anyone on. That said, suspects, yeah, ten, maybe an even dozen. All members of what's left of the Dodder Demons. The past year, maybe a year-and-a-half, has seen the Demons numbers greatly decrease. In the end, there simply weren't enough people to maintain control of their territory with all the pressure coming in."

"The Byrne Gang and Bell were putting all the pressure on them?"

"That's what we think, and that's what I'd like the two of you to take a look at. As I mentioned, the pressure started with infringements, drives through Dodder territory, the occasional physical assault, and graffiti spray-painted on homes. That grew into not only shootings but also homes set on fire, destruction of vehicles, more assaults, and in two instances, we suspect, a local bank forcing the owners, both Dodder members, into foreclosure. The Byrne Gang literally pulled the rug out from underneath anyone who was associated with the Dodder Demons. Don't get me wrong, not a complaint on my part because they left the area. Except that nothing's really changed. The Byrne Gang stepped right in and now seems to be increasing the drug problem we're facing. That's only going to get worse unless we do something. The first thing we have to do is put the brakes on any payback escalation. Then we have to find out where this added incentive is coming from and neutralize it. I'm hoping you can help," O'Brien said.

"I think we can," Suel said. "The first thing I'd like to do is take a look at the scene of the Bell murder."

Dillon nodded.

"Let me get someone to take you there now," O'Brien said and picked up the phone.

NINE

The officer in the squad car they were following was named Shannon Yates. She was a slender woman, no more than thirty years old, and drove like a bat out of hell. "For God's sake, we'll get pulled over for speeding," Suel said.

"Paddy, we're following a squad car. I don't think—"

"Are you joking, lad? This is Tallaght. It's probably a setup. They'd like nothing better than to pull over and ticket someone from Special Branch so they could spread the word that no one is above the law in Tallaght. Meanwhile, we'd—"

The siren and flashers suddenly came on the squad car as it slowed and approached an intersection.

"See, I told you," Suel said, but Yates drove through the intersection and took a right on the second street, Ferndale. They followed her around a bend in the road for the better part of a mile. She eventually pulled up onto the grass boulevard. She stopped in front of a unit on the righthand side of the street, essentially parking against the flow of traffic, although there hadn't been a car coming toward them since they went through the intersection. Suel pulled in behind her, blocking the driveway entrance to a two-story attached house.

The place had a pebbled exterior, which suggested some form of exterior insulation had been attached, most likely within the past five or six years. There was a three-foot wall running across the front of the property and no gate on the car entrance. What had originally been the front garden was now completely paved with hexagonal concrete pavers. Two plastic trash bins were pushed up in front of the picture window, and the drapes inside had been pulled closed. The address on the house was number 13, an unlucky number not lost on either Dillon or Suel.

They climbed out of the car and followed Yates into the paved area. "Okay, so here we are. Ding-Dong had pulled his car in against the sidewall," she said and pointed at an oil stain on the hexagonal pavers. "The first report was of shots fired. That call was made about ten minutes after midnight. The mail had been dropped through the slot in the front door just after 10:00 that morning. The mail was still on the floor when officers opened the door, suggesting Ding-Dong hadn't been back home since he'd left sometime before 10:00 that morning."

"You said the first call was shots fired. Was he shot more than once?" Dillon asked.

She shook her head and gave him a look. "No, only once, close up between the eyes. Residue from the weapon suggests the shooter was outside the vehicle but right up against the driver's door. The driver's window was down on the car, and it was a chilly night, so the thought is the shooter may well have been someone he knew. An individual he was comfortable enough with to lower his window and talk to."

"Response time?" Suel asked.

"About three minutes. When the street name came across the radio, a squad was aware of Ding-Dong's residence. The department does, or rather did, regular patrols through this neighborhood because of Ding Dong. The squad that night was just around the corner."

"Any idea who killed him?" Dillon asked.

Yates shook her head. "No, the list is long of people who would be happy to see the end of him. You can probably start with all the neighbors. Would you like to be raising children with a neighbor like Ding-Dong on the lane? I can let you inside if you'd like to take a look around," she said, pulling a key from her pocket and moving toward the front door.

"How come there's no Garda security tape on the door?" Suel asked.

"We had some here originally, as you would, but after the fourth time it had been removed, we stopped. My sense is the neighbors are just happy to see the last of Ding-Dong and his friends. I know they held an evening celebration just across the lane in one of the homes when they learned he'd been killed."

"Can't say as I blame them," Suel said.

"Gloves on just to play it safe. I've more in my car if you need some," she said, slipping on a pair of latex gloves. Dillon and Suel did the same. She opened the door, and an alarm system immediately started to beep. Yates stepped to a keypad on the wall, punched in a code, and the beeping stopped.

The layout looked similar to the O'Shea house. A short hall leading past the staircase to a kitchen and dining area. The sitting room with a fireplace was off to the left. Dillon stepped into the sitting room, and Suel and Yates followed. There were a half-dozen small logs neatly piled alongside the fireplace, and a pile of ashes and a fire screen in front of the fireplace. A brown leather couch and a coffee table were positioned on a black and gold Oriental rug on the opposite side of the room. What appeared to be a framed oil painting of a naked woman on a couch, in more of an impressionistic rather than a sexually suggestive style, hung above the fireplace. There was a TV on a small table across from the couch and two remotes rested on the coffee table.

A framed black and white photo, apparently of Ding Dong Bell as a young boy eleven or twelve, with two younger girls, probably sisters, and two adults, most likely the parents, rested on the fireplace mantel. Dillon took out a notebook and wrote.

"What are you writing?" Suel asked.

"Looks like those may be his sisters. It would be interesting to talk to them. You know anything about the family?" he asked Yates.

She shook her head. "Not really. There's another picture like that upstairs in the bedroom. As far as I know, there's been no contact with the family. I know the father passed from cancer two or three years ago, and the mother was killed in a car accident back ten years ago or so."

"Probably a good thing they weren't around to learn their son was murdered," Suel said.

Yates nodded. "Kitchen is back this way. You can check with DCI O'Brien, but all indications were your man lived alone. Nothing was found that suggested a relationship with anyone. No women's articles in the house. A small quantity of cocaine along with, I think, seven thousand Euros were found upstairs in the bedroom behind a dresser. Otherwise, nothing out of the ordinary. Oh, they did get a laptop computer, and I believe that's in our Tech Lab. Shall we take a look at the kitchen?"

Dillon headed for the kitchen as Suel asked Yates if she had been here for the initial investigation. Dillon figured Suel was just making conversation, attempting to get on a more personal level with her. As he stepped into the kitchen, he shook his head. The kitchen layout was virtually identical to the O'Shea house. The cabinets were a lighter colored wood, possibly a birch veneer, and the countertops were a gray Formica as opposed to the granite at O'Shea's, but the windows, the sliding door, the sink, stove, and refrigerator were essentially the same.

Dillon opened the refrigerator door. Nothing out of the ordinary, although the loaf of bread in the plastic bag had dots of green mold on the crust. He pulled open the freezer door; frozen fruit, a box of ice cream bars, two pizzas, and a tray of ice cubes. The cupboards were filled with the usual items: pasta boxes, rice, flour, sugar, and salt. The everyday plates and bowls were a matched set of six. Tea, tea mugs, four or five glasses most likely stolen from pubs, and a half-dozen wine glasses filled up the last cabinet.

"I'm going to head upstairs and look around," Dillon said.

"Join you in just a minute," Suel said and proceeded to tell Yates about a case they'd worked two or three years ago.

Dillon headed up the stairs. Just like the O'Shea place, there was a landing twelve steps up and then a ninety-degree turn and two more steps to the upstairs hallway. The bedroom was the same as O'Shea's, except that the bed was up against a different wall. The bed was also stripped, and Dillon figured the Forensic team had probably taken the sheets to be examined.

He opened the wardrobe and glanced at the shirts, jeans, and two suits hanging inside. A half-dozen pairs of shoes were arranged on a rack. The dresser was pulled away from the wall, which made sense based on what Yates had told them regarding the cocaine and the cash found. He still went through the dresser drawers but didn't find anything out of the ordinary.

The second bedroom was set up to be an office. The desk had a large empty area where a desktop computer once rested. A surge protector with eight outlets was on the floor beneath the desk. Three cords were plugged in and ran up onto the desk where the computer had been. There was a two-drawer file cabinet next to the desk, but both drawers were empty. No doubt the contents were somewhere in the Tallaght station.

Dillon checked the bathroom but didn't find anything unusual. He went down to the first floor just as Suel and Yates were coming out of the kitchen. "Find anything?" Suel asked.

Dillon shook his head. "Nothing out of the ordinary. Looks like Mr. Ding Dong led a rather solitary life. But I just have the sense that much like O'Shea's place, it almost seems to be staged."

"There's a shed out back if you lot want to have a look," Yates said.

"Lead on," Suel said, then turned and gave Dillon a wink.

TEN

The back garden was only as wide as the unit but fairly long. There was a brick patio and a table for six with an umbrella. Two lawn chairs were positioned on either side of a gas grill. A boxwood hedge, trimmed to a height of eighteen inches, ran along the end of the patio. A brick path led from the patio to the shed in the rear of the lot.

"Oh, that is really funny," Yates said in reply to whatever Suel had just told her and then laughed.

"Honest to God, it's the truth," Suel said.

Dillon walked down toward the concrete shed. The wooden door to the shed was painted black with a simple sliding lock holding it in place. Dillon slid the cylinder over and pulled the door open. The ceiling consisted of sheets of plywood and the shed was only about six and a half feet high. Three large beams, four feet apart, ran across the ceiling from front to back. Dillon stepped around a lawnmower with a bag attached, ducked beneath a beam, and looked around. Nothing out of the ordinary; the lawnmower, a wheelbarrow, a shelf with grass and hedge clippers, shovels, plastic trash bags, a spare umbrella for the patio table, a garden hose, and two paintbrushes resting on cans of paint. Nothing more than the usual sorts of things you'd expect to see in a garden shed. Dillon turned to go back to the door, and there, on the side of the beam facing the far wall, was a nail, and hanging from the nail was a chrome key. Clearly not for a door lock. It was cut almost like a skeleton key, except that it was flat.

"Hmm-mmm, interesting," Dillon said and pulled out his cell phone. He took two photos of the key hanging from the nail. "What do you two make of this?" he said, holding the key in his gloved hand as he showed it to Suel and Yates.

"Maybe some kind of safety deposit box. You know, in a bank or a private vault storage company," Yates said.

Dillon and Suel looked at one another. "You know of any private vault storage companies?" Suel asked.

She nodded. "Oh yeah, there are at least two here in Tallaght that I know of, along with a number of banks. I've never checked, but there are probably more private storage companies in Dublin."

"Do you have an evidence bag in your squad car?" Dillon asked. Yates grinned and pulled an evidence bag from her pocket. Dillon placed the key in the bag and said, "We'll take this back to DCI O'Brien. It may be nothing, but then again, who knows."

Dillon sealed the bag and wrote the time, date, and his name on the top of it. They walked back into the house. Yates closed and locked the rear door, then followed Dillon and Suel out the front door.

"I'll wait for you in the car, Paddy," Dillon said. "Shannon, it was nice to meet you, and thanks for your help. Hopefully, we'll see more of you in the coming days," Dillon said and raised the evidence bag with the key. He got a nod from Yates and headed to the car. Suel and Yates slowly made their way to the cars, talking as they went. They stopped in front of the squad car, and Suel handed her a business card. She opened the door to the squad car, reached in, and then handed Suel what looked like her card. They shook hands, maybe holding hands a little longer than normal, and Suel walked over to Dillon waiting in the car.

Yates climbed into the squad car, buckled up, and drove off.

"Oh, she seemed nice enough," Suel said as he settled behind the steering wheel.

"You think?" Dillon said. "Did you see anything of interest in there besides her?"

"Well, if you must know, I was busy getting the lowdown from her on your man Ding-Dong and what the word is in the ranks on the situation between the Byrne Gang and the Dodder Demons. By the way, named after the river running through Tallaght, in case you were wondering."

"Well, there you go, a fount of useless information. Let's head back to the Tallaght station. I want to hand over this key to O'Brien and let him know we were on top of things."

"I know what I'd like to be on top of," Suel said as he started the car and pulled back into the street.

"Don't even go there, Paddy."

"Just saying, mate, just saying."

This time, Suel pulled into the front visitor's lot, and they entered through the front door. They showed their warrant cards and then waited for a detective to come down and escort them up to O'Brien's office. There were two detectives at their desks in Homicide, but not the same two they'd seen earlier. They walked to O'Brien's office but stopped when they heard him on the phone in what sounded like a somewhat heated conversation.

His phone call was apparently finished once they heard him say, "I said, no, damn it!" followed by the sound of the receiver getting slammed back onto the base.

Suel whispered into Dillon's ear, "Let me count to thirty, first," and proceeded to move his lips, counting. He eventually gave a nod, and they stepped forward and knocked on the doorframe.

"Come in," O'Brien said without looking up.

"Just back from the scene of the crime, sir."

"Take a seat and tell me what you think," O'Brien said. They sat down, and O'Brien said, "So?"

"Interesting place. Obviously, your team has been through. The desk computer was gone. Dust in places where they had been checking for fingerprints," Suel said.

"It reminded me of the O'Shea residence we went through the other day," Dillon said.

"O'Shea?" O'Brien said.

"The murder in Finglas. He was killed with an automatic weapon. LR 22 rounds, five to be exact, in his back garden."

O'Brien nodded. "An American, wasn't he?"

"Yes, but he had dual citizenship, so an Irish passport as well. Although we never found that. His home gave off the sense of having been staged. It didn't appear to be lived in. The man was twenty-five years old, and there wasn't a computer or a tablet in the house. No identification, no wallet, mail, nothing of that sort. On top of all that, as an apparently unemployed twenty-five-year-old, he was driving a 2021 E300 Mercedes Benz."

"Maybe family money coming from the States?"

"Possibly, but we've not been able to find anyone. He's from Boston. Parents are dead. He's been over here for two years. Anyway, I had the same sense of the place being staged going through the Bell residence today. We did find this, however," Dillon said and handed the evidence bag with the key across the desk to O'Brien.

O'Brien studied the key for a moment and said, "This looks like a key to a safety deposit box."

"That's exactly what we were thinking, or well, actually hoping."

"We had a team go through that place top to bottom for three days, and they missed this?" O'Brien said.

"Actually, it wasn't in the house. It was in the shed in the back garden. Hanging from a nail on the back of a beam, easy to miss," Dillon said. He pulled out his phone, brought up the image, and showed it to O'Brien.

O'Brien nodded and said, "I suppose life would be far too simple if you happened to know where the box for this is."

"Unfortunately, that is the case. Still, we're lucky to have found the thing. There must be a way to narrow down the location based on the serial number on the key," Dillon said.

"With any luck, we'll find out soon enough. Anything else?" O'Brien said.

"No, sir," Dillon said.

O'Brien looked at Suel and raised his eyebrows. "I think that's about all for now, sir," Suel said.

"Very well, lads, keep me posted if you learn the location of the safety deposit box."

"You can see the serial number on the photo," Dillon said. "Once we get back to Special Branch, I'll have the Tech Lab do a search on it. Hopefully, they'll be able to come up with something."

O'Brien nodded and said, "Well, don't let me keep you."

They all stood, shook hands, and then Dillon and Suel headed out of the office. They gave nods to the two men at their desks, both on the phone. They headed down to the lobby and out the door. Twenty minutes later, Suel had pulled into the lot at Special Branch.

Once inside the building, Dillon headed over to the Tech Lab, and Suel took the elevator up to Special Branch.

ELEVEN

Dillon pressed the intercom button next to the door marked Tech Lab. A moment later, a female voice said, "How can I help you?" In the background, Dillon heard a noise that sounded like boxes being stacked.

"Hi, Emily, Jack Dillon. I've got a little project for you."

"Oh, gee, I can hardly wait," she said, sounding like she meant anything but that. The door buzzed, and Dillon walked into the Tech Lab. Emily was standing at a distant counter in the back of the lab. She was dressed in her standard white lab coat, latex gloves, and a face mask. A half-dozen stacks of large books were lined up on the counter.

"Hi, Emily. Are you looking for the next great read?" Dillon said.

"I only wish," she said and set four more books on the counter. "No, someone out there was attempting to be clever," she said and held up what looked like a thick college textbook. She opened the book, turned the first few pages, and held the book open for Dillon to see. The center of the book had been cut out.

"Transporting drugs?" Dillon asked.

"Cocaine, to be specific. Bringing them in on a ferry from France. Kids, students, they'd carry three or four of these, usually in a backpack. God only knows how long they'd been doing this. From what we know, they got a free ferry ticket and maybe a hundred euros. They would hand off the books to some fool in the parking lot, who would pay them a hundred euros. They were caught just by chance. Someone dropped one of the books, and a brick of cocaine fell out and literally landed at the foot of one of the Garda officers, if you can believe that."

Dillon looked at the stack of books, twenty-four already on the counter and another box that hadn't been unpacked. He guessed it probably represented the potential for maybe a million euros worth of illegal drugs that had been hidden in that many textbooks.

"You mentioned you had a little project," Emily said.

"Oh, yeah, sorry, just doing the math in my head on how much was confiscated," he said, nodding at the stack of books.

"Yeah, and that's just the ones they caught. Whoever is behind this could have been doing this for years."

"Nothing short of amazing. Okay, so here's what I've got," he said, handing her the evidence bag with the key. He went on to give her the short version of obtaining the key. He left out Suel's interaction with officer Shannon Yates.

Emily nodded. "Hopefully, we can trace the location of the box from the serial number. Let me unload this last box, and then I'll run a search on the serial number. If no one else comes in, I might be able to have something for you later this afternoon or tomorrow morning."

"Oh, God, finally something that isn't going to take a month. That would be great, Emily. Call me when you're finished, and I'll come down. I promise I'm not going to call and bother you."

"I'd appreciate that," she said and set the bag down next to the keyboard on the counter.

Dillon made his way up to Special Branch. Suel was on the telephone. The lights were off in DCI McCabe's office. Dillon walked to the office and knocked on the door, just to be sure McCabe was indeed out of the office. When he didn't hear a response, he sat down at his desk. A light was blinking on his phone, signaling a message waiting.

Dillon phoned McCabe's office and, after three rings, got dumped into voice messaging. "Yes, DCI McCabe, this is Marshal Dillon. DI Suel and I met with DCI O'Brien in Tallaght. Based on our meeting, we went through the house belonging to Dennis Bell, the individual murdered the other night in Tallaght. We recovered what we believe to be a key to a safety deposit box. We informed DCI O'Brien of this, and the key is now in the possession of the Tech Lab. Using the serial number on the key, they will attempt to trace the key to a facility, either a bank or a vault storage company. As soon as we have an update, we'll let you and DCI O'Brien know."

Dillon disconnected and then listened to the message waiting for him. "Yeah, Jack, Eric Bergman. Hey, we got a phone number in the States, Boston actually, for Patrick O'Shea's brother. His name is Sean O'Shea. I've left a message asking him to call but have not heard back from him yet. That said, they're five hours behind us, time-wise, so it's only mid-morning in the States. Feel free to give me a call. If I hear anything, I'll get in touch. Thanks."

Dillon punched in Bergman's number. After four rings, a woman said, "U.S. Embassy, how may I direct your call?"

"I'd like to speak with Eric Bergman. This is Marshal Jack Dillon, attached to Dublin Special Branch."

"One moment, please, while I see if Mr. Bergman is available."

It was more like four minutes while Dillon waited, but finally, the woman came back on the line. "I'll connect you now, sir."

There were a couple of clicks on the phone, and then Bergman said, "Hi Dillon, thanks for calling me back."

"Sorry I wasn't here for your call, Eric. We got assigned to another case. This time a shooting down in Tallaght."

"Another American?" Bergman asked.

"No, thankfully. Initial observations suggest a gang-land hit. They requested Special Branch assistance, and Suel and I drew the short straw."

"Good luck with that," Bergman said.

"Yeah, thanks. I think we're going to need it. Have you gotten a response from the brother in the O'Shea murder?"

"Not as of yet. It's what, about 10:30 in the morning over in Boston. I made the call about two and a half hours ago. It's possible that's an office number or a home line, and he's out. Who knows, the man could be on vacation for a week. I've made the call, policy is I call again in forty-eight hours. If I don't get a response after forty-eight hours, we make two more attempts and then send a notification via certified mail. If that's returned to us, we chalk it up as no current address. We'll have to alert Dublin City Morgue, and I believe they will bury him at some point. That could be a year down the road."

"Yeah, I talked to a guy over there," Dillon said. "They hold the body for up to a year, then bury him if there's no contact. They don't cremate in case the body has to be exhumed for medical or legal purposes."

"How often does that happen?" Bergman asked.

"To my knowledge, almost never, but they're just playing it safe."

"If I hear from the brother, I'll let you know. Everything else going okay?"

"Same shit, different day," Dillon sighed.

"I get it," Bergman said and disconnected.

Dillon revisited the Dennis Bell file. Bell had been involved in an assault on two suspected members of the Dodder Demons gang. Their names, Desmond Connell and Justin McArdle, along with their addresses, were in the file. Dillon brought up the records on both individuals. Neither one was a newcomer to Tallaght An Garda Síochána. Two assaults on Connell's record, plus a few illegal drug charges and a stolen car at age fifteen. McArdle had three assaults, two robberies, suspicion of offering underaged girls for sex but never charged, and drugs. Just the sort of people you'd want living next door to you. Dillon copied down their addresses and headed over to Suel's desk.

Suel was in the process of going through a file. He looked up as Dillon approached and said, "Whatever it is, I'm not interested."

"Wait until you hear what I have to say."

"Do I have a choice?" Suel said.

"Not really. Ding-Dong Bell apparently put two members of the Dodder Demons in the hospital. Both were released the day before his murder. Wouldn't it seem logical we'd speak to both of them?"

"The file said they were released but also suggested they were not in any physical condition to offer harm to Bell. They were both home on bed rest. One has a brace on his leg, knee damage, and is using a walker. The other is dealing with pinched nerves between the L4 and L5. That's the lower back and makes it virtually un—"

"Unfortunately, I'm very familiar with pinched nerves between the L4 and the L5. I've been there. We should still talk to them. They may be incapable, but they probably know someone or a number of people who aren't incapacitated and were more than willing to deal with Ding Dong Bell.

Suel nodded. "Okay, you can drive."

TWELVE

It was a twenty-minute drive down to Tallaght at this time of the day. Dillon was using his GPS to provide directions to Desmond Connell's home on Heather-view Avenue. The street was a replay of the attached units where Dennis Bell lived. Small, attached, two-story stucco structures. Each one with the exact same floor plan as Bell's place, except in the case of Desmond Connell's, the front door was on the opposite side of the unit.

Once again, a three-foot wall ran across the property, with an opening to allow a car to pull in and park on the concrete pad up against the unit. Dillon pulled off the street and up onto the drive, essentially blocking any exit of the gray 2018 Audi A3 parked up against the house.

A patch of moss-covered grass in need of cutting was next to the concrete pad. A rusted child's dump truck and a broken plastic sword were scattered across the grass. Dillon led the way along a small sidewalk to the front door. He rang the doorbell and pulled out his warrant card. The doorbell was answered a moment later.

A heavy-set blonde woman opened the door, took one look at Dillon and Suel, and said, "Not the bloody Gardai again. Might as well come in. Des is parked in front of the telly." She took a long drag from her cigarette and shook her head.

As they stepped into the entryway, she leaned into the sitting room and said, "Oh, Des, darling," meaning anything but. "More friends here to have a little chat. Keep it down, lads. No shouting, we've two wee ones napping upstairs at the moment."

"Thank you, ma'am," Dillon said as they stepped into the sitting room. Desmond Connell was a heavy-set, dark-haired man, with the final remnant of a black eye on the left side of his face. He was wearing a light-blue jersey touting Dublin's rugby team and red plaid boxers. The knee on his right leg was wrapped in a black molded plastic brace with foam padding. The knee appeared red and swollen.

Connell was stretched out on the black leather couch. Two partially crushed beer cans were on their side in front of the couch. Off to the side was a walker. Two small white plastic bottles with what looked like prescription pain pills rested on the seat of the walker.

Connell picked up the remote, lowered the sound on the game show, and said, "Now what? I told you lot everything I know when I was in the hospital. It was that fecking bollox Ding-Dong and his mates. They went after meself and Justin with a Hurley just for the fun of it. Enjoyed themselves they did. We were just having a pint when they show up and knock the hell out of us for no reason at all. Told us to get our asses out of Tallaght. We been here our whole life, and we're supposed to leave? I don't suppose you arrested the bastards, did you?"

"No need to. Your man Ding-Dong is dead," Suel said.

Connell didn't appear to be surprised. He leaned back and smiled, "Yeah, God bless. There's still some good in the world."

"Why do you think he did this?" Dillon asked and nodded at Connell's knee.

"I've no idea. I'd never met the man before. He and his two mates struck me as the sort just looking for trouble."

"You know the names of the two men with Bell?" Suel asked.

"Believe me, if I knew, I'd tell the likes of yous. I've no idea. Really, I don't."

"It's too bad he's dead. We'd love to arrest him," Dillon said.

"Bastard deserved to get what little brains he had blown out."

"Oh, gee, and here we thought you didn't know he was shot," Suel said.

"Shot? Well, no, I, I didn't. It was just a saying I was using, you know? Honest."

"You know, Desmond, we're getting the sense you may know a bit more than you're letting on," Suel said.

"Might be helpful if you had any idea who shot your man, Ding-Dong."

"Let me know how that would help me. You've no idea what I'm dealing with. And look at this, my fractured kneecap. Do yas know how long it's going to take me to get back to walking, if ever? For Lord's sake, I'm liable to be walking with a limp for the rest of me life, and you lot is gonna tell me what the hell will be helpful? Do you follow the news at all? You ought to be out arresting every single one of those knackers in the Byrne Gang. Lock the bastards up and throw away the damn key."

"You want to help us do that?" Suel asked.

Connell shook his head. "You really are out of touch. I got a wife and two wee ones. Go on, get the hell out of here. You're wasting me time." With that, Connell picked up the remote and turned the sound back on.

Suel tapped Dillon on the shoulder and signaled the door with a nod of his head.

"Always a pleasure to chat with you, Mr. Connell," Dillon said. He tossed a business card next to the two prescription bottles on the walker, and they headed out the door.

"How'd you think that went?" Suel said as they headed toward the car.

"Actually, better than I expected. At least we got to talk to him. You never know. Maybe the wife will put some pressure on him."

"I think if the wife thought she could get away with it, she'd strangle your man. You can imagine the pressure she's feeling. What if the Byrne Gang went after her or the kids? They're perfectly capable of doing that."

"Comes with the territory," Dillon said. "Let's see if we can get anything from your man McArdle. He lives just a couple of streets over."

THIRTEEN

Justin McArdle lived on Bawnville Avenue. Not surprisingly, his home was at the end of the lane overlooking gorgeous athletic playing fields in Dodder Park and, beyond that, the Dodder River, although the river was hidden by trees. The park itself had a paved walking path that went on for almost two miles.

The houses along the lane were all attached until you got to McArdle's home. His place was the last house on the lane, next to the park, and unattached. It also appeared to be twenty or thirty years newer than all the attached homes on the lane. Dillon pulled up into the driveway, then backed out and parked against the curb, with the car facing the far end of the lane. They climbed out, Dillon pressed the fob to lock the car, and they headed to the front door.

Dillon rang the doorbell. After a long moment, he rang it again. Eventually, a male voice shouted from inside. "What do you want?"

"An Garda Síochána, Special Branch," Suel said.

"Put your ID through the mail slot."

"Open the bleeding door, McArdle, and we can show you our IDs. Can't take the chance of the likes of you running off with them." Suel shouted, and then they waited a bit. Suel looked at Dillon and said, "What do you think?" Suddenly the door opened an inch or two. A brass security chain was still attached to the door and pulled taut.

"Let me see your ID," the voice said. Presumedly, it was McArdle hiding behind the door.

Suel pulled out his warrant card and held it in the two-inch opening between the door and the doorframe.

"All right, all right. Yas know I can't be too careful," McArdle said as he unhooked the chain, opened the door, and stared wide-eyed at Dillon. Dillon held his warrant card up in front of McArdle. "So what does the likes of yas want?"

"Just a moment of your time, sir. We'd like to see if we could find out what happened to you and Desmond Connell. We heard you all were assaulted," Suel said.

McArdle opened the door wider. He would normally be about five-nine or ten, but he was leaning forward and clearly uncomfortable. A large black and blue bruise, at least three inches long, ran across his forehead above the right eye. "All right, come in if you must. I've to sit and quickly, me back, you know," he said, grimaced, and headed into the sitting room.

The room was clearly larger than the ones in the attached homes they'd been in. The fireplace was half-again as large with a massive mantel. A couch and coffee table were positioned across from the fireplace on a red and blue oriental rug. A red leather wingback chair sat on either end of the coffee table.

McArdle slowly settled onto the couch with a groan. He adjusted the pillows behind him and then took a sip from the mug of tea resting on the coffee table. He grimaced, shook his head, and said, "Now me damn mug is cold," clearly casting the blame on Dillon and Suel.

"You were assaulted a few nights ago, spent the night in hospital," Suel said.

"I wasn't just assaulted. The bastards tried to kill me, they did. I'm lucky I can even walk, for God's sake. Came at us, me and Connell, with a Hurley no less. Desmond will walk forever with a limp, and I'll be lucky if I can ever stand up straight again. We reported it to the Gardai. You lot are just the latest to come and ask the same questions. I can save yas the time because not a damn thing is going to happen. You ought to take the bastards out and shoot 'em is what you should do."

"What can you tell us about Dennis Bell?" Dillon asked.

McArdle shook his head and sighed. "I'm not surprised. I can barely walk, Desmond has to use a walker, and the likes of you come around to ask me about Ding-Dong Bell. All I can say is the bastard got what he deserved. When I heard the news, it absolutely made me day. If I knew who did it, I'd send 'em a bottle of Paddy's whiskey, I would. And no, before you ask, I don't know who did it. I'd give them more than a pat on the back, and I'd gladly buy them a pint, but I've no idea who in God's name committed that wonderful act."

"What can you tell us about the Byrne Gang? Who are the ones causing trouble?" Suel asked.

"Who are—Now you can't be fecking serious. Really? Who is causing trouble? The whole lot of them are causing trouble, for God's sake. One bad apple after another, and rotten to the core, as they say. Don't think you can fool me. The likes of you are letting 'em get away with it. It's sinful is what it is. Have you arrested the knacker with the Hurley what done this to me? I'll save yas the trouble of answering. Yous have done shite all. They've gotten away with a vicious assault, in broad daylight, in the middle of the day, and you just give 'em all a free pass. Well, the hell with yas. Looks like we'll have to deal with this ourselves, and deal with it, we will."

"Well, sir, we'd like to caution you on that. You see, let's be honest for a moment. You've spoken to officers before us. You've already said as much. But you haven't given us any names. How are we supposed to get them if you know who they are but you won't tell us? Who was with Ding-Dong Bell?" Dillon said.

"Oh, so now you're thinking I'm a snitch, is that it?"

"No, I'm thinking things are going to explode, and next time, instead of getting hit with a Hurley, you're going to be killed, and then there'll be no point in asking you questions because you won't be able to respond."

"Go on, the both of yas. Get your dumb asses out of me house. Do yas hear? Go on, get the hell out," McArdle shouted, then grimaced from the back pain.

"You give us a call if you decide we can be of help," Dillon said and tossed a business card onto the couch next to McArdle. "We'll see ourselves out."

Dillon stood and walked out of the room. Suel was right behind him. "What an absolute waste of time," Dillon said as they stepped outside.

Suel closed the door behind them. "Did you really expect anything else?"

"No," Dillon said as he shook his head. "You know what's going to happen to these Dodder idiots. They're outmanned, outgunned, and they're too damn stupid to do anything about it. I don't like Connell or this fool McArdle, but I don't want to see either one of them murdered. It's an absolute shame. Okay, that's enough for me today. Let's head back to Special Branch."

"Probably the smartest thing you've said all afternoon," Suel said as he climbed into the passenger seat.

FOURTEEN

They were back in Special Branch twenty minutes later. DCI McCabe was still out of the office. The light on Dillon's phone was blinking. He listened to a message from Emily in the Tech Lab and called her.

"Hi, Dillon. Got an address for you on that key for the safety deposit box."

"Is it even in Ireland?" Dillon said.

"Oh yeah, as a matter of fact, it's in the city center. A company called Merrion Vaults. They're located on Burlington Road just off of the Grand Canal."

"You're sure the box is there?"

"That's where the key is registered. Box number is 2643. It would be very strange if it wasn't there. The company would know it was missing."

"I'll be down to get the key in just a minute. Thanks, Emily." Dillon hung up and googled Merrion Vaults. According to their website, they were scheduled to close in twenty minutes. Given the rush hour traffic, there was no way they could get down there in time, and then there was the potential trouble with the whole privacy issue.

He walked over to Suel's desk. Suel held up three fingers, signaling he'd be on his current call for at least another three minutes. Dillon nodded and turned to head back to his desk.

"Yes, Shannon," Suel said. "That sounds like it would be fun. I'd love to go. If I pick you up at 7:00, does that give you enough time? Oh, well, don't let me keep you then. See you later and looking forward to it," Suel said and hung up. "What did you need, Dillon?"

Dillon turned around and headed back to Suel's desk. "Setting up something with Shannon Yates?"

"Never you mind, she had a legal question, and I'm going to help her, is all."

"Yeah, sure, Paddy. Hey, speaking of legal questions, do you know anyone in the legal department?"

"What seems to be the problem?" Suel asked.

"Potential problem," Dillon said and went on to explain about Emily tracing the safety deposit key to Merrion Vaults down on Burlington Road. "I want to get into that safety deposit box just as soon as possible."

"Well, you can certainly tie the key and, therefore the potential contents in the safety deposit box to Dennis Bell and quite possibly his murder. Hang on, let me check something," Suel said and opened a desk drawer. He pulled out a leather-bound notebook, turned a couple of pages, and said, "Yeah, here we go. Ultan Leary, he's a solicitor in the legal department, extension 335. He's probably still at his desk. Give him a call. He'll be able to write the request, and you could possibly have the search warrant by sometime tomorrow."

"Extension 335, you said?"

"Yeah, Ultan Leary, tell him hi from me. He's a good apple," Suel said.

Dillon hurried back to his desk and punched in 335. "Ultan Leary," a deep voice said after the second ring.

"Hi, Ultan. This is Marshal Jack Dillon. I'm with Special Branch, and I'm hoping you might be able to help me out. We're in the process of investigating the murder of an individual named Dennis Bell and—"

"Is this the lad who was shot in the head over in Tallaght the other night? Supposedly associated with the Byrne Gang?"

"Yeah, that's him."

"You automatically have right of access to his home and automobile," Leary said.

"Yes, and we've been through both. While going through his home, we came across a key to a safety deposit box. We've traced the box using the serial number on the key. The box is located in Merrion Vaults down on Burlington Road. I'd like to get a search warrant allowing us to go through the safety deposit box and gain custody of anything possibly connected to the murder and, or, the Byrne Gang."

"That shouldn't be too difficult," Leary said. "What I would need would be the serial number on the key, the number of the safety deposit box, the property office record on the key, the case number on Bell's murder, and that should pretty much do it."

"Are you going to be at your desk for another thirty minutes?" Dillon asked.

"Oh, yeah, I'll be here for at least another hour," Leary said.

"I'll be down there shortly," Dillon said.

"You know where we are?"

"Second floor," Dillon said.

"I'll be waiting for you," Leary said and disconnected.

Dillon gave Suel a wave and hurried out of the office. He took the elevator down to the main floor and almost ran through the halls to the Tech Lab. He crossed his fingers as he pushed the intercom button. He was about to push it again when Emily's voice said, "Tech Lab."

"Hi, Emily, it's Dillon. I need to get that key and take it over to the legal department. They're going to apply for a search warrant on that safety deposit box."

"I'm in my office," Emily said and buzzed the door open.

Dillon hurried inside. The piles of hollowed-out textbooks were still lined up on the back counter. He hurried past the first two counters and into Emily's office. She was seated behind a stack of files. The copy machine on her desk was whirring away.

"I'm just printing off some forms they'll need," she said. "Who are you dealing with in legal?"

"Ultan Leary, do you know him? I got his name from Paddy Suel."

"Oh, he's really good. Easy to work with. You shouldn't have any trouble. Especially with Bell being murdered, they'll pretty much let you check out anything."

"That's what I'm hoping. Any problem doing your search on the key?"

Emily shook her head. "No, it's almost as if the address was printed on the key. Between the banks and the companies like Merrion Vaults, things are pretty tightly controlled. That doesn't stop people from locking up illegal items, contraband, drugs, and the like, but the basic system is tightly controlled."

The printer stopped, and Emily stacked six sheets together, signed and dated the top sheet, placed them in a manila file folder, and handed the folder to Dillon. "Here you go. Good luck. Oh, and the key," she said and held out the plastic bag containing the key.

"Thanks, Emily, much appreciated," Dillon said. He grabbed the evidence bag, placed a business card in the file folder, and hurried out of the lab. He took the elevator up to the second floor, hurried down a hall, realized he'd taken a wrong turn, and backtracked. He stepped into the legal department a minute later.

A woman at the front desk, Dillon pegged to be around fifty, was just pushing her desk chair in. A large cloth bag with a shoulder strap was resting on the desk, and she was in the process of placing a pair of black shoes into the bag. She looked up at Dillon and started to say something.

"I'm Jack Dillon from Special Branch. I'm here to see Ultan Leary. He's expecting me. I was on the phone with him not fifteen minutes ago."

"Oh, well, umm, let me check. Please have a seat," she said and indicated two faux leather couches against the opposite wall. Dillon headed for one of the couches. "Yes, Mr. Leary, I have a gentleman here from Special Branch. He said you're expecting him. Yes, that's the name. Very well. Yes, you too," she said and hung up.

"Sir, if you'll go down this hall," she said, pointing to the only hall leading out of the reception area. Third door on your left."

"Thank you," Dillon said. He flashed a quick smile and hurried down the hall.

FIFTEEN

The third door on the left was also the first door that was open. Dillon knocked on the doorframe as he stepped in.

The office wasn't overly large, but there was a good-sized desk with a credenza behind it. Two chairs were positioned in front of the desk. Ultan Leary was a sandy-haired guy, maybe forty-five years old. He wore a dark blue tie and a light-blue button-down shirt with the sleeves rolled up to his elbows. A gray suit coat hung over the back of his desk chair. At least a dozen files were scattered across the desk, three of which were open. He smiled as he stood and held out his hand.

"Good Lord, Dillon. You must have run all the way over."

Dillon shook his hand and said, "Just anxious to get this moving and didn't want to hold you up."

"Not to worry, I'm here for a while. Under the circumstances, the victim having been murdered, you're pretty much granted access to anything you can think of."

Dillon handed him the file Emily had put together. Leary quickly paged through it. "Yeah, not a problem.

Twenty-four to forty-eight hours, and we'll have that warrant for you. You happen to know DI Paddy Suel in Special Branch?"

"I do. In fact, we're partners. I just spoke with him on my way out of the office. In fact, he's the one who gave me your name and number. Said to say hi for him."

"So if this goes to hell in a hand basket, he's the one I should blame," Leary said.

"Exactly," Dillon replied, and they both chuckled.

"You're the American that was caught up in that incident out at Terminal Two some years back, aren't you?"

"Yeah, that was me."

"Hell of a mess," Leary said and shook his head.

"I have a couple of photos on my phone of where we found the safety deposit box key. It was in a garden shed on Dennis Bell's property, more or less hidden on a beam running along the ceiling."

Leary opened a desk drawer, pulled out a business card, and handed it to Dillon. "Send a copy of those images to my email address. We don't necessarily need them, but it certainly won't hurt."

"I'll do it now," Dillon said and proceeded to email the images to Leary. A minute or two later, as they were chatting, Leary's computer signaled two emails coming through. Leary moved his mouse, brought up the emails, and clicked on one of the images. "Oh, yeah, perfect. I don't see any problem with this request."

"Anything else you need from me?" Dillon asked.

Leary shook his head. "No, this will be over there first thing in the morning. I'll give you a call just as soon as I know something."

Dillon extended his hand across the desk, shook hands with Leary, and left. He was back up in Special Branch five minutes later. Suel's desk was cleared off, and Suel was nowhere to be found. No doubt getting ready for his hot date with Shannon Yates.

Dillon left a message for DCI McCabe explaining the request for a warrant for Dennis Bell's safety deposit box. He cleared off his desk, locked the drawers, and went out to his car.

Rush hour was still running strong, and rather than listen to the news, he set the radio on a classical station with few commercials and headed home. He stopped at the Grape Vine, his local wine shop, purchased three bottles of Sean Minor Sauvignon Blanc, and drove home. He turned off Pappen's Road onto his lane. As he drove past Tara's house, she was just climbing out of her car, and she gave Dillon a wave. He waved back, pulled into the parking area in his front garden, and entered the house. Lucifer met him at the door. Dillon let him out into the front garden, placed the wine bottles in the refrigerator, and went upstairs to change into comfortable clothes.

He dined on leftover chicken and french fries from two nights earlier and had just settled onto the couch in the sitting room when the doorbell rang. He debated answering, thinking it would probably be someone looking for donations of some sort. The doorbell rang a second time, and he made his way to the door, prepared to deliver a polite "No thank you," to whoever was out there.

"Well, it's about time," Tara said when he opened the door. "I was beginning to think you weren't going to answer." She was wearing a very short powder-blue skirt and a matching top with spaghetti straps. The form-fitting stretch fabric left nothing to the imagination. She smiled, lifted her empty wine glass, and said, "Are you going to invite me in?"

"What? Oh, yeah, sorry about that. Come in. Come in. Perfect timing. I was just about to have a glass of wine," he lied. "Can I talk you into joining me?"

"Thought you'd never ask," she said and stepped into the entry. A lovely perfume scent drifted over Dillon as he closed the door behind her. He made a mental note of the sparkly pink sandals with four-inch heels and headed into the kitchen.

He took a wine glass from the cabinet, pulled a bottle of wine from the refrigerator, and twisted off the cap. He filled both glasses, raised his glass, and they clinked glasses. "Let's go into the sitting room. It's much more comfortable," he said and followed her into the sitting room. Along with admiring the view of her exposed back and skirt, he suddenly realized he was unable to detect the outline of a thong or any other undergarment.

Tara settled onto the couch next to Lucifer, and Dillon took up residence in one of the wingback chairs. As they chatted, he thought about her, apparently, now former boyfriend whom she'd been arguing with last week when he'd seen her.

"More wine?" Dillon asked sometime later.

"Sure," Tara said. She drained her glass and held the empty out to Dillon.

"Back in a minute," he said as he hurried out to the kitchen. The first bottle was empty, and the second bottle was only half full. Dillon refilled the glasses and rushed back out to the sitting room.

Tara's pink sandals were on the floor, and she was curled up on the couch, leaning toward the wingback chair Dillon was about to sit down in. "So, are you seeing anyone now, Dillon?" she asked as he handed her the glass.

"Seeing? You mean dating? No one, actually. I've been so busy, all of a sudden, I put my head up, it's been another month, and I just haven't had the time, I guess."

"I know all about that," she said and took a long sip of wine. "Mmm-mmm, this is nice wine. Where'd you get it?" He told her. They talked about the Grape Vine for a while before Tara asked another question about who he was dating. They drank more wine, chatted, and laughed.

Dillon woke up. They were on the floor in front of the fireplace. Tara was snoring loudly. A leopard print fleece blanket was partially covering her. Lucifer was on the couch, sleeping on Tara's powder-blue top with the spaghetti straps. Dillon's jeans, jersey, and plaid boxers were on the coffee table. He carefully reached over and pulled his cellphone from a pocket on his jeans. He pushed the button and checked the time, 3:57. His head began to pound.

He rolled away from Tara and stood. He gathered up the empty wine glasses and tiptoed into the kitchen. In case he had any doubts, the clock on the stove confirmed the time, 3:57. The three empty bottles of Sean Minor Sauvignon Blanc and a half-finished bottle of Pinot Noir added credibility to his headache. He pulled the aspirin bottle from the cabinet and tossed two into his mouth. He filled the lipstick smeared wine glass with water and washed down the aspirin. He debated getting a pillow for Tara or taking her upstairs into his bed but decided against both options. Instead, he quietly climbed the stairs and crawled into bed.

His alarm woke him, and he quickly reached over and turned it off, almost knocking the clock onto the floor in the process. He brushed his teeth, shaved, and showered, keeping the door closed so as not to wake his guest. He pulled on his bathrobe and made his way down to the living room. Lucifer was still asleep on the couch, on top of Tara's top, but Tara was nowhere around. He checked the kitchen, the spare bedroom, and even the bathroom. Apparently, Tara had gone home at some point without her top.

SIXTEEN

Dillon took two more aspirin for breakfast. Once he coaxed Lucifer back into the house with a biscuit, he grabbed Tara's top. Despite Lucifer sleeping on it last night, he could still catch a hint of the lovely perfume. He tossed the top in the front seat of the car and backed out onto the street. He drove forty feet, slowed in front of Tara's house, and decided it was too early to ring her doorbell. Hanging the top on the front door didn't seem like a very good idea, so he drove to Special Branch.

"So, how was your night?" Suel asked as Dillon poured himself a coffee in the break room.

"Hey, I'm right here. You don't have to shout," Dillon said.

"Oh, well, pardon me. Would we happen to be nursing a bit of a hangover?"

"I think it's safe to say it's not a bit of a hangover. It's a major hangover, and I've no memory of the best part of the evening."

"So who was she? Or did you pay someone?"

"For God's sake, Paddy. I didn't pay someone. It happened to be a woman who just can't get enough of me. Although after going through three bottles of wine, it might have been cheaper if I just paid her outright. Speaking of last night. How was your night with Shannon? Were you ever able to answer her legal question?"

"Legal question? What in the hell are you—Oh yeah, that's right, I told you she had a legal question. The night was nice. A quiet dinner, a pint afterward, and then we went our separate ways."

"That was it? Dinner and a pint?" Dillon asked.

"It was our first date. She had to prove she isn't a slapper. Now she's done that. Our next night out will be both of us proving we're well behaved and not in it just for sex. Once that's done, we'll have our third night out where we can both get down to what we want."

"I've been through that routine uncountable times," Dillon said and took a sip of coffee. He grimaced when he swallowed. It felt like battery acid entering his stomach, and in case he had any doubt, his stomach let off a loud growl.

"Sounds like you might be better off with some food before you risk drinking more of that coffee. Go back to your desk. I'll step outside and get something for you at one of the food trucks in the park."

"You don't have to do that," Dillon said.

"Yes, I do. Until you get some food in you, preferably with high sugar content, you're going to be worthless. Dump the coffee and settle in at your desk. I'll be back in ten minutes."

It was closer to fifteen minutes before Suel returned with a white bakery bag and a tray with two cups. He reached inside, pulled out a large caramel roll, and set it in front of Dillon. Then he pulled one of the cups from the tray and set it next to the pastry.

"There you are. Now eat that caramel roll. They're delicious. And drink that cup. It's hot chocolate, by the way, with marshmallows. Much better, and the sugar content will speed up your recovery time. Anything on the search warrant?"

Dillon shook his head. "No, and I promised Leary I wouldn't harass him with phone calls."

"I wonder if I should give him a call?" Suel said.

"Let's give him some time. It's not even 10:00. He may not have even submitted it yet."

Suel nodded and said, "You're probably right."

As Dillon inhaled the caramel roll, he phoned DCI O'Brien in Tallaght. "O'Brien," was how he answered in a no-nonsense manner.

"Good morning, sir. Marshal Dillon with Special Branch here. Just wanted to let you know we submitted a request for a search warrant on Dennis Bell's safety deposit box. We hope to have approval later today or to-morrow."

"Excellent, good work. What, exactly, do you hope to find?"

"Actually, we're not sure what we'll find, sir. But it's part of the process of not leaving any stone un-turned."

"Good move. Let me know how things work out. I'm curious, which bank is the box in?"

"It's not in a bank, sir. It's in a private business called Merrion Vaults. They're located on Burlington Road, close to the Grand Canal."

"Merrion Vaults. I've heard of them but never been there. We had a case six or eight months ago where someone robbed a jewelry store and dumped everything in a box there."

"Were they easy to work with?" Dillon asked.

"Oh, yes, very easy. In fact, based on the report I read, they were easier to work with than a couple of banks we've had to deal with over the years."

"Hopefully, that will continue, sir. I'll keep my fingers crossed."

"Anything else on the Bell case?"

"Not really. We spoke to Desmond Connell and Justin McArdle yesterday. Both of them are clearly in pretty bad shape from the beating they received from Bell and two others. To say they were uncooperative would be a bit of an understatement. In fact, McArdle said he'd like to find whoever it was that murdered Bell, give him a pat on the back and buy the guy a pint."

"Well, there you go. No surprise, I guess. Let me know what you find, if anything, in the safety deposit box."

"Good or bad, I'll keep you up to date, sir."

"Thank you, Dillon. Best of luck," O'Brien said and hung up.

The caramel roll and the hot chocolate did actually help, and by noon, Dillon was feeling much better. He didn't grab lunch, but there was a tray full of chocolate chip cookies in the break room, and he ate two of those when no one was looking.

Ultan Leary phoned just after 2:00. "Yes, Marshal Dillon. I've your search warrant signed, sealed, and delivered. It's sitting on my desk whenever you'd care to pick it up."

"Thank you for the call. I'll be down in the next fifteen minutes," Dillon said and hung up. He hurried over to Suel's desk.

"You need another caramel roll?" Suel asked.

"No, just got the call from your man Ultan Leary. He's got our search warrant for Dennis Bell's safety deposit box. You want to go down there with me? We'll pick it up and then go over to Merrion Vaults."

"Give me a moment to reply to this email, and I'll join you," Suel said.

Dillon glanced at Suel's computer screen as he headed back to his desk. The email was from Shannon Yates.

Ten minutes later, Dillon and Suel were knocking on Ultan Leary's office door. Suel carried a briefcase with a camera and camcorder.

"Oh, Lord. Just when I thought things couldn't get any worse," Leary said, looking up as they entered.

"Good to see you again, Ultan," Suel said, stepping forward and shaking hands.

"Good to see you, Paddy. You're looking rather dapper today," Leary said, nodding at Suel's sweater and pressed trousers instead of the usual jeans and jersey he wore.

"Just looking my best in the hopes I'd be allowed down here with Dillon to pick up the warrant."

"Yeah, record time on this one for a change. I didn't expect to see it until the end of the day at the earliest," Leary said

"Thanks for getting it," Dillon said and gave a nod to Leary.

Leary picked up the file folder Dillon had left yesterday. The warrant was attached to the file with a paper clip. "Here you go. Hope it's a successful trip. If I can give you one additional piece of advice. If possible, have a uniformed officer drive you in a squad car. You shouldn't have a problem, everything is in perfect order, but the uniform and the squad car add a degree of authority. It gets people smiling, nodding, and saying "yes sir" to any request you may have."

"Thanks, we've already got someone lined up to drive us." Suel said.

Dillon hoped he didn't appear too surprised at Suel's response. "Well, we best be on our way," Dillon said. He stepped forward and shook hands with Leary. Suel did the same. Everyone said goodbye, and they headed out of the office.

SEVENTEEN

Once they were out in the hallway and heading toward the staircase Dillon asked, "You think we should line up a squad car?"

"Were you even listening?" Suel said. "I told Ultan I've got a squad car and a uniformed driver lined up. This isn't my first dance, Dillon."

"I thought you were just saying that. I didn't realize you'd actually set it up. Good, glad I don't have to drive."

"Not half as glad as I am. The last thing I want is to sit in the passenger seat, fearing for my life. How's the head, by the way?"

"I hate to admit it, but the caramel roll and the hot chocolate got me going in the right direction. I snuck a couple of those cookies someone put out in the break room, and they helped too."

"Glad to be of assistance," Suel said as they headed down the stairs to the main floor.

"You going to call our driver?" Dillon asked.

"Already sent a text message. The driver should be waiting out front for us."

They walked through the main lobby, nodded, and said hello to the two guards seated at the front desk. As they stepped outside, a squad car pulled up in front of the building.

"Perfect timing," Dillon said.

"I'll grab the front seat, you can stretch out in back and close your eyes," Suel offered and opened the rear door for Dillon.

Dillon began to crawl in and stopped halfway. "Oh, hello, Shannon. Good to see you again. Who did you piss off to end up with this duty?"

"Nice to see you, Marshal. You feeling all right? You don't look too well."

"Feeling better, actually. Busy evening, up working until very late last night."

"Well, if this isn't a pleasant surprise. How are you, Shannon?" Suel exclaimed as he settled into the passenger seat and grinned.

"Just fine, Paddy. Good to see you again," she smiled. Once Suel closed the door, she put the car in gear and headed out of the parking lot.

Dillon noticed a box full of evidence bags on the floor of the vehicle. He exhaled a long breath realizing, with the previous evening's experience, he'd completely forgotten to get any bags. No one spoke for the next few minutes. Finally, Dillon broke the silence and asked, "Shannon, are you planning to go in with us?"

"Whatever you want. Is there a restriction on the warrant regarding who or how many can be there?"

"No, but I'm thinking along the lines of what Leary said. Having a uniformed officer does provide a stronger sense of official presence. I think it would be a good idea if you came in with us."

"Be happy to do that," she agreed.

Suel turned around and mouthed the words "thank you."

Dillon just shook his head. It was about a fifteen-minute drive to Burlington Road. The Merrion Vaults building was a six-story brick structure next to the Mespil Hotel. A four-star hotel just on the corner of Burlington Road and Mespil Road. A car was pulling out of a parking place as they approached. Shannon pulled ahead and quickly backed into the spot. Everyone climbed out of the squad car. Shannon placed her uniform hat on her head and grabbed the box of evidence bags. They entered the building and made their way to the reception counter.

"Good afternoon. How may I help you?" the woman behind the counter asked.

"An Garda Síochána. We're here to open a safety deposit box. We have a warrant that allows this, and we will probably need to see a supervisor or a manager," Dillon said.

The woman didn't even blink, suggesting this probably wasn't the first time she'd been through this. "If you'll take a seat, I'll inform our manager, Mr. Nolan."

"Thank you," Dillon said and smiled. They headed toward two small couches facing each other in front of the window, looking out onto the street.

"So far, so good," Suel said as he and Yates settled onto a couch. Dillon sat down opposite them.

"So, Shannon. Have you been involved with anything else regarding the Dennis Bell case?" Dillon asked.

"No, nothing. From what I understand, his parents and both sisters have refused to cooperate. I'm not sure they'd be much help anyway. Ding-Dong Bell was a rising star in the Byrne Gang, and, in my opinion, they either supported him, in which case they won't provide any information, or they were very much against his participation, in which case they probably wouldn't have any information to provide."

Dillon couldn't argue with her logic. He was about to ask another question when a man in a dark suit stepped over to the receptionist's counter. The woman behind the counter nodded in the direction of Dillon, Suel, and Yates, and he hurried over.

"Good afternoon, I'm Thomas Nolan, Manager for Merrion Vaults. You have a warrant to open a safety deposit box?"

"Yes, we do," Dillon said. As he stood, he handed over the file with the warrant attached to the front of the folder. "I'm Marshal Jack Dillon. This is DI Paddy Suel and Officer Shannon Yates. We have the key to box 2643, registered to Dennis Bell, a gentleman murdered last week in Tallaght. We would like to examine the contents of the box and possibly take some or maybe all of the items into our possession. Depending on what, exactly, we find."

Nolan nodded and said, "If you would follow me to my office. I'll need to see your warrant cards along with a personal item of identification."

They followed Nolan down a hall and into a rather large office. The desk was neatly arranged with three computer screens displaying the interiors of a number of rooms lined up with safety deposit boxes of all different sizes. Dillon, Suel, and Yates had their warrant cards and a personal ID card in their hands as they entered Nolan's office.

Nolan glanced at Dillon's and then Suel's and said, "Very good." He took a long moment looking at Yates' cards, then smiled and said, "Thank you." He set the file on his desk, examined the search warrant, flipped through the pages Emily in Tech had copied, and nodded. "Very well, everything appears to be in order. This will be one of our larger boxes, Twenty-two by sixteen by twenty-four. You do have the key, don't you?"

"We do," Dillon said and held the evidence bag with the key for Nolan to see.

"Perfect, if you'd follow me, please."

With Nolan leading, they headed back down the way they'd just come, walked through the front lobby, and through a set of security doors. They passed two uniformed guards and entered a vault. The open stainless steel door was about eighteen inches thick. The vault wasn't just a small room. It actually went on and on. The walls were covered with doors of different sizes leading to large or small safety deposit boxes. The floor was covered by red carpeting with an eight-inch wide marble slab running the length of the walls containing the boxes. The boxes were numbered. Each door required two keys to open the door before you could remove the box from the wall. Nolan stopped halfway along the wall at box 2643 and bent down to where the larger boxes were held, approximately two feet off the floor.

Suel got the camera ready, and Yates turned on the camcorder and began filming. There were two lock plugs on the door. He placed his key in the smaller of the lock plugs then stepped to the side. Dillon placed the key he had in the larger of the lock plugs. Nolan reached down, turned both keys, opened the door, and stepped back. Dillon grabbed hold of the metal handle attached to the box with his left hand and pulled the box out. It was heavy, and he placed his right hand beneath the far end of the box as he pulled it out.

"You got it?" Suel asked and clicked two more photos.

"Yeah, relax, I got it."

"It might be filled with gold bars," Nolan joked. "If you'll follow me, we'll put you in a private area where you can review the contents. It's our policy that I now inform you that the room is under round-the-clock secu-rity. Anything you do is filmed and stored in a digital format, available for eternity. Any questions?"

They all shook their head.

"Now, if you'd follow me, please." Nolan led them along the far wall of the vault, and just when Dillon was thinking he might have to hand the box to Suel, they entered a small cubical with two chairs and a counter attached to the wall. The cubical was still in the vault. Dillon set the box on the Formica counter. Shannon set the box of evidence bags next to the safety deposit box.

"Officers, I'll leave you to it. Should you need assistance, or once you've finished, simply press two-two on the keyboard, and I'll be alerted. Thank you."

"Thank you," they replied in unison.

Nolan stepped out of the cubicle, and Dillon said, "Well, I guess we should take a look. Paddy, you want to get the camera out and start taking pictures. Who knows what the hell we'll find in this thing? Shannon, if Paddy's taking pictures, would you take a video as I open this and remove items from the box? The box was heavy, so there's a lot in there."

"Maybe Nolan wasn't joking, and it's full of gold bars," Suel said. He pulled the camcorder from the briefcase and handed it to Shannon. He pulled the camera out, turned it on, and gave Dillon a nod. Shannon nodded and focused the camcorder on Dillon. Dillon pulled a pair of latex gloves from his pocket and slipped them on.

EIGHTEEN

Dillon gave a nod. Yates clicked on the camcorder again, and Suel took a picture.

"All right, here we go. This is Marshal Jack Dillon with Special Branch. I'm with DI Paddy Suel, also with Special Branch, and officer Shannon Yates with Tallaght An Garda Síochána. We're at Merrion Vaults on Burlington Road in Dublin. Our IDs and our search warrant have been accepted by Mr. Thomas Nolan, the Manager at Merrion Vaults." Dillon added the time and date and lifted the lid on the safety deposit box.

"Holy shit," Suel said and clicked the camera button four times.

"Oh my God," Yates said at the same time.

"You getting this, Shannon?" Dillon asked.

"Yes, loud and clear."

"Okay," Dillon said. "I'm going to remove this first layer." With that, he began to remove the bundles of hundred euro notes. Each bundle was wrapped with a paper band labeled 10,000 with a green stripe running across it. Dillon did a quick count. There were eighteen bundles, which amounted to a hundred and eighty thousand euros. As he began removing the bundles, the level below became exposed. "Oh, Jesus, you still getting all this on the video, Shannon?"

"Yes, keep going."

"More money?" Suel said.

"Check this out," Dillon said and pulled out what looked like a brick covered in duct tape.

"Cocaine?" Suel said.

"I would guess so. It certainly isn't baking flour."

Over the course of the next three or four minutes, Dillon emptied the safety deposit box. Along with the eighteen bundles of hundred euro notes, there were twenty duct-tape-covered bricks of what they suspected was cocaine.

"Shannon, come over here and film the empty safety deposit box. Paddy, take a couple photos of this thing empty as well. I think we'd better call someone to come and get this stuff. It doesn't make sense to haul it back to Special Branch in a squad car."

"I think that's a very good idea," Suel said.

Dillon pulled out his phone, but he couldn't get a signal in the vault. He pressed the number two button on the keypad twice. "I guess now we just wait."

Nolan arrived a couple of minutes later. "All set to—Oh dear," he said, looking at the stacks of currency and the bricks of powder stacked on the Formica counter.

"I need to step out and make a phone call. We're unable to haul this sort of thing in a squad car. We need to get some assistance. I want to have a security team and a secure vehicle hauling these contents," Dillon said.

Nolan nervously nodded and said, "Yes, but of course. I understand perfectly. If you'll just follow me, please."

"You two okay on your own for a moment?" Dillon asked.

"Yeah, just get someone over here to take possession of this stuff," Suel said.

Dillon followed Nolan out of the vault. They walked past the two guards seated outside the entrance. Nolan stopped and said to the guards, "Stop anyone from entering for the next thirty or forty minutes until I give you the all-clear."

Once they stepped into the hallway, Dillon pulled out his cellphone and got a signal. "I can call from here," he said to Nolan.

"I'll just wait down the hall and then escort you back to the cubicle."

Dillon phoned McCabe's number and crossed his fingers.

"DCI McCabe," was the response he heard after the third ring.

"Oh, glad you're there sir. This is Marshal Dillon. I'm with DI Suel and a uniformed Tallaght officer at Merrion Vaults. We've just opened the safety deposit box belonging to Dennis Bell. The individual murdered—"

"Murdered in Tallaght. Yes, I'm aware of the case. If you're calling, I would guess you've found something?"

"We've found a couple of items. A good deal of cash, a hundred and eighty thousand euros to be exact, and along with the cash, there are twenty duct taped covered bricks of what we suspect is cocaine." McCabe was silent. "Sir?"

"Yes, yes. Sorry, you said a hundred and eighty thousand euros?"

"Yes, sir, along with twenty bricks of what we suspect is cocaine. We'd like some security to transport this out of here. We've photographed and filmed the opening and emptying of the safety deposit box. We're currently in a cubicle in the vault, but transporting that amount of cash and contraband is—"

"I understand completely. I'll get a unit over immediately. I want you and the other officers to remain in the secured area. Who is the point of contact there?"

"The manager's name is Thomas Nolan."

"Nolan, got it," McCabe said a moment later, causing Dillon to think he wrote the name down. "You just relax and remain in the vault, and Dillon, damn good job. Well done to all three of you."

"We'll check in once we're back at Special Branch."

"Stay safe," McCabe said and disconnected.

"Mr. Nolan," Dillon called to Nolan, who was standing at the end of the hall.

Nolan hurried back to Dillon. "Everything all right?"

"Yes, they'll be sending security. I've given them your name. With any luck, they'll be here in the next ninety minutes. Can you escort me back to the cubical?"

Nolan nodded and headed back toward the vault, with Dillon following. They stopped just outside the cubicle, and Nolan said, "As soon as your team arrives, I'll bring them to you."

"Thank you, Mr. Nolan. I have to ask, has this happened before?"

Nolan nodded. "On occasion, maybe every eighteen months or so. Usually, it's related to some sort of stolen items. Jewelry more often than not. Your particular situation is unique given the quantity of cash and the drugs. I'm unaware of a situation with more drugs, but given our business, I suppose it's possible. I'll let you get back to your project."

"Thank you. We'll be confiscating the drugs and cash. I can send you a copy of our film and the photographs if you'd like," Dillon said.

"Yes, please, and if you could include an official statement on a letterhead, that would be much appreciated."

"Will someone else rent that box?" Dillon asked.

"In due time. Mr. Bell paid for it through the end of the year. Even under these circumstances, we'll lock it up, and it will remain empty until his contract expires."

"We'll keep the key to the box."

Nolan nodded. "I have your paperwork, name, address, and phone number if we need to get in touch. It's standard procedure to change the lock with a new owner."

"Thank you for your assistance. My apologies for things ending this way. At some point, there's liable to be a press release. I'll do everything in my power to ensure your name, along with Merrion Vaults, isn't mentioned. If you would be so kind as to send us a list of the dates Mr. Bell accessed his box that would be a big help."

"But of course and we would appreciate any help you can give in not mentioning our name," Nolan said.

Dillon stepped into the cubicle. Suel and Yates were seated in the chairs, chatting away. Suel turned and said, "They going to send someone?"

"Yeah. I got hold of McCabe. He's sending a team out. I'm thinking we leave everything just the way it is until they get here, and then we film and photograph it being packaged and taken out. Nolan said Bell paid the rent on the box until the end of the year, so it will remain in the vault, empty, and then they'll rent the thing."

"Any idea of the value we're looking at?" Yates asked.

Dillon shook his head. "It depends on the quality and how many of those bricks you're buying. Once the lab checks it out, we'll have a better idea, I guess. Before we leave, remind me to check with Nolan and see how often Bell was in here. I'm curious if he kept this for backup or if he was in here every other day or weekly taking from or adding to the stash."

"Either way, it's now off the market," Suel said.

NINETEEN

A voice outside the cubicle said, "Just in through here."

Suel and Yates rose from their chairs, and Dillon stood up from the floor as Nolan stepped to the side and four officers entered. The officers were dressed in black and wearing black protective vests with a tag in yellow letters that read GARDA Armed Support Unit. Each officer carried an automatic weapon.

"For God's sake, Liam Duncan, as I live and breathe," Suel said and extended his hand to the first officer.

"Ah, Paddy, if I knew it was you we were coming to arrest, I would have worn me dress uniform," Duncan said and laughed. "So this is it, your man's secret stash? What was his name, Bell?"

"Yes, Dennis 'Ding-Dong' Bell."

"Charming," Duncan said and chuckled.

"It's what we've found thus far. Oh, Liam, this is Marshal Jack Dillon, my partner in Special Branch, and this is Shannon Yates, with Tallaght Gardai."

Duncan shook hands with Dillon and Yates and then said, "This is our team," and that was it for the introduction.

Dillon took the hint and said, "Did you bring anything to transport the evidence? We have evidence bags, but I—"

"Not a problem," Duncan said. "Jake, you have the duffels?"

One of the other officers handed a series of black nylon bags to Duncan. The bags were about two feet long with handles and a zipper along the top. Either side of each bag was emblazoned with An Garda Síochána in bold yellow letters.

"That will be perfect," Dillon said. "If it's all right with you, I'll load the bags up. We'll be filming that process and taking photos. Are you guys okay with being photographed?"

"We can do that as long as there aren't any facial shots. We don't need some knacker posting an image online or looking for us."

"I get it," Dillon said. "Paddy, Shannon, if you would do the honors of recording this, I'll fill up these bags. Duncan, if you guys want to stand behind me with your weapons at the ready. If you're wearing a ring or a watch, maybe remove it so it can't be used for future identification."

As it turned out, none of them wore a watch or jewelry. They lined up behind Dillon. He gave the date, time, and location. He mentioned himself, Suel, and

Yates and referred to Duncan's team simply as Garda Armed Support. It took little more than five minutes for Dillon to fill one of the duffel bags with the two evidence bags of cash and place the suspected bricks of cocaine into four evidence bags, two evidence bags each into a duffle bag. Once they were finished and the cameras were turned off, Dillon pressed the number two key on the keypad twice, summoning Nolan once again.

He appeared almost immediately. "All set?"

"Yes, sir, thank you for your cooperation. We'll leave you in charge of the empty safety deposit box, and if you'd lead us, we'll be out of your hair."

"Then follow me, please," Nolan said.

The Armed Support officer, who was not carrying a duffel bag stepped in behind Nolan. The other three spaced themselves between Dillon, and Yates, with Suel bringing up the rear.

Nolan led them out of the vault and to the building entrance. A reinforced patrol van was parked on the sidewalk in front of the building. As they stepped out of the building, the officer seated behind the wheel hurried out and opened the side door. The officers quickly tossed the duffel bags in behind the front seats and moved to the rear and the front of the vehicle to watch for any potential problems. Fortunately, there weren't any, and they quickly climbed into the van. The flashing lights and the siren were turned on, and they disappeared around the corner.

"Let's head back to Special Branch and wrap this up. I'll buy the first round tonight," Suel said.

"I might be drinking fizzy water, but it sounds like a good idea. I need to bring DCI McCabe and O'Brien up to date and get those cameras back to the property room."

"I'll deal with the cameras. You can deal with getting the word out to the powers that be," Suel said.

"Shannon, I hope you'll be able to join us," Dillon said, which led to a smile on her face as well as Suel's.

TWENTY

illon knocked on DCI McCabe's door. "Dillon, come on in. Everything work out?"

"Yes, sir. The ASU team arrived, and it couldn't have been more than fifteen minutes from start to finish before they drove off to the Crime Laboratory. The drugs will be housed there pending any potential lawsuits, although since Dennis Bell, the guy who essentially had possession, is dead, I can't foresee a lawsuit. Under the Proceeds of Crime legislation, the cash will eventually be forfeited to the state."

"A very nice day's work. Well done, Dillon."

"Thank you, sir. I have to say we couldn't have done it without DI Suel, Officer Yates from Tallaght, and the Armed Support Unit."

McCabe nodded and said, "Make sure you bring DCI O'Brien up to date."

"I'll be making that phone call in just a moment, sir."

"Well, don't let me keep you, and again, well done, Dillon."

Dillon returned to his desk and phoned DCI O'Brien in Tallaght. "DCI O'Brien."

"Yes, sir, Marshal Dillon with Special Branch. Just calling to bring you up to date on the safety deposit box belonging to Dennis Bell."

"What did you find?"

Dillon went on to describe the drugs and cash in the box and the Armed Support Unit carrying everything away to the Crime Laboratory.

"Good, well done."

"Thank you, sir, and thank you for lending us Officer Yates. She did a stand-up job."

"Glad to hear it. Actually, I was a little surprised she volunteered."

Volunteered? That figures, Suel, Dillon thought. "Well, the presence of a uniformed officer made it all that much easier. We had wonderful cooperation from the manager of Merrion Vaults, and part of that had to be because of her presence in uniform."

"I'll pass on the compliment. Anything on Ding-Dong's murder?"

"Not at this stage. He was involved with an assault on Desmond Connell and Justin McArdle, both Dodder Demons, but neither one of them was willing to provide any real information. We'll keep looking, but I fear there's bound to be an attempt at payback."

"You don't think Ding-Dong Bell's murder was payback?"

"It certainly may have been. My fear is that whoever assisted him is a likely target for a similar result, and that would only serve to escalate things."

"Hopefully, you'll uncover something. Keep me posted and let me know if there's anything I can do to help."

"Will do, sir, and thank you."

"Thank you, Dillon. Well done," O'Brien said and disconnected. Dillon walked over to Suel's desk. Suel had pulled over a desk chair on wheels from an unoccupied desk. Yates was sitting alongside Suel, the two of them laughing and chatting away.

"Sorry to interrupt but did you get the cameras returned?"

"We did once we downloaded the tape and the images. I've sent copies to the property room. We were just watching the tape. Here take a look," Suel said. He clicked on a link and turned his laptop toward Dillon. The images of the cubicle and the safety deposit box were suddenly displayed. A new image came on the screen every four seconds and went through Dillon emptying the box and arranging the contents on the counter. Once it was finished, Suel clicked on another link, and the video Yates had taken with the camcorder began to play. When the video was done, Suel said, "We've got more photos and a tape of you loading the stuff into those bags if you want to see that."

"I've seen enough. Good job, you two. I was thinking of maybe making a stop at the Autobahn. I'm buying, if you're interested."

"Sounds as though you've made a complete recovery from how you felt this morning," Suel said.

"Well, to be honest, I'll be sticking with sparkling water and a twist tonight, but I'd be happy to supply the beverage of your choice if you'd care to join me."

Suel gave a look in Yates' direction.

She nodded vigorously.

"We'll see you there, Dillon. See if you can't secure some comfortable seating and a table for us."

"I'll do just that," Dillon said. He walked back to his desk, cleared it off, locked it, and headed out the door. He walked out to the parking lot, climbed into his car, and that was when he noticed Tara's powder-blue top with the spaghetti straps lying on the passenger seat. There was something slightly erotic about her waking up, probably still drunk, and walking topless across the lane to her house.

He thought about that for a moment, debated calling her and asking her to join them. He immediately labeled the idea as possibly his most stupid thought of the day. He drove home, let Lucifer out into the front garden, and then coaxed him back into the house with a biscuit. He pulled in front of Tara's house, but her car wasn't in the drive, so he drove the three blocks to the Autobahn.

Suel and Yates were nowhere in sight. Dillon ordered a sparkling water with a twist of lemon and settled in at a table in the bar. Suel and Yates arrived twenty minutes later. As soon as they sat down, a server was at the table and took everyone's orders. Everyone purposely avoided talking business for the next sixty minutes. Dillon placed a second order for drinks, and once those were finished, everyone left to go home. Although based on looks and glances, Dillon figured either Suel was going to her place or she would be going to his.

Dillon headed home, happy with himself for not drinking any alcohol. He turned onto his lane and drove down to his house. Tara's car was in the drive as he passed her house. He debated for a brief moment and decided to just get it over with.

He pulled a few of Lucifer's hairs from her top, climbed out of the car, and walked over to her place. The curtain was pulled, but the sitting room lights were on. He gave a brief touch to her doorbell. She answered a few seconds later.

"Oh, Dillon, stopping by for a repeat of last night?"

He smiled and said, "You seem to have left this at my place."

"Oh my God. I was still intoxicated when I left. I don't even remember walking home."

"Well, apparently, it must have been quite the scene," he said and handed the top to her.

"You have time to come in for a minute?"

He nodded and said, "Yeah, for a minute."

"It'll save me the trip," she said and handed him a navy-blue windbreaker with 'An Garda Síochána' in yellow letters over the left breast.

"Oh, God, I didn't even know this was missing."

"I don't know where I left my top. I probably looked for it, never found it, and apparently grabbed your windbreaker and left."

"Lucifer was sleeping on your top on the couch. I checked on you around 4:00, and you were sound asleep in the sitting room. I checked again around 6:30, and you'd gone home at some point."

She shook her head. "My apologies for inviting myself over. I didn't mean to intrude. I just—"

"Oh, please, you didn't intrude, Tara. It's always enjoyable when you come over. Oh, wait, that maybe came out wrong. I didn't actually mean…well, it was just very nice to see you and—"

"Maybe you should stop while you're ahead, Dillon."

"Yeah, probably."

"Can I offer you a glass of wine? I'm actually just having a sparkling water but feel free to have some wine."

"Actually, if you have any more of that sparkling water, that would be perfect. No reflection on you, but after last night, I'm making an effort to behave."

"Oh, you behaved and followed direction," she said. "Let me get that water for you. You want some ice?"

"Yes, please, that would be great."

"Coming right up. Grab a seat. I'll be right back."

They chatted for forty-five minutes, and then Dillon said he had to get home. He thanked Tara for the water. She replied with a peck on the cheek, and he left. He watched the 10:00 news with Lucifer asleep on the couch. They went up to bed once the news was over.

TWENTY-ONE

Dillon woke before his alarm, showered, shaved, and headed downstairs dressed for work. Lucifer went out forty-five minutes later. Dillon placed his breakfast dishes in the dishwasher and coaxed Lucifer back inside with a biscuit.

He backed out of the front garden, glanced at Tara's house as he drove past, and headed to Special Branch. He wasn't the first person in the office, but he was there before Suel, and that was all that mattered.

Suel washed up on shore an hour later with a smile on his face, whistling a tune Dillon recognized but couldn't recall the title. "You seem to be in a good mood. Things go okay for the rest of the evening?"

"Could not have been better," Suel said. "Your woman is quite the energetic little thing. What are you working on?"

"I'm going over the Bell file, trying to find something that might point to whoever killed him. It almost had to be someone he knew. Someone he was comfortable enough with that he lowered the window on his car to talk to them."

"I've been wondering about that," Suel said.

"Here's what I'm thinking. What if it wasn't one of the Dodder Demons? We know Connell and McArdle were still in hospital, so they're off the list. What if it was someone in the Byrne Gang?"

"But Bell was in the Byrne Gang. In fact, he was up and coming."

"You're right, as always. So what if it was someone in the gang who possibly viewed him as competition? Possibly someone who was passed over and Ding-Dong Bell got the promotion they thought should have been theirs?"

"Humph. I never considered that. I guess it certainly could be a possibility," Suel said.

"Exactly. It could also be that everything we took out of that safety deposit box yesterday represented funds and product that Bell stole from the gang. It strikes me as strange he'd have all of that stored in a safety deposit box if it was just a temporary holding place for a couple of days or a week. Just transporting that quantity in and out would be risky. It took three guys to haul all that out of there yesterday. What if Bell had been grabbing the occasional brick or a handful of bills? If he was someone involved in regular transactions, maybe he was always taking a personal cut."

"Not far-fetched," Suel said.

"Let me take it a step further. Someone finds out Bell is taking a personal cut, and they put the word out. His killing serves as a warning to anyone else who might have similar ideas. They get reminded that even an up and coming guy is going to be eliminated if he's cheating the organization."

Suel seemed to think about that for a moment. "So maybe we need to chat up someone familiar with the Byrne Gang. You recall who was heading up the investigation on Bell's murder at the Tallaght station?"

Dillon nodded and paged to the front of the file. "Yeah, I saw the name in the file. Here it is, DI Ward Tiernan. Did you talk to him at all? I haven't."

Suel shook his head. "I haven't talked to him. Don't really know him other than I think he has a brother who played for Dublin rugby maybe five or six years back."

"If I can set something up this morning, you want to come with?"

"Yeah, count me in. We've been drawing blanks thus far. God forbid he'd have something for us."

Dillon picked up his phone and called Tallaght station. "Hi, Marshal Dillon with Special Branch, can you connect me to Ward Tiernan, please. Yes, thank you." He looked over at Suel and said, "I think he's there, and we—"

"DI Tiernan," a voice said, and Dillon pulled the receiver away from his ear for a half-second.

"Hi, Good morning, DI Tiernan. This is Marshal Dillon with Special Branch. I was wondering if—"

"You're the one who went through the safety deposit box, right? We just finished watching the tape not thirty minutes ago. Nice work. DCI O'Brien said you found the key to the box on-site?"

"Yeah, that's right. We found it out in the shed in the back garden. Just a lucky find. It was hanging from a nail on the back of one of the ceiling beams. Easy to miss. I told that to DCI O'Brien."

"Well, we went through the place for the better part of three days and never found it. What can I do for you?"

"We're looking at suspects on the murder of Dennis Bell, and to be honest, we're coming up empty-handed. I was wondering if we might take a bit of your time this morning and get any ideas you might have."

"More than willing to chat. We can do it here if that works. You interested in coming down here to the station? I have to be honest. We've been drawing blanks as well. The logical thought would be someone from the Dodder Demons, but we're not hearing a word. Our sources are coming up empty-handed. No one seems to have anything to share."

"You think someone's putting pressure on them?"

"No, actually, we don't. If someone was putting pressure on them, we'd be able to pick up on it. They've been on the back foot for some time. My sense is they'd love to take credit for offing Ding-Dong, but the facts seem to suggest they didn't do it, and right now, no one would believe them if they said they did do it."

"Sounds like we're more or less on the same page," Dillon said. "You have some time this morning? We could be down there in the next half-hour."

Tiernan seemed to think about that for a moment. "If you can come down, I'll make time. Oh, and I'm partial to scones."

Dillon laughed at that and said, "We'll see what we can do. See you in thirty minutes."

"That was fast," Suel said as Dillon hung up his phone.

"Yeah, well, they're coming up empty-handed just like us. Let's go. The worst that can happen is we end up no wiser than we are now. Your man said he was partial to scones, so we can pick some up from one of the trucks in the park."

TWENTY-TWO

Dillon pulled out of the parking lot and drove into Phoenix Park. There were a half-dozen food trucks lined up a mile into the park. He pulled to the curb, and Suel hurried out of the car. He didn't return for almost ten minutes.

"What took you so long?" Dillon asked when Suel finally climbed back in.

"There was a line of eight people waiting ahead of me. Wouldn't you know, the woman just in front of me has all the time in the world to read the sign of what they have available. But did she? When she moves her fat arse up to the counter, she can't make a damn decision. One of this, one of that. What does that taste like? Is that one gluten-free? I don't know who wanted to kill her worse, me or the poor guy working the counter. Anyway, I got four scones, just in case someone is with your man Tiernan."

After showing their warrant cards to the guard at Tallaght station, Dillon pulled into the security parking lot. He found a spot in the back of the lot, and they hurried to the door. Dillon brought up the security code that

O'Brien had given him and he'd stored on his phone. He punched it into the keypad, and they entered the station.

They took an elevator up to the Homicide section and stepped into the office. Two of the six desks were occupied. As they entered, the older of the two men looked up and called, "Dillon?"

Dillon gave a nod, and they headed toward the desk as the man stood. "DI Tiernan?" Dillon said, extending his hand.

They shook hands and Tiernan said, "Please, call me Ward. Very nice to meet you, Dillon." He had salt and pepper hair, a square chin, and blue eyes.

"This is my partner, Paddy Suel," Dillon said.

Tiernan nodded and shook hands with Suel. "I've heard about both of you. Sounds like you're keeping busy in Special Branch."

"Never enough time. Oh, we brought you some scones," Suel said.

Tiernan opened the bag Suel handed to him and smiled. "Let me get some teas, and we can have a pleasant chat." He set the bag on his desk and walked over to a counter littered with tea mugs. He filled the kettle and set it to boil. He was back two minutes later with three steaming mugs. "Take a seat, lads, and thank you for these scones. I'll guard them with me life. Now, help yourselves and tell me what's on your mind," Tiernan said and indicated the two chairs in front of his desk. Dillon had the sense they'd been recently placed there.

"Well, we wanted to talk with you about the Bell murder. You have any leads you're working on? I'd love to tell you we interviewed Desmond Connell and Justin McArdle, but that's too strong a term. They barely spoke to us."

"Very brief conversations with the two of them. It was like pulling teeth to get any information," Suel added.

Tiernan nodded. "Oh, yeah. They're a couple of pieces of work, probably at no surprise to the two of youse. You know what we've been dealing with. You learn anything from them?"

"Only that they wanted to buy a pint for whoever shot Ding-Dong Bell."

"No surprise there."

"So, you said on the phone you hadn't come up with any suspects," Dillon said.

Tiernan nodded. "Even worse than that. Let me be perfectly honest here. Normally in a situation such as this, with a little bit of positive or negative interaction, we'd have a list of at least three or four names. But, with this case, we've got absolutely nothing. Not so much as an anonymous phone call. A bit strange, to be honest."

"You pick up any response from them on the contents of Bell's safety deposit box?" Dillon asked.

Tiernan shook his head and said, "No, but it's still early. Give it twenty-four hours, and the information will get out there. We've got an informer we'll mention it to, and he'll be eager to spread the word. I'm getting the sense you might have an idea."

"It's just an idea, but since we all seem to be grasping at straws, we can at least consider it. We're not getting any information from anyone. It's possible Bell was murdered because of what we found in the safety deposit box. But here's the problem we have with that. If the organization knew about it, wouldn't they do something like offer to forget about his *indiscretion* if he returned the cash and drugs? Then once he returned everything, they'd make an example of him, kill him, and spread the word that this is what happens if you rip off the organization."

Tiernan seemed to think about that and slowly nodded. "Yeah, I can see your point. But he was still murdered, and apparently by someone he felt comfortable enough with that he lowered the car window to chat."

"Maybe a woman," Suel said.

"Mmm-mmm, maybe," Tiernan said. "But Bell wasn't an idiot. He was always on his guard. It had to be someone he knew, someone he trusted. The Dodder Demons put the word out that one of their lot was responsible, but it doesn't stand the test. That, plus the fact they've no evidence to back the statement up. No name of a specific individual. The few things they've said have been blatantly wrong. He wasn't killed by a shotgun blast. He wasn't shot numerous times. He wasn't intoxicated and had his guard down."

"We're thinking pretty much the same thing. It had to be someone he knew, someone he was comfortable with. What about this as another option. Someone in the Byrne organization, a friend, a coworker, if you will. The two of them are up for a promotion or maybe a larger section of town where they're in charge of the profits. Maybe one of them is considered to interact with a major client or distributor. Something like that, but Bell ultimately gets the nod, and the other person is by-passed."

"You're suggesting someone in the Byrne organization, who is jealous of Ding-Dong's success, decides to eliminate him?"

Dillon and Suel nodded in unison. "That's exactly what we're thinking. Given the size of the Byrne Gang, there could be three or four, maybe even more people, who feel that Ding-Dong got the nod and they deserved whatever he got," Suel said.

Tiernan nodded. "That certainly makes sense and would fit nicely into what we've been dealing with. I can think of two, possibly three, individuals who would fit that scenario."

"Maybe put the word out you picked up a set of prints on the car door," Suel said.

"Or, better yet, DNA, just in case they were wearing gloves. That way, the DNA could have come from bumping against the car or reaching in with the gun and touching the doorframe, or even touching Ding-Dong himself. Maybe going through his pockets," Dillon said.

Tiernan nodded and said, "I like it. DNA from someone. Let me pull the names of the likely suspects." He spun his chair around, pulled a file drawer open, and took out three files. "Right off the top, these three would be the most likely."

He handed the files to Dillon. The files were labeled by name, Kevin O'Neill, Brennan Hogan, and Dara Boyle. Dillon handed the O'Neill file to Suel and opened the Hogan file. A black and white photo of Brennan Hogan was the first item in the file.

The photo had been taken on the street. Hogan stood on the sidewalk chatting with two other men. He was a heavy-set man in what looked like a large black t-shirt stretched tight over his massive stomach and jeans. In his left hand, he held a dog leash with what appeared to be a black Labrador on the end of the leash. Hogan had close-cropped hair, three chins, and a Celtic cross tattooed on the bicep of his right arm. The arm was large but not necessarily muscular.

"Besides eating a lot of pizza and candy, what does Brennan Hogan do?" Dillon asked.

Tiernan chuckled and said, "He never met a meal he didn't like, never missed a meal for that matter. What does he do? He basically is in charge of the day-to-day collections for the Byrne protection racket. He has a team of very efficient individuals who collect funds, payment if you will, and theoretically provide protection to businesses in the district. It's no secret that he was hoping to move up the ladder. Your man Ding-Dong definitely bypassed him. That said, the two of them spent a good deal of time together socially. Rumor has it Ding Dong was instrumental in providing companions for Hogan, if you get what that means."

"Companions? You mean women?" Dillon said. Tiernan nodded. "Good Lord, can you imagine the likes of Hogan rolling over on you in the middle of the night?"

"I'd prefer not to," Suel said. "And this knacker, Dara Boyle." Suel set the open file on the desk. The file photo showed a thirty something year old man, blonde hair, heavy but not fat, more of a solid muscular build. He had a large tattoo on the left side of his neck.

"Yeah, Boyle. He's one of the enforcers for your man Jimmy Byrne. He's a tough guy. Involved in at least twenty assaults over the years. Those are just the ones that have been reported. God only knows how many he's actually committed. He's been instrumental in taking over the Dodder Demons' territory, threatening the people who'd been paying them. Definitely someone looking to move up in the ranks. Dennis Bell isn't, or rather wasn't, capable of being part of the muscle of the Byrne Gang. That said, he'd moved up to the next level, and Boyle is still dealing with folks on the street."

"Which leaves Kevin O'Neill," Dillon said and opened the third file.

Tiernan shook his head. "He's the strange one. I say that only because he's university educated. Very bright lad. Comes from a good family. He's been employed for the past three years by Robert McCain. That's actually the name of a small accounting agency. They have one client, namely Jimmy Byrne. Byrne encouraged McCain to hire Kevin O'Neill. Byrne is actually Kevin O'Neill's uncle. O'Neill keeps his hands clean as far as action on the street goes. That said, he's no doubt learning the ropes as far as cooking the books for Jimmy Byrne. I added O'Neill to the list only because all four were at the same level up until Ding-Dong Bell got promoted. Of the three, he would be the least suspect but still a possibility."

TWENTY-THREE

They were driving back to Special Branch. Dillon was behind the wheel.

"What do you think?" he asked.

Suel had an open file on his lap with copies of the three photos and pertinent information on each individual. "My initial thought is we check out either Dara Boyle or Brennan Hogan. Just based on the activities they're involved in, they would seem to be the more likely individuals. Of course, this is all speculation, so who knows? But let's at least take a look at those two."

Dillon's phone suddenly rang. He ignored it, and eventually, the ringing stopped. A moment later, the phone signaled someone had left a message. Traffic was picking up, and the last thing he needed was to pull his phone out and attempt to talk. Besides, they were only ten minutes from Special Branch, and he could check the message then.

"My money is on Hogan," Dillon said. "Based on his history of collecting payments for the protection racket, it looks as though he has a tendency to let his temper get the best of him. He's had a number of assault charges. Although interestingly, most of the cases were dropped. In the two most recent cases, the victims didn't show up for the hearing. Both of those cases were dismissed. It all suggests an individual who's comfortable threatening people and making good on the threats if he has to."

Suel nodded. "He's my first choice, too, with Boyle running a close second. Let's put our time and effort into Hogan. With any luck, we can get a handle on him and then check out Boyle. Are you thinking of bringing him in for questioning?"

"We could do that, but my fear is he'll show up with a solicitor and refuse to answer anything we ask."

"Yeah, although he could get so pissed off, he'd shout something we could use or threaten us, but that's a long shot. Might be better to track him down and see where it goes. Worst scenario is he refuses to talk, and then we can haul him in. He'll get his solicitor, but even if he doesn't tell us anything, we'll be no further behind."

Dillon pulled into the secure parking area, and they headed up to Special Branch. As they stepped into the office, DCI McCabe was just coming out of the break room. He gave them a wave, signaling they should join him in his office.

"Shite," Suel said under his breath as he flashed a smile, and they headed for McCabe's office.

"Take a seat, gentleman, and bring me up to date. You met with DCI O'Brien?"

Dillon shook his head. "No, sir. We met with DI Ward Tiernan. He's heading up the investigation on the

Dennis Bell murder. They're coming up empty-handed as well, and we shared our thoughts about the murderer possibly being a contemporary of Bell's, someone in the Byrne Gang."

"And what did he think?" McCabe said.

"He thought it was worth a try. Up till now, no one has come up with anyone credible from the Dodder Demons. The possibility of an in-house execution by a contemporary makes sense, and by the end of today, the information regarding the contents of Bell's safety deposit box will be out there, and a search for whoever killed him is going to slow down if not stop altogether," Suel said.

"Any idea who may fit the bill?"

"We've got three names. Two seem to be more likely than the third, but we'll check them all out."

"I'd say that's at least a little better than our last conversation."

"One can only hope," Dillon said.

"Thank you for the update. Please continue to keep me posted," McCabe said by way of dismissal.

Back at Suel's desk, Dillon said, "You interested in finding this fat ass Hogan and chatting him up?"

"Let's do it. His file lists him as a permanent resident of The Manhole."

"That's the name of a pub?"

"Can you think of a better place to find the likes of Brennan Hogan?"

"I see your point. You know how to get there?"

Suel nodded. "I'm sorry to say, in my much younger days, I wandered in on a rare occasion. Let me just say the place is well-named."

The Manhole Pub was located in a two-story building at least a hundred years old. The corner of the building was actually at a forty-five-degree angle, with the second story supported by an iron post. The black door entrance was just behind the iron post. The pub name, minus the letter H, was in black letters across the front of the building: MAN OLE PUB.

"That actually might be an improvement on the name of this place," Dillon said as he climbed out of Suel's car.

"That letter has been missing as long as I can remember," Suel said.

Suel pushed the wooden door open and stepped inside. A bar ran the length of the narrow room. Worn bar stools were arranged along the bar. Two older men sat at the bar talking to one another. Half-finished pints of Guinness rested in front of them. At the far end, a guy, maybe fifty, sat on a bar stool with his back against the wall. His eyes were closed, and Dillon thought he could hear a mild snore.

The gray-haired female bartender behind the bar didn't seem to mind. "What'll it be, lads?" she said, raising her eyebrows, leaning forward, and resting her elbows on the bar. She smiled and moved her elbows, exposing a little more cleavage.

"We're looking for Brennan Hogan," Suel said.

She stood, shot a quick look toward a booth in the far corner of the room, and said, "Is he expecting youse?"

"He said he'd love to chat," Suel said and headed toward the booth. A black Labrador was stretched out on the floor, asleep. As they approached, two muscular men slid out of the booth and stood facing them. One of them had what looked like a tire track tattooed from his neck up to his hairline on the left side of his face. The other guy had a shaved head and wore a nose ring.

"Well, as I live and breathe. Connor Ginty, when did you get out?" Suel said to the guy with the nose ring.

"DI Suel? I swear on my mother's grave. Whatever it is you're investigating, I wasn't involved."

"Ah, now, Connor, not to worry. I checked, lad. You've been on the straight and narrow for almost a week, at least I think so. I just stopped by to tell you to keep up the good work."

Ginty seemed to relax and nodded. "Honest, I have. Thanks for the kind words."

The man standing next to him gave Ginty a look and shook his head.

"Say, Connor, as long as we're here, we'd like to chat with your friend, Mr. Hogan. It'll just take a moment. Would you let him know we're here?"

"I heard you. Just when I thought I was having a nice day. It's okay, lads. Maybe get me another Guinness and some pub grub. This won't take long."

Once they moved toward the bar, Dillon and Suel slid into the booth opposite Brennan Hogan. His large stomach was pressed up against the table. It seemed clear to Dillon that the photo in the file was taken at least a hundred pounds ago. Hogan now had four chins, and his fingers looked like bratwurst sausages. He was centered in the middle of the booth, eliminating any semblance of room for someone on either side. He wore a gray sweatshirt that was grimy around the collar and his wrists. A number of what looked like gravy stains dripped down the front of the garment.

"Whatever happened, I wasn't there," he said as they slid into the booth.

"Interesting, your name came up when we were talking about Dennis Bell," Suel said.

"No surprise. We were friends. Worked together from time to time. I miss the lad. Really, I do."

"We heard you might be taking his place," Dillon said.

Hogan studied him for a moment. "You an American? Things here getting that bad?" he said, looking at Suel. "To answer your question, I've no idea what it is you're going on about. Dennis was a good friend, and we were both between employment opportunities."

"Between employment opportunities? Really? That's not what Jimmy Byrne told us. He said you were doing a hell of a job. Spoke very highly of you."

"Who can blame him?" Hogan said. "Look, lads, anything I can do to help you catch the bastard what done

Dennis in, you just let me know. We've no idea who's responsible yet. But we'll find out. Until then, I would suggest you get on with your investigation and find the knacker before we do. Because once we find him, justice will be quick and sweet."

"Anyone in particular you think might be good for it?" Dillon pressed.

As Hogan shook his head, his chins jiggled back and forth. Once he stopped shaking his head, they jiggled a second or two longer. "Ahh, just in time. A little snack to keep me going," Hogan said as the muscle-bound thug, Ginty, placed a large bowl of mashed potatoes with plenty of melted butter on the table. The thug with the tire track tattoo set a pint glass of Guinness down. Hogan slid the glass across the table, picked it up, and drained almost half.

"Nice chatting with you, Brennan. We'll be in touch," Suel said.

Dillon slid out of the booth, and Suel followed.

"Mind yourself, Connor," Suel said to Ginty.

"We'll be back, Mr. Hogan," Dillon said.

They headed out of the pub. A blue plastic bag with what appeared to be a fairly fresh dog dropping rested beneath the windshield wiper on the driver's side of Suel's car.

"Mother of God," Suel growled. "I ought to take this back into the pub and feed it to Hogan." He lifted the wiper, grabbed the bag, and tossed it onto the curb.

"I thought they were nice guys," Dillon laughed.

TWENTY-FOUR

Back at Special Branch, Dillon and Suel were paging through the file on Dara Boyle, another contemporary of Dennis Bell who had been by-passed for a higher position in the Byrne Gang. It was now after 5:00, and they were still coming up empty-handed as far as finding a place where Boyle hung out.

"Let me give a call to Ward Tiernan at Tallaght station. Maybe he knows of a place," Dillon said and took out his phone. "Oh, Jesus, I completely forgot about this."

"What?" Suel said.

"When we were driving back after talking to Tiernan. I had a phone call and let it drop into voice messaging. The call was from Noel Leonard at Dublin Morgue. God, I can't believe I forgot about it. He called me hours ago."

"He left a message, didn't he?"

"Yeah, hang on a second. Let me see if I can reach him." Dillon brought up the number for Dublin Morgue on his cell and tapped the screen. The phone rang at least a half-dozen times, and he thought he was about to be dropped into voicemail when a familiar voice answered, "Dublin City Morgue."

"Hi, Noel?"

"Dillon, glad you called back. You got my message?"

"It's on my phone, but I haven't listened to it yet. I was driving when you called and then got involved in a case, the Dennis Bell murder, actually."

"Oh, well, that's interesting, only because we had a call from Rom Massey just after the noon hour. They—"

"Rom Massey? The funeral directors?" Dillon said.

"Yeah, they removed Patrick O'Shea's body. They were here right around 1:00 this afternoon."

"What?" Dillon said, half-shouting and leaning forward on his desk. Suel looked over from his desk and hurried over. "Where did they take the body? Is there a funeral? Who in the hell authorized this?"

"Calm down, Dillon. Everything was by the book. Next of kin contacted them. I've got the paperwork here. A man listed as Sean O'Shea. He's apparently the next of kin, a brother, I believe."

"Did they take the body to a funeral home? Rom Massey has a number of locations. I wonder if—"

"No, that's one of the reasons I called. First, I wanted to let you know Rom Massey was here to transport the body and the other reason was they were taking O'Shea to Mount Jerome."

"Mount Jerome? I'm not following. What am I missing here?"

"It's a cemetery and a crematorium. The body is going to be cremated. In fact, it may well have been by now. I've no information regarding a funeral service, but that's not unusual."

"Mount Jerome, you said?"

"Yes, but I'm—"

"Thanks, Noel. I'm going to try to call them now. Chat tomorrow," Dillon said and disconnected.

"I'm bringing Mount Jerome up on my phone now," Suel said then placed his cell phone against his ear. After the better part of a minute, he said, "Yes, this is DI Paddy Suel with An Garda Síochána calling regarding the cremation of a body delivered early this afternoon. Patrick O'Shea. Please call me," he said then gave his cell phone number and disconnected.

"No answer?" Dillon said.

"No, but we just might be able to catch someone there before they shut down. Let's head over. I'll drive. I know the place."

"God, I could kick myself for not returning Noel Leonard's call sooner. Damn it."

"Relax, Dillon. Beating yourself up isn't going to do any good. Besides, that's my job, and I enjoy it. Come on, let's get over there. It's in Harold's Cross, right next to Rathmines. With any luck we can be there in ten minutes."

They hurried out of the building and into Suel's car. Apparently, they'd run out of luck. Due to rush-hour traffic, it was closer to twenty minutes before they arrived at the cemetery.

"This is a Victorian cemetery, established back in the 1830s," Suel said. "I guess the cemetery business was falling on hard times forty-some years ago, so they set up the crematorium, and evidently that turned things around."

As Suel turned into the entrance, a man was in the process of padlocking the front gate. "Oh, for the love of—" Suel screeched to a stop and hurried out of the car.

"Sorry, sir. We officially close at 4:00. Gates are locked at 5:00. I'm actually almost an hour late. We open tomorrow at 8:00."

"We're with An Garda Síochána," Suel said and held out his warrant card. "We need to talk to someone at the crematorium."

"Did you have an appointment? I just locked up that building. Everyone is gone."

"No, no, we didn't have an appointment. Damn it, are they open at 8:00 tomorrow morning?"

"Yes, they are. It's a busy place. If you can believe it."

"Actually, I can. Thanks for your time. We'll be back tomorrow," Suel said.

He climbed back into the car and started the engine. "They're shut down for the day. They open at 8:00 tomorrow morning."

"What do you think the odds are they've already cremated, O'Shea?"

"Probably a hundred percent. But so what? We don't need the body. We just need the contact information on the next of kin. Put a call into your man at the American Embassy. Maybe he knows something."

"Good idea," Dillon said. As Suel pulled back onto the street and headed toward Special Branch, Dillon took out his cellphone and called Eric Bergman.

After three rings, a man's voice said, "United States Embassy."

"Hi, Eric Bergman, please."

"I'm sorry, but he's left for the day. Would you care to leave a message in his voicemail?"

Damn it, Dillon thought. "Yes, please."

"One moment, sir,"

Dillon heard a couple of clicks, and then Bergman's recording came on. "Eric Bergman. I'm sorry, but I'm unable to take your call at this time. Please leave a message, and I'll get back to you just as soon as possible."

A moment later, there was a beep, and Dillon said. "Hi, Eric. Jack Dillon calling. The time now is 5:50. Apparently, the body of Patrick O'Shea was moved from the Dublin Morgue this afternoon and delivered to Mount Jerome to be cremated. The paperwork was signed by next of kin, Sean O'Shea, Patrick's brother. Do you know if Sean O'Shea is in Ireland? And, if he is, might there be a way we could meet with him? I'm sure he has questions regarding his brother's murder, and we would like to learn anything we can regarding who was responsible. Thanks, I look forward to your call," Dillon said and disconnected.

"You interested in a pint?' Suel said.

"You mean you've got time? I just presumed you'd be linking up with Shannon Yates."

"Well, I just might be, but not until later this evening. I could buy you one. The way things seem to be going, it may be the only positive event that happens to you today."

"No doubt. You want to stop for one at the Autobahn?"

"It's a bit out of my way, but okay."

"Drop me off in the parking lot, and I'll meet you there."

Twenty minutes later, they were halfway through a pint of Guinness at a back table in the Autobahn. "I'll buy the next round if you've got the time," Dillon said.

"It's such a rare occasion when you offer to buy that I'll make the time."

"Not funny," Dillon said and gave a wave to a server just walking past. "Two pints of Guinness, please," he said.

She nodded and hurried toward the bar.

"What do you say to us meeting at Mount Jerome tomorrow morning? The moment they open the gates, we can get into the crematorium."

"I'm fine with that. What if he's still there?" Suel said.

"I don't think that's our concern. I'm more interested in the paperwork. Maybe we can determine if the brother is actually here in Dublin. I'd like to talk to him and see what he knows about his brother. For example, how was he living here? Was he making money, or was he on a trust fund or something? I still have the sense his place looked like it was staged. It just didn't have the appearance of having been lived in. Especially by a guy."

Suel nodded. "Yeah, it would be nice to talk to him. You know what else strikes me as strange? Whether he's here or not, I don't understand why we haven't been contacted. If you had a brother killed where you lived or halfway around the world, wouldn't you want to know about the investigation? Has anyone been arrested? Is there some way you could help? We haven't heard feck all from anyone."

The server arrived with the pints of Guinness. Dillon handed her a twenty euro note and said, "Keep the change."

"Aren't you the big tipper," Suel said and held his glass up for a toast. Ten minutes later, the glasses were empty, and they headed out the door.

Dillon was just two minutes from his place. As he turned onto the lane, he thought about walking over to Tara's with a bottle of wine, but then he drove past her house and recognized the car parked in front. The former boyfriend.

He pulled into his drive, let Lucifer out, dined on leftovers for dinner, and went to bed after the evening news. So much for a fun evening.

TWENTY-FIVE

Dillon was up before his alarm went off. He'd finished breakfast and was reviewing the O'Shea file on his laptop when Lucifer made his way downstairs. Dillon let him outside, filled a travel mug with coffee, and then coaxed Lucifer back in the house with a biscuit. He was parked at the front gate of Mount Jerome Cemetery a full half-hour before it was scheduled to open. Suel arrived twenty-nine minutes later. The man Suel spoke with the night before suddenly appeared, unlocked, and opened the front gates.

Both Dillon and Suel gave him a wave as they drove past and made their way to the crematorium. They parked next to the entrance, stepped inside, and headed to the receptionist counter. The woman at the counter was just removing a tea bag from her mug.

"Good morning. How may I help you?" she said, apparently unable to hide the surprised look on her face at the appearance of visitors this early in the morning.

"An Garda Síochána," Suel said, holding out his warrant card. "We'd like to talk to someone regarding a cremation yesterday. We need to look at the paperwork."

"Was there a problem?"

"If we could speak with whoever is in charge, please," Suel said.

"Let me see if Mr. Murphy is available," she said and punched some numbers on the phone. "Yes, good morning, sir. I have two gentlemen out here with An Garda Síochána. They have some questions regarding a cremation done yesterday." As she said that last bit, she looked up at Suel.

Suel nodded and smiled.

"Yes, sir. I will. Thank you." She disconnected and said, "He'll see you now. If you'll follow me, please." She stepped out from behind the counter and led them down a short hall. An open office door was at the end of the hall, and she stepped inside. Dillon and Suel followed.

A man with dark, curly hair stood and stepped out from behind the desk. "Thank you, Megan," he said, dismissing the receptionist and focusing in on Dillon and Suel. "I'm Jim Murphy, manager." He smiled and extended his hand. As they shook, he said, "Is there a problem with licensing or equipment updates? We've been in business for almost forty years."

"No, sir. Nothing like that. We believe a cremation was performed yesterday on a gentleman by the name of Patrick O'Shea."

"Oh, yes, the American. Tragic, a murder victim, I believe."

"Yes, that's correct. We'd like to look at the paperwork if we may. We've had a devil of a time trying to connect with family, and it's our understanding that the paperwork was signed by O'Shea's brother."

"I believe that's correct, but if you'll follow me, we can take a look," Murphy said, leading the way out of his office.

"Did you or anyone actually meet the brother?" Dillon asked.

"No, in fact, the payment for service was made by a credit card in the United States. That includes the cremation and then placing the ashes in the columbarium."

"I'm sorry, what exactly is the columbarium?" Suel said.

"It's a room or building with niches for funeral urns to be stored. Along with payment for the cremation, the next of kin, in this case, a brother, I believe, paid for the space in the columbarium."

"Is there a funeral service scheduled?" Dillon asked.

"Not that I'm aware of," Murphy said as he shook his head. He opened a door that was labeled records, and they stepped inside. A redheaded woman seated at a desk looked up.

"Gemma, these gentlemen are with An Garda Síochána. They would like to examine the O'Shea paperwork from yesterday," Murphy said.

"Is there a problem?" she asked, stepping over to a counter. She pulled three manila file folders from a multi-tiered shelf. She took the middle file from the stack and handed it to Murphy, who in turn handed it to Suel.

"That's the entirety of our records. If you want copies, everything is online, and we can email the file to you."

Suel opened up the file, glanced over the first page, and turned to the next page. He pointed at something and handed the file to Dillon.

Dillon looked at the signature Suel had pointed to, Sean O'Shea, written in black ink with the name spelled out in block letters below the signature. "So, Mr. O'Shea. Sean O'Shea was here," Dillon said.

Murphy shook his head. "No, he was not. That paperwork is from Rom Massey. But I follow the gist of your question, and Mr. O'Shea would have been there to sign the paperwork. The paperwork accompanied the body of," Murphy glanced over Dillon's shoulder at the file, "the body of Patrick O'Shea."

"And this would have been done yesterday?" Dillon said.

"No, I believe," Murphy scanned the paperwork. "Yes, based on the date, the paperwork was completed forty-eight hours ago. The following day, yesterday, the Rom Massey hearse obtained the body from Dublin Morgue and delivered it to us. We performed the cremation late yesterday. Mr. O'Shea's ashes will be interred in the columbarium later today."

"Is there a service, some sort of formal procedure?" Dillon said.

"Oh, there certainly can be, and from any one of a number of religious faiths, although nothing is scheduled, which is not usual. Usually, we see this when someone born here in Ireland lived abroad and wanted to be returned to the isle. Cremation is the logical method and, dare I say, the most affordable."

"So no one here saw or dealt with Sean O'Shea?" Dillon said.

"That is correct. You may want to check with Rom Massey. The paperwork is from their facility on Mobhi Road if you know where that is," Murphy said.

"I do, as a matter of fact. Right next door to the Grape Vine wine store," Dillon said.

"Yes, exactly," Murphy said.

Dillon handed a business card to Gemma and said, "If you would be so kind as to email me a copy of this file, I would appreciate it."

"I'll do it right now," she said and began running her fingers across her keyboard.

"Mr. Murphy, thank you very much. You've been a big help, and thank you for the education," Suel said.

They both shook hands with Murphy, thanked Gemma, and headed out the door and down the hall. They called "Thank you" to the woman behind the reception counter and hurried to their cars.

"You know where this place is?" Dillon asked.

"Yeah, not far from your home. I might stop in the Grape Vine and buy some wine afterward if we've got a moment. I'm entertaining this evening," Suel said and grinned.

"I'll see you at Rom Massey. First one there waits for the other," Dillon said.

Suel nodded and climbed into his car. Dillon watched him take off before he slid behind the wheel of his car. He was about to start his car when his cellphone rang. He pulled it out, Eric Bergman calling.

"Hi Eric, Thanks for calling."

"Sorry I wasn't in last night. We've got four folks from the House of Representatives in town, so I'm on a short leash. You said in your message that paperwork had been signed regarding the body of Patrick O'Shea. Don't quote me, but can't that be done electronically?"

"I presume so, but Suel and I just left the cremation site. We reviewed their file, and the paperwork appeared to have actually been signed by someone in person."

"I've got a call into passport control. They're checking their records for a Sean O'Shea passport. I may not hear back from them until late today or tomorrow."

"Let me know as soon as you know anything," Dillon said. They chatted for another half-minute and then disconnected.

TWENTY-SIX

Dillon pulled in behind Suel's car. They were parked in front of the hardware store next to the Rom Massey funeral home on Mobhi Road. The wine shop, the Grape Vine, was at the other end of the building. Suel was leaning against the back of his car, watching Dillon as he pulled in.

"Well, it's about time," Suel said as Dillon stepped out of his car.

"Yeah, sorry about that. I got a phone call from Eric Bergman just as you pulled away."

"Bergman? What did he say? Did he have a line on O'Shea's brother?"

"I only wish. He placed a call to Passport Control, but it will be the end of the day or tomorrow before he hears anything."

"That figures. Well, let's get this over with. If the brother was here, we'll probably find out he flew back to the US yesterday."

Dillon led the way into Rom Massey. The windows were tinted on the facility, so it was impossible to see inside. They stepped into a small lobby with three couches arranged around a coffee table. A young woman was seated at a desk against the far wall. She flashed a bright, sparkling smile as they approached.

"Good morning, and welcome to Rom Massey. How may I help you?"

"Hi, we're with An Garda Síochána, and we would like to talk with someone regarding the transport of a body from Dublin Morgue to the Mount Jerome facility yesterday afternoon."

The sparkling smile immediately disappeared. "Let me get our manager for you," she said and punched in two numbers on the desk phone. She glanced up at Dillon and Suel as she spoke, "Yes, sir. There are two gentlemen with An Garda Síochána in the lobby, and they would like to talk to you regarding the transport from Dublin Morgue yesterday. Yes, sir. Very well. Thank you." She hung up the phone, flashed a quick smile, and said, "Mr. Fulham will be out in just a moment."

She wasn't kidding. About ten seconds later, a man in a dark suit stepped into the lobby, nodded, and held out his hand. "Good morning, I'm Dennis Fulham. What seems to be the problem?" he said as he shook hands with Dillon and then Suel.

"Nice to meet you," Dillon said and handed his warrant card to Fulham.

"Thank you, not necessary," Fulham said.

"Actually, there isn't a problem. We're hoping you might be able to help us. The transportation of Patrick O'Shea yesterday to Mount Jerome was apparently arranged by his brother Sean O'Shea. We're trying to locate Mr. O'Shea and provide him with an update on his brother's, umm, passing."

"Yes, that dreadful shooting over in Finglas."

"Yes, would you have any contact information for Sean O'Shea?"

Fulham seemed to think for a moment. "Let's go back to my office. I've got the file. I'm not sure we have what you're looking for, but it would be best for you to make that determination. This way, please," Fulham said and headed back the way he came.

Dillon and Suel followed him down a hall, past what appeared to be a large reception room with an open coffin at the far end. Two large flower arrangements were positioned at either end of the coffin. Just now, the room was empty, with the exception of a man running a vacuum cleaner over the carpet.

Fulham stepped into an office and closed the door behind them. "Have a seat, gentleman," he said as he stepped behind his desk. He paged through a half-dozen files on a credenza. "Yes, here we are. Payment in full, American Express. Sean O'Shea. No address but there is a phone number," he said, handing the file over to Dillon.

Dillon opened the file. There were a total of four pages. One was the payment receipt for transporting Patrick O'Shea's body to Mount Jerome. Two pages were Rom Massey's policy with Sean O'Shea's signature at the bottom. The last page had an email address for Sean O'Shea and a phone number.

"Would it be possible to get a copy of this page?" Dillon asked as he handed the last page with the phone number to Fulham.

"Not a problem," Fulham said. "Bear with me while I bring this up on the computer and print it off." He ran his fingers across the keyboard, clicked on the mouse a couple of times, and suddenly the printer next to his desktop screen began to hum.

"You met Mr. O'Shea?" Suel asked.

Fulham nodded. "He was here for about a half-hour. This would have been three days ago. Nice enough lad, although, how can I say? He was definitely in charge. We got along just fine, but I wouldn't want to cross him."

"Did he mention anything regarding his brother's murder or home, anything on a personal note?" Dillon asked.

Fulham shook his head. "No, nothing like that. I did find it interesting that he referred to me as "sir" a number of times. A bit formal, but then, we see all sorts of reactions and behaviors in this business."

"And the credit card he used was his?" Suel asked.

Fulham nodded and opened the file. "Yes, in fact, we have an image of it on the back of the receipt. I'll print a copy of it for you," he said and handed the receipt to Suel. The image of O'Shea's American Express card was printed in color. The card was gray, American Express Platinum. The name above O'Shea's was Bridge Street Capital.

Once copies of O'Shea's email address, phone number, and credit card were printed, Dillon and Suel left their business cards with Fulham, who then led them back out to the lobby. They shook hands and left.

"We're still grasping at straws," Suel said as they headed back to their cars.

"I'm going to call his number now. Sooner or later, something has to click in this case. Keep your fingers crossed that he's still in Dublin," Dillon said and pulled out his cellphone. He punched in the number for Sean O'Shea and waited. A moment later, there was an odd sound and then a recording, "We're sorry. The number you have dialed is not in service. Message number 22595" Click.

"Busy? You didn't leave a message?" Suel said.

"Just a recording that says the number is not in service."

"Maybe he's got it turned off because he's over here and doesn't want to pay the price for an international call."

"Yeah, maybe. Or what's more likely is he got a burner phone that he used for about thirty-six hours until his brother was cremated, and once that was done, he tossed it in the trash."

"You're making him sound like some kind of criminal."

"I'm beginning to wonder. He was at Rom Massey three days ago and never contacted anyone regarding our investigation," Dillon said.

"I'm thinking there's a good chance your man O'Shea has already headed back to the States. We're only a few minutes from the club where Byrne's enforcer, Dara Boyle, hangs. Might be worth a stop to see if he's there. Otherwise, we've got feck all to look at."

"How 'bout I drop my car at Special Branch, and you drive?" Dillon said.

"Happy to be your chauffeur," Suel said.

TWENTY-SEVEN

Dillon parked in the security lot at Special Branch and climbed into Suel's car. Tallaght Trainers was a boxing club Dara Boyle regularly visited. It was the only place listed in his file. The boxing club was a one-story gray stucco building in a quasi-industrial park. The stucco walls were covered with graffiti, making most of it impossible to read.

"Of all the places to spray paint shit, this would seem to be one of the worst ideas," Dillon said as Suel parked.

"Can you imagine what some of these guys would do if they caught you spray painting on their boxing club?"

"Maybe that's why it hasn't been covered up. They're hoping it attracts graffiti artists, and then they get to beat the hell out of them. Let me look at that picture of Dara Boyle again," Dillon said.

Suel pointed at the file wedged between the console and the passenger seat. Dillon opened the file and studied the image of Boyle. He was a solid-looking, muscular man in his mid-thirties with blonde hair and a large tattoo on the left side of his neck. Given the angle of the photograph, it was impossible to make out what the tattoo was.

"Let's see if he's here," Suel said, and they headed into Tallaght Trainers.

There was nothing like a reception counter, a smiling receptionist, or a separate door leading to the gym area. They stepped into a large room with four boxing rings. Three of the rings had guys sparring in them. Off to the side were a half-dozen boxing bags and two weight machines. A number of guys were standing around the rings, watching the sparring.

Dillon was aware of more than one person saying something to the men standing around and then everyone glancing over at him and Suel. A couple of heads shook, and one guy didn't run but quickly walked toward a back door. It took a good ten seconds, but the word was out that the Guards were here.

"Over there on the left," Suel said. "Your man with the brown leather jacket leaning on the ring. I think that's him."

Dillon glanced over to the far ring. Sure enough, it had to be Dara Boyle against the base of the ring, talking to one of the boxers who was nodding politely. The tattoo on Boyle's neck was obvious from where Dillon stood, a human skull with what appeared to be a snake wrapped around it. *How charming*, Dillon thought.

He headed toward the ring with Suel behind him. As they approached, two men next to Boyle said something to him and hurried around to the far side of the ring.

Boyle gave a quick glance at Dillon and Suel, frowned, and said something to the boxer in the ring, who walked over to a stool in the corner and sat down.

"Dara Boyle?" Dillon said.

"That'd be me," Boyle said without looking at Dillon.

"We'd like to have a word with you. No problem where you're concerned. It's simply a question regarding Dennis Bell."

"Well, in case you haven't heard, some bastard shot Ding-Dong a week ago."

"We're aware of that. We were wondering if you had any idea who might have done it."

Boyle looked over at Dillon and scoffed. "Jaysus, who in the hell do you think did it. Those Dodder bastards had to be the ones. Everyone loved Ding-Dong, except for those planks. Give me a pass for forty-eight hours, and I'll grab the little twat and string him up, right and proper like."

"If you know who's responsible, we can—"

"Were you even listening? I told you, the bleedin' Dodder bastards, for Christ's sake. No wonder youse are always behind the pitch. You've no idea. Now, if you'll excuse me, I'm trying to help a lad out here."

"Good talking to you, Boyle. Mind yourself," Suel said and smiled when Boyle looked over and glared at him. "We best be off, Dillon. There's feck all to get here."

Dillon studied the skull and snake tattoo on Boyle's neck for a second, nodded, and they headed back out the door. At least this time, there wasn't a bag of dog poop under the windshield wiper when they got to Suel's car.

"Any thoughts?" Dillon said as they climbed into the car.

"Yeah, we don't seem to be getting anywhere."

"You think your man's anger was legit?" Dillon said.

"I'd say it was. Either that, or he's an awfully good actor. He seemed justifiably upset. I'm thinking if I got one of those tattoos, it might attract all kinds of women," Suel said.

"Yeah, and not the kind that would be worth anything. Who in their right mind gets a skull with a snake wrapped around it on their neck?"

Suel shook his head. "Hey, you mind if we take a quick detour on the way back to the office?"

"Don't tell me you want to go back to Rom Massey and buy wine at the Grape Vine."

"No, nothing like that. You got a phone number for Ronan Mullen in Finglas?"

Dillon nodded. "Mullen, yeah, I got his number. What are you thinking?"

"What if O'Shea's brother was actually here? Wouldn't it make sense that he paid a visit to his brother's house? Maybe he even slept there. You'd think there'd be personal items there. Photos of the family, jewelry, something along those lines."

"You know, that's a damn good idea. Hang on, let me see if I can get him," Dillon said. He took his phone out, made the call, and put his phone on speaker.

Mullen answered on the second ring. "Dillon, great to hear from you. Tell me you've got something on the Patrick O'Shea murder."

"We've got an idea," Dillon said. "Are you aware the body was moved from Dublin Morgue to Mount Jerome for cremation?"

"What? When the hell did this happen?"

"A couple of days ago. Apparently, O'Shea's brother ordered it. He was here in Dublin and contacted Rom Massey to transport the body. Paid for cremation with an American Express credit card. We're hoping we can catch up with him and talk to him if he's still in Dublin. But we've no idea where he might be. We thought it might be a good idea if we checked out O'Shea's place. Maybe he's there or was there."

"I can't believe this. We had no idea. Why the hell didn't anyone contact us?"

"The only way we found out is one of the docs at the Morgue, an intern actually, let me know." Dillon didn't mention he left the phone message unanswered for hours and didn't learn of the cremation until the following morning. "Anyway, we're thinking of heading over to the O'Shea house. Can you meet us there with the keys? We're leaving Tallaght now."

"I can be there in ten minutes. See you then," Mullen said and disconnected.

"Good idea, Paddy. Mullen had no idea the body was cremated."

"Yeah, I just hope to God we find something."

"I hope we find this brother," Dillon said.

TWENTY-EIGHT

They pulled up to the O'Shea house. Mullen's car was parked in front.

"He's probably inside," Dillon said as they hurried up the sidewalk. Dillon recalled the Blue 2021 Mercedes Benz E300 that had been parked in the driveway his first time here. The front door was open maybe an inch. As Dillon stepped inside, he glanced into the empty sitting room and called, "Ronan, DI Mullen?"

"Is that you, Dillon?"

"Yeah."

"I'm back in the kitchen," Mullen said, stating the obvious.

They walked past the staircase leading up to the second floor and through the open door into the dining area. The first thing Dillon noticed was that the bottom wooden panel covering the shattered glass door leading into the back garden was pulled away from the doorframe. Mullen was leaning against the kitchen counter. He gave them a nod. He was wearing latex gloves and was on his cellphone. "No, I need forensics out here today. I got word not thirty minutes ago that a brother from the US was in Dublin. I suspect it may have been him.

Yes. All right. Thank you. I'll be here waiting," he said and shook his head as he ended the call.

"Ronan, do you know my partner, DI Paddy Suel? Paddy, this is DI Ronan Mullen with Finglas. He's in charge of this investigation," Dillon said.

"Nice to meet you," Mullen said and shook his head. "We've got a kitchen sink full of dirty dishes. Someone made a pot of coffee, and as you can see, they pulled the panel away from the backdoor and got in that way."

"Logic would suggest it was the brother," Dillon said. "He didn't contact the station asking what was happening in the investigation?"

"Absolutely not. The first I heard of him was your phone call. I came over here and found this mess. Look at this place."

An empty ice cream carton was on top of a pile of trash in the wastebasket. Dillon walked over to the kitchen sink and looked at the stack of dishes and mugs. "Five plates. I would guess he was here for at least two or three days. Could he have gained access to that Mercedes that was parked in the drive?"

"He could, but he hasn't. I called them just before I called forensics. The car is still locked up in the impound lot."

"You check upstairs?"

Mullen shook his head. "Just a quick look to make sure no one was up there. I'm still going through the kitchen. Looks like two chicken breasts, a pork steak, potatoes, coffee, pizzas, and some ice cream. That's the packaging I found in the wastebasket. It was empty last time I was here. Oh, and at least part of a bottle of Paddy's whiskey. I checked the freezer, just ice cubes and a bag of frozen veg left in there."

"We'll check upstairs," Dillon said. He pulled a pair of latex gloves from a box on the kitchen counter.

Suel slipped on a pair of gloves, and they headed upstairs to the two bedrooms. Everything looked the same in the larger bedroom based on what Dillon could remember. The sheets, blanket, and pillows were missing from the bed, but Dillon had told Mullen about the thong he'd discovered in the bed, and Mullen had contacted forensics to grab the bed linens.

"Everything looks the same," Dillon said. "This is the bed where I found the thong. Forensics are checking the sheets. I know they searched the drawers and the wardrobe. There really wasn't anything out of the ordinary up here except for some condoms in a bathroom drawer."

Suel stepped out of the bedroom and into the smaller bedroom. "Hey, Jack, check this out," he called.

Dillon hurried into the other bedroom. The bed, which he recalled as having been made, was now disheveled as if someone had slept in it. The other thing was a series of small cloth squares, maybe two inches by two inches, half crumpled up on the floor.

"Check this out," Suel said and nodded at the mess on the floor.

"Oh, Christ," Dillon said. He picked up one of the squares and sniffed it. "Yeah, gun cleaning patches. Whoever was in here was cleaning a gun. I'd guess a pistol."

"I'm thinking the brother, Sean was staying here. Low profile, obviously no receipt trail from a hotel or bed and breakfast."

"We might want to check the airport car rentals," Dillon said. "If he's been cleaning a gun, it's not a huge leap to suggest he intends to use it."

"You think he brought it over from the States?"

"I suppose it's possible, but it wouldn't be easy unless maybe he disassembled it or somehow had it shipped over. It might make more sense that he purchased it once he got here. Maybe he had a tighter relationship with his brother than we realized, and it was hidden here somewhere. If he's still in the country, my guess is he'll be looking for whoever killed the brother."

"Hell, we can't find out who did it. How in the hell is some guy coming in from the States going to know? Has he ever even been here before?"

"Let's see what we can find out," Dillon said and pulled out his phone. He pressed the screen twice and put the phone to his ear. "Yes, this is Marshal Jack Dillon with Dublin An Garda Síochána, Special Branch. I'd like to speak with Eric Bergman, please." A moment later, Dillon said, "Thank you."

"Is he in?" Suel said.

Dillon nodded and suddenly said, "Hi, Eric, thanks for taking my call. Some things have come up in the Patrick O'Shea murder investigation. We're in O'Shea's house, and someone has been sleeping here and cooking meals, maybe two or three days' worth. We suspect it's his brother, Sean O'Shea. On top of that, we've found what appears to be remnants of gun cleaning. What? No, but patches on the floor and the smell of gun cleaning solvent. Yeah, I'd appreciate that. As soon as you hear anything, let me know. Also, if you could email his passport image to me once you get it. I think we had better get the word out. Okay, thanks. I'll catch you later."

"Did he have anything on O'Shea's arrival?"

"No, not yet, but he's going to put some pressure on."

"O'Shea was in the army, wasn't he?" Suel said.

"Yeah, three tours in Afghanistan. Special Forces."

"Oh, God. So he knows his way around weapons."

"Yeah, for sure, and not the sort of person you'd want to mess with."

They checked the bathroom and didn't find anything. They went downstairs, talked with DI Mullen for a few minutes, and told him about the unmade bed and the gun cleaning.

Mullen just shook his head. "Forensics promised to be here within the next two hours, which probably means it will be three hours. I want to be here when they arrive. I'll have them check out that mess upstairs. I don't like the sound of all this. I've got the uncomfortable feeling we may be dealing with someone who knows exactly what he's doing."

Dillon nodded. "The American embassy is checking with passport control. Hopefully, we'll get a handle on when Sean O'Shea arrived and how often he's been here. Keep your fingers crossed and pray he's not familiar with Dublin."

"Who knows what kind of contact he had with his brother. We still haven't found a cellphone, a computer, or any semblance of mail," Mullen said.

"Please keep us in the loop, Ronan. We learn anything, we'll pass it on," Dillon said, and they headed out the door.

"What do you think?" Dillon said as Suel started the car.

"I think we had better find this guy and fast. I don't like the sound of any of this," Suel said and pulled away from the curb.

Back in Special Branch, Dillon searched for online information on Sean O'Shea. He didn't find a thing. He phoned Chris Becker, a pal with the US Marshal's back in the States, and ended up leaving a message.

Suel strolled over to Dillon's desk. "Any luck with your friend over in the States?"

"Had to leave a message. It's the noon hour over there, so with any luck, he'll call me back today. I left my cellphone number."

"I'm at a stopping point and going to head out. You hear anything, give me a call."

"You meeting up with Shannon tonight?"

"We might have a conversation."

"Yeah, that's what you want, a conversation."

"She's coming over for dinner, so we'll see how it goes."

"Well, good luck. Hopefully, it will be a quiet night on this end. I'm heading home in a bit. I'll see you in the morning," Dillon said.

Suel grinned and hurried out of the office.

Dillon was headed home forty-five minutes later. He debated grabbing a quick dinner at the Autobahn, decided against it, and turned onto his lane. No former boyfriend's car in front of Tara's house tonight, and her car was in the drive. He thought a visit to her after dinner might be just the thing.

He let Lucifer out into the front garden, found a pork steak and a potato that didn't appear to be spoiled in the back of the refrigerator, and ate dinner in front of the TV.

He showered, splashed on some aftershave, pulled on a clean shirt, grabbed a bottle of red wine, and knocked on Tara's door.

"Oh, Dillon, what a pleasant surprise and perfect timing," she said just as his cellphone rang.

"Oh, sorry, let me just get rid of this call," he said, handing her the bottle of wine. "This is Dillon," he said into his phone.

"Dillon, DCI O'Brien. Sorry to interrupt your evening but thought you should know. We're at the Manhole

Pub. There's been a shooting, three shootings, to be exact. Your man Brennan Hogan and two compatriots have been killed."

"You're at the Manhole?"

"Yes, just got here. This happened forty-five minutes ago."

"I'll see you in fifteen minutes," Dillon said and disconnected. "Sorry, Tara, I've got to run. You can keep the wine," he said.

"But I was hoping we—"

Dillon had already disappeared around the hedge, literally running to his car.

TWENTY-NINE

Dillon had to park almost a block away from the Manhole Pub. He took his ID with the lanyard from the glove compartment and headed toward the Manhole. The street was blocked by police vehicles, a forensics van, and a number of unmarked cars. Uniformed officers were keeping a curious crowd at bay. He worked his way through the crowd, saying, "Excuse me, pardon me, thank you."

"Sorry, sir, no further. We have an investigation underway," a uniformed officer said to Dillon.

He suddenly realized he still had his ID with the lanyard in his hand. He quickly draped it around his neck and held out his warrant card.

"Oh, beg your pardon, sir. I wasn't aware. Please, go ahead,"

"Hey now," a man shouted. "What's with the likes of that bastard, and the rest of us can't—"

Dillon turned and held up his ID on the lanyard.

"Oh, sorry lad, good on ya," the man said to chuckles throughout the crowd.

Dillon got a look from most of the officers as he walked past, but no one said anything. Two officers were standing at the door. One of them studied the ID around Dillon's neck and then looked at his warrant card for a good half-minute. "All right, sir," he said as he handed the warrant card back to Dillon.

"Is DCI O'Brien inside?"

The officer nodded. "He was last time we checked unless he snuck out the back entrance."

Dillon stepped into the bar. The first thing he saw was the gray-haired woman who had been tending bar when Dillon and Suel talked to Hogan yesterday. She was seated in a booth with her back to the bodies at the end of the room. She was sipping what looked like whiskey and talking to two officers who were taking notes. A bottle of Jameson 18 that went for somewhere around a hundred and twenty-five euros a bottle was on the table next to her. *Good for her*, Dillon thought.

The bodies, there were three, were back next to the booth where Dillon and Suel had talked to Brennan Hogan for all of five minutes. He recognized Connor Ginty, the man Suel knew. He was lying on his back with a bullet hole in the middle of his forehead. A splatter of blood and brain matter had coated the wall where Ginty must have been standing. The thug who had the nose ring and the tire track tattoo was leaning against the back wall with his legs stretched out in front of him. His eyes had a glassy stare, and the left side of his chest was covered in blood.

Brennan Hogan was lying face down on the floor. Based on the rubble beneath him he'd apparently fallen onto a chair. Given his massive weight, the chair had disintegrated. One of the broken chair legs was protruding out the back of his left side. Dillon counted three bullet holes just above Hogan's left ear.

At the moment, three officers in white hooded scrubs, shoe coverings, and masks were examining the bodies. Two more officers were photographing the scene.

"So, what do you think?" a voice said.

Dillon turned to see DI Tiernan. "Ward, God, I'm sorry about this."

"You aren't kidding. Whoever did this was in and out in less than thirty seconds. Had to be professional."

"Dillon?" someone called, and Dillon turned to see DCI O'Brien coming toward them. "That was fast. You said fifteen minutes, and you weren't kidding." O'Brien wrinkled his nose and leaned toward Dillon. "Aftershave?"

"I was just out of the shower when you called. God, I can't believe this. Suel and I just spoke with Hogan in that very corner booth yesterday."

"You learn anything?"

"All we learned was Hogan had no intention of providing any information. You can see where that got him."

"Pardon me, but I've got to check with some folks," Tiernan said and hurried off.

"Hell of a mess," O'Brien said. "Whoever did this, it sure as hell wasn't their first dance, that goes without saying."

Dillon glanced around the room. "They have any security in this place? I don't see any cameras."

"No, damn it. That's why fat boy settled in and conducted all his business here. No record of who in the hell he talked with. We've no idea who arrived to pay him and now who in God's name did this. We got nothing."

"What about the bartender? I saw two men in the front booth interviewing her."

"You mean Lizzy Byrne? She's been around the block too many times. Besides, Jimmy Byrne is her nephew. They'll ask her questions and let her drink that whiskey, hoping it might loosen her up, but at the end of the day, we're not going to get anything. Whatever she knows, she's saving for her nephew, that plonker Jimmy. You have any thoughts on this?"

"Just a rough idea and a name. There was a shooting over in Finglas a week or so ago."

"Was that an American?"

"Yes, by the name of Patrick O'Shea. Anyway, I have a sense his death in some way was the cause of Dennis "Ding-Dong" Bell's murder. But that's just a guess. We haven't got anything to prove it. Just a gut feeling. That said, we just found out O'Shea's brother, Sean, was and maybe still is in Dublin. He had Patrick's body transferred from Dublin Morgue to Mount Jerome and cremated a couple of days ago. This Sean O'Shea never contacted Finglas Garda with any questions about his brother's murder. We suspect Sean broke into his brother's house and stayed there for at least two or three days. What we do know is that whoever stayed there cleaned a gun, probably a pistol. The brother Sean was in the US army, in Special Forces, and served three tours in Afghanistan. He would be very proficient with firearms and quite capable of creating this event," Dillon said.

"Where is he now? We need to bring him in and question him. Find out where he was this afternoon."

"We don't know where he is. We don't even know if he's still in the country."

"When did he arrive here?"

"We're checking on that now. I was hoping to hear from passport control or the embassy, but that's not going to happen until tomorrow. I've got a call into contacts back in the States, and hopefully they'll be able to provide some information. But right now, I'm afraid we're just marking time."

"There must be something we can do. What if I made some calls?"

"Maybe if you contacted passport control and explained the situation, they would speed things up. The man's name is Sean O'Shea. We suspect he would have arrived four to seven days ago. Quite possibly flying out of Boston, Massachusetts, in the US."

"Sean O'Shea, Boston. Let me make the call now," O'Brien said. He pulled out his cellphone and walked over to the far corner of the bar.

Dillon crossed his fingers and hoped maybe O'Brien could provide the break they so desperately needed.

O'Brien was back two minutes later. He did not look happy. "Just when you need 'em, I end up leaving a damn message. I'll eat the head off 'em tomorrow when I call. God help 'em if they don't call me back."

Dillon hung around for another two hours and was no further ahead than when he first arrived. He looked around for DCI O'Brien but couldn't find him, so he walked back to his car and drove home. He debated calling Suel, but what was the point? As he turned onto his lane, he thought about going over to Tara's but almost immediately decided that was a bad idea. Besides, her car was gone.

He let Lucifer out into the front garden, and then the two of them watched the evening news. There was only a brief, thirty-second bit on the Manhole Pub. The incident was described as "an ongoing investigation into a shooting at the Manhole Pub." No further information was given. Dillon turned off the news, and he and Lucifer headed up to bed.

THIRTY

Dillon was up and cooking scrambled eggs for breakfast while listening to the news when Suel phoned. "Hi, Paddy," was how he answered the phone.

"Dillon, turn on the damn news. There was a shooting last night at the Manhole Pub."

"Yeah, I know. I was down there. I figured you—"

"What? You were at the Manhole?"

"Yeah, I got a call from DCI O'Brien."

"You should have called me. What the hell did—"

"Paddy, just think of what you were involved in last night. Oh, and by the way, it wouldn't have made a bit of difference. I spoke with Tiernan and O'Brien at the scene. They've no idea who did it. If I was watching the same news as you were, they didn't release any victim's names. By the way, it was Hogan, along with your man Connor Ginty and that guy with the tire track tattoo on the side of his face. No security cameras in the place. Oh, and get this. That woman bartender in there?"

"They didn't shoot her, did they?"

"No, they did not. But she wasn't talking much to the two officers interviewing her, and O'Brien told me that Jimmy Byrne is her nephew."

"Oh perfect, no doubt she'll be saving whatever she knows for him."

"I did see the bodies, Paddy. Your man Ginty was shot right between the eyes. The guy with the tattoo was hit in the heart, and Hogan had three rounds just above his left ear."

"Any idea on the weapon?"

"No, it was way too soon for that. My educated guess is a pistol. I was there a little more than two hours, and other than telling O'Brien the little we know about Sean O'Shea, I wasn't adding a thing."

"I'm thinking we should get down there," Suel said.

"Yeah, give me a couple minutes to eat some breakfast, and I'll meet you there. See if you can get a line on the photos and film they were taking of the scene last night. I'd like to see them. You never know what might turn up reviewing those images."

"I'm heading out now. I'll see you down there," Suel said and disconnected.

Dillon wolfed down his breakfast, coaxed Lucifer in with a biscuit, and was on his way ten minutes later. Things appeared to be a lot calmer this morning. An area was taped off in front and on either side of the Manhole, but now there were only two officers and two squad cars parked in front of the pub. The crowd from yesterday was no more. Dillon was wearing his ID around his neck and was able to hold up the ID and nod at one of the officers as he pulled into the parking lot. Another half-dozen police vehicles were parked in the lot, as was Suel's car, along with four others. He parked, walked around the building, and entered through the front door.

He spotted Suel immediately, leaning against the bar, talking with DI Tiernan. Tiernan looked over as Dillon entered and gave a nod.

"Good morning. You ever get home last night, Ronan?"

Tiernan shook his head. "Caught three hours sleep at the station. Then back here."

"Any updates?"

"All shot with a pistol, close range. We're guessing the same weapon, but that will be confirmed later today. Autopsies on all three are scheduled for 11:00 this morning."

"Any witnesses surface?"

"As it stands now, no. Right now, the only person in the place, other than the shooter, was the bartender."

"That's Lizzy?"

Tiernan nodded. "Claims she was in the backroom getting bottles and didn't see anyone."

"And Jimmy Byrne is her nephew?"

"She's a dead end. Won't be telling us anything but her name. Obviously upset last night and still didn't talk. I'm sure she's got a solicitor by now, and he'll be answering any questions we have."

Dillon glanced over at Suel.

"O'Shea?" Suel said.

Dillon nodded.

"Be interesting what they find on the rounds. I'm guessing a nine-millimeter, maybe a Beretta or a Glock. It seems funny they never found a weapon on any of the victims. You think your man was that fast that they never had the chance to draw?" Tiernan wondered.

Dillon thought for a moment. "Probably. I'm guessing he searched them and took their weapons once they were down. That would only take a couple of seconds. Hogan was lying on the floor over there," Dillon said and pointed toward the general area. "He was so fat and wedged into that booth I can't see him jumping out in a hurry. He was probably already on his feet. Maybe they were going somewhere in the car."

"Or maybe he was just heading to the Jacks," Tiernan said.

Suel said, "Yeah, and Connor Ginty and Tire Track were going to follow. Their backs were turned toward the shooter and—"

"Except that Ginty was shot between the eyes, and Tire Track looked to take one in the heart. But still basically the same deal. They're caught off guard. Bang, bang," Dillon said, moving his arm as if he aimed a pistol. "One, maybe two seconds, and then three rounds into Hogan, who doesn't even have the time to process what just happened. If it was O'Shea, and odds are he's the shooter, he kills them, collects at least two, maybe three weapons, and leaves."

"And where in the hell does he go?"

"What if, along with the guns, he grabs a set of car keys?" Tiernan said.

"Hogan's car was gone?" Dillon asked.

"It is, but only because it was impounded. But the other two had to have some way to get around. I can't see them driving around in Hogan's vehicle every day of the year. We'll have vehicle information on both of them," Tiernan said. "I'll have someone double-check the lot here in a minute."

"Did Hogan have anything like an office here?"

"That booth in the corner served as his office," Tiernan said. "He was here seven days a week. The place is owned by an investment group. Jimmy Byrne just happens to be the ranking member of the group."

They chatted for another few minutes, and then Tiernan stepped away to make some phone calls. Suel looked at Dillon and said, "Do you find it a bit strange that they don't have a handle on who owns the cars in the parking lot? They knew which one belonged to Hogan, although I can't imagine anyone the size of Hogan being able to squeeze behind a steering wheel."

"And Tiernan said Hogan's car has already been impounded."

"Yeah, but the other two, what about their cars? I don't know, there isn't a lot to go on. No cameras in the place. God, it has to be just about the only pub in town without cameras. But I'm starting to get the sense that maybe they aren't really rushing to find whoever shot these guys."

"What? Come on, Paddy. I think under the circumstances, they're doing the best they can. They're shorthanded, for starters. Tiernan said he's going on about three hours sleep."

"Yeah, I get all that, but what if they're thinking, as awful as this situation is, it eliminated three individuals who were not contributing a lot of positive energy to the community."

"The community? Paddy, are you going "Happy Thoughts" on me? Are you thinking as long as it's bad guys being shot, they're not looking too hard to find the shooter?"

"I'm just suggesting a hypothetical, is all."

"Interesting thought," Dillon said.

Eric Bergman phoned while they were still at the Manhole. "Yeah, Dillon, got your message, and believe it or not, I actually heard back from passport control."

"What'd they have to say?"

"Your man Sean O'Shea was a regular visitor. He arrived in Dublin every couple of months. He usually stayed three or four days. Listed himself as a tourist."

"He give any indication where he was staying during those tourist visits?"

"No record of that."

"Anything else?"

"No, that's all for now. The stateside address we have for him is out of date. But interestingly, that address was a Boston condo that sold for four-point-five million two years ago."

"And O'Shea was the seller?"

"Appears to be. It's a little sketchy because the unit was actually owned by a hedge fund, Bridge Street Capital."

"That rings a bell. If I remember correctly, they purchased the house in Finglas where Patrick O'Shea lived, although he was listed on the title as the owner. I'll have to check on that to be sure."

"I sent you a copy of the email from Passport Control. Oh, and they included a passport image of Sean O'Shea. He's been here often enough that he probably knows his way around town."

"Okay, Eric, much appreciated," Dillon said, and they disconnected.

"Tell me something positive, please," Suel said.

"I don't know if it's necessarily positive, but it's another bit of information. A group called Bridge Street Capital actually purchased the home for Patrick O'Shea in Finglas. They also purchased a Boston condo for Sean O'Shea that was sold two years ago. More importantly, Sean O'Shea has been over here for three or four days every couple of months for the past few years. So, to answer our earlier question, he probably knows his way around town. Take it a step further, and a couple of years would be more than enough time to establish a group of friends or business partners."

"Yeah, regardless of what kind of business you were in," Suel said.

THIRTY-ONE

Dillon and Suel headed back to Special Branch. Suel went up to the office, and Dillon headed along the first-floor hallway to the Tech Lab. He pushed the button on the keypad, and Emily answered a moment later. "Tech Lab."

"Hi Emily, Jack Dillon. I'm trying to find someone and wondered if you could help," he said.

"Oh, I can hardly wait. This will be great because I don't have anything else to do," she said. The door buzzed a second later, and he hurried into the lab.

Emily was at the back counter working on a computer. The computer screen was five feet by four feet and mounted on the wall. Different names and dates were on the screen, none of which Dillon recognized.

"So, how can I help you?" Emily said without looking at Dillon. She continued to type, adding more names onto the screen.

"I'll wait until you're finished," Dillon said.

"I'm not a guy, Dillon. I can multitask," she said. She typed for a few more seconds and then stopped and faced him. "Okay, what do you have?"

"Thanks. I'm trying to find someone named Sean O'Shea. I think he may be staying in a Dublin Hotel and—"

"And you want me to do a search on current hotel residents."

"Well yeah, but—"

"You know if he's in a BnB, I'm not going to be able to find him."

"Actually, I'd like you to look under two names. He's—"

"Two names, his and a woman's?"

"No, if you'd let me finish. His name, Sean O'Shea, and then a business name, Bridge Street Capital, they're both out of Boston."

She seemed to think for a moment and then said, "Okay, I can do that."

"You want to write down those names?"

No. I'll remember them. If he's in a hotel, it shouldn't take long."

"Thank you. Okay, I'm out of your hair."

"Thank you," she said.

Up in Special Branch, Dillon turned on his computer and checked his email. A message from Eric Bergman at the embassy was the third email and the first one Dillon opened. Two sentences from Bergman and then the passport image of Sean O'Shea. Dillon studied the photo for a moment. Based on what he could remember, Sean O'Shea appeared to look similar to what he recalled of the younger brother, Patrick. Both had red hair, fair skin, and blue eyes. Based on the passport information, he was thirty-five years old.

Dillon's desk phone rang. "Dillon," he answered.

"Found him," Emily said. "He's staying at the Merrion Hotel in the main building. Under Bridge Street Capital. Checked in two days ago. You need the address?"

"No, I know where it is. Does it say how long he's there or what his room number is?"

"Sorry, just that he has a room there and checked in a few days ago. You want the phone number?"

"Yeah, just in case, but we'll be going over there in person in a few minutes," Dillon said as he looked over toward Suel's desk and gave him a wave. He wrote down the phone number, thanked Emily profusely, and hung up.

"What do you have?" Suel said.

"Maybe a break. What do you think about paying a visit to Sean O'Shea?"

"O'Shea? Does Tallaght have him in custody?"

"No, but he's got a room at the Merrion Hotel. Checked in a few days ago. Made the room reservation under the name Bridge Street Capital."

"This is the best news so far. Let's go. I'll drive if you want," Suel said.

"That's okay. You've done enough of that. My turn is way overdue." Dillon placed the copy of O'Shea's passport photo in his jacket pocket, and they drove into the city center, headed to Merrion Street Upper. He pulled to the curb just past the Merrion Hotel, a four-story red-brick building. He placed a sheet of paper with the Garda Logo and beneath that the words OFFICIAL BUSINESS on the driver's side of the dashboard, and they climbed out of the car. Dillon pressed the fob, locking the car, and they headed into the building.

The hotel actually consisted of four houses built in the 1760s. The Mornington House, leased in 1769 to the Earl Of Mornington, is the most important and, not surprisingly, was the house where O'Shea was supposedly staying.

They walked up the four steps and entered through the massive black door with the large brass knob. Just inside stood a doorman wearing a double-breasted gray coat that went to his knees, along with gray trousers, black shoes, and a top hat. Everything in the lobby was painted white. Suel said, "An Garda Síochána," to the doorman as they entered and took a right turn heading across the marble floor to the reception desk.

Both of them had dealt with hotels uncountable times, and rather than ask for O'Shea's room number, they simply showed their warrant cards, asked to speak to a manager, and then waited.

It wasn't a long wait, maybe four or five minutes, but under the circumstances, it felt like twenty minutes to Dillon. Once in the manager's office, they simply explained there had been a death in the family, and they were there to inform Mr. O'Shea. The manager checked their warrant cards and looked up the Bridge Street Capital's room number. At no surprise, O'Shea was in one of the larger suites.

"Does he have a car?" Dillon asked.

"He's not provided that information, and we allow free parking for our residents, so I would say that no, he does not have a vehicle. Shall we see if he is in the room?"

The manager escorted them up a marble staircase with purple carpeting and down a hall to the room. He knocked on the door twice, but there was no response. "I'm afraid Mr. O'Shea isn't here," he said.

"Would you unlock the door, please?" Suel said.

"Unfortunately, that would be in violation of our privacy policy and—"

"His brother died of a rare tropical disease," Dillon said. "It's highly contagious, and if he's in there and dead, there's no telling what the danger is to your other residents."

"Not to mention the negative news reports," Suel added.

The manager seemed to think about that for a brief moment and then nodded as he inserted the master keycard into the slot, pushing the door open as he knocked.

Three large windows with open drapes were on the far side of the room. Two upholstered couches and a chair were positioned in front of a fireplace. A coffee table with six empty wine bottles and three glasses was in front of the fireplace. Dillon heard a soft moan coming from a distant corner of the large room.

"Mr. O'Shea?" the manager said and received another slight moan in response.

The manager, Dillon, and Suel looked to the right and focused on the kingsized bed. Two naked women were lying in bed. A redhead and a blonde. The redhead was lying on her stomach with a pillow partially pulled over her head. The blonde was on the opposite side of the bed. A shapely leg was stretched over the bedsheet, and her right arm was draped across her eyes.

"Mr.O'Shea," Dillon said, raising his voice.

The blonde groaned and rolled onto her back. "Oh, God, please shut the hell up and get me some aspirin."

"I think we can handle things from here," Suel said.

"But our privacy policy, umm, I don't think—"

"I doubt we're looking at registered guests. We'll only be a minute if you'd care to wait out in the hall," Dillon said.

The manager nodded and hurried out of the room.

"Let me check the bathroom," Dillon said. He walked past the bed just as the blonde pulled the sheet up and over her head. The bathroom was at the end of a short hall. The door was partially open, and the light was on. Dillon peeked in. The room was easily larger than his guest bedroom. Everything in there was marble, the tub, the shower, the double sink, the jacuzzi. Two crumpled towels were on the floor. The room was gorgeous and empty. No sign of O'Shea. Dillon walked back to Suel, shaking his head.

"Are you joking? You mean to tell me he left these two for a morning walk?"

"I suppose we could ask them," Dillon said.

Suel shook his head. "I doubt they can remember their own names. Let's go before your man decides to report us. Still, a wonderful view in the room."

"Might be a good time to do a quick search," Dillon said.

Suel nodded and headed for the bedside table on the blonde's side of the bed.

Dillon walked over to the eight-foot-tall mahogany wardrobe and opened it. Four shirts, a suit, and a sports coat were on hangers. Dillon checked the empty pockets in the suit and the sports coat, then turned to the four drawers. He opened them to find the usual underwear, socks, and t-shirts. The bottom drawer held three pairs of shoes. Suel was looking beneath the bed, and Dillon walked back to the bathroom. Other than a comb, razor, shaving cream, and skin moisturizers, there wasn't any-thing.

The women's outfits were piled on the floor next to the fireplace. Their purses were on the floor in front of the two couches. Dillon quickly checked the outfits and purses but didn't find anything like a gun.

"Gentlemen? I really must insist," the manager said as he stood in the doorway, holding the door open.

At the sound of his voice, the blonde made a little noise and rolled over on her side. The redhead appeared to take a deep breath but otherwise didn't move.

"Please," the manager said.

Suel nodded, gave a last look at the women, and walked toward the door. Dillon took a final quick look around and followed Suel out of the room.

"Thank you for your patience," Dillon said.

"I would appreciate it if you kept this little episode to yourselves. I fear it really was in violation of our policy."

"We won't tell a soul," Suel said.

THIRTY-TWO

The manager escorted them to the front door and gave the doorman a nod. He immediately stepped over to the door and held it open for them.

"Can't thank you enough for your cooperation," Dillon said.

"Yes, it's been rather interesting, gentlemen. I wish you all success in your endeavor. Enjoy the rest of your day."

"Oh, say, before we go, just one more question. Do you happen to have a restaurant in your facility?"

"Yes, we do, rated four stars, by the way. You must come try it out sometime. Best to make a reservation in advance. It's always quite busy."

Dillon nodded and looked at Suel. "What do you say to a coffee and some pastry before we leave?"

"Pastry?"

"Relax, I'm buying."

"There's a coffee shop just around the corner. I'm sure you would find it more to your liking," the manager said.

"I think coffee and a pastry are just the thing. After all your assistance, the least we can do is make a purchase. If you could just point us in the right direction, we'll find our way," Dillon said.

"But of course. If you'll just follow that hallway," he said, pointing. "It will be on your right. You can't miss it."

"Thank you again," Dillon said and held out his hand. He received a limp handshake in return.

Halfway down the hall, Suel said, "What in God's name are you thinking, Dillon? Who the hell wants to have coffee at the most expensive place in Dublin? Let's hit that coffee shop around the corner."

"Trust me," Dillon said as they stepped into the half-filled restaurant a moment later. A woman in a starched white blouse and black skirt smiled and said, "Good morning, gentleman. Do you have a reservation?"

"Thank you, but we're joining a friend. Ah, yes, there he is," Dillon said and began walking toward the far corner of the room.

"Tell me that's him with the red hair," Suel said.

"I hope so, or it's going to be embarrassing. You take the left side, Paddy. I've got the right." They headed for the corner table.

Sean O'Shea watched as they approached but didn't make a move. Once they were in front of his table, he smiled and said, "An Garda Síochána, I presume."

"Pleased to meet you, Sean. You're a difficult man to find," Dillon said and held out his hand.

O'Shea ignored the hand. "Apparently not as diffi-cult as I'd hoped. You may as well have a seat. No point in causing a scene."

"Thank you, don't mind if we do. First off," Dillon said as he pulled out a chair, "please accept our deepest condolence regarding the loss of your brother, Patrick. I mean it. We're in the midst of an ongoing investigation into who is responsible."

Other than giving a slight nod, O'Shea didn't dis-play any reaction.

"Do you have any questions we might answer?" Dil-lon said.

"No, I don't think so. A very tragic event. Patrick loved Ireland, and I believe he would be pleased to know that his remains will be here for eternity."

"Yes, certainly. If you don't mind my asking, how long do you intend to stay?"

"Not much longer. I've a bit of business to wind up. Looking at an opportunity, as a matter of fact. With a little luck, I believe the current owners may be persuaded to part with that aspect of their business. But then, one never knows."

"Isn't that always the way?" Dillon said. "Listen, we'll let you get on with your day. Here's my card. If I can be of any assistance, don't hesitate to contact me. Under the circumstances, it's the least I can do."

O'Shea smiled and picked up Dillon's card. "You're a US Marshal? Here, in Ireland?"

"Yeah, I won't bore you with the details, but I've been attached to An Garda Síochána for a few years. I rather like it here. As I said, if I can be of any assistance, please let me know, and again, our condolences," Dillon said and stood.

"Nice to meet you. I'll be sure to keep an eye out," O'Shea said.

"So will we," Dillon replied, and they headed out of the room.

Once they were in the hallway, Suel said, "Okay, that was probably the strangest meet I've ever been involved in, and I didn't utter a word."

"I'll tell you one thing, he's got a plan laid out, and that little visit did nothing to discourage him. I'm convinced he did Hogan and those other two, and he's so sure he got away with it that he celebrated with that blonde and redhead last night."

"You have any ideas?"

"Yeah, I'm going to stay here and keep an eye on him. You're going to taxi back to Special Branch, bring DCI McCabe up to date, and get a team set up on O'Shea twenty-four-seven. Whatever he has planned is not going to be good."

"I'll be back just as soon as I can. Mind yourself until then."

"I plan to," Dillon said as they stepped into the lobby, and the doorman opened the door for them. They headed toward Dillon's car. He looked around and waited for an older couple to walk by. Once they were past the car, he pushed the fob on his car key, and the lid on the trunk rose four inches. He lifted it and glanced around once more. He input a four-digit code into the lockbox next to the spare tire and took out a nine-millimeter Beretta. He quickly shoved the pistol against the small of his back and pulled the image of O'Shea from his coat pocket. "Make copies of this for everyone."

"Good luck, back as soon as I can," Suel said and stuck out his hand to hail a taxi. A moment later, the taxi drove down the street, turned at the corner, and disappeared. Dillon crossed the street and settled onto a bench a little further down. From where he sat, he could watch the door to the hotel as well as the entrance to a parking garage around the corner. Theoretically, if O'Shea left, Dillon would be able to spot him. Maybe an hour later, a taxi pulled up in front of the hotel and waited with its flashing lights on. The driver turned on the light on the roof of the taxi, signaling that the vehicle was occupied.

Dillon watched for the next five minutes, checking the taxi with the flashing lights and the entrance to the parking garage. Suddenly, the front door to the Merrion Hotel opened and out stepped first the redhead followed by the blonde. At least now they were dressed. They appeared none the worse for wear, climbed into the taxi, and disappeared around the corner.

THIRTY-THREE

It was after 1:00 when two members of Special Branch arrived at the Merrion Hotel and took over. Dermot Roach introduced himself, and Dillon headed back to Special Branch. He and Suel reviewed the images taken at the Manhole Pub that DI Tiernan had forwarded.

"We need a break," Suel finally said. "It's like reading the same paragraph a dozen times."

"Let me give a call to Noel Leonard. With any luck, they've completed the autopsies on the Manhole group."

"You thinking the same weapon?" Suel asked.

"It's almost a given. Still, it would be nice to have a confirmation." He picked up the phone, called Noel Leonard at Dublin Morgue, and ended up leaving a message. "Yeah, Noel, Jack Dillon. We're involved in the investigation of the three men murdered at the Manhole Pub. I believe the autopsies were scheduled for this morning. Just checking to see if you have any results. Please give me a call when you're able."

"They're probably still at it," Suel said.

"I'm not expecting anything other than a confirmation of the same weapon. The least we can do is—" Dillon's phone rang. "How's that for a quick reply? This is probably Noel."

"Dillon," he answered.

"Dillon. Ward Tiernan. I'm afraid we've got another one."

"Another shooting, Ward?"

"Yeah, a young girl, twenty-six years old. Nora Lynch. Get this. Her uncle is Jimmy Byrne."

"What? Byrne? Where are you?"

"We just arrived at her house in Tallaght. Happened maybe forty minutes ago. Just got here but thought you should know. This has to be linked to the three at the Manhole."

"Oh, God, we're on our way. What's the address?"

"Alderwood Green, number 1A."

"Okay, Ward, we're on our way. Shit," Dillon half-shouted as he hung up.

"Don't tell me," Suel said.

"Yeah, and it gets worse, some young girl, and her uncle is Jimmy Byrne." Dillon pulled out his cell and pressed speed dial. "Let me call that team at the Merrion Hotel and—Yeah, Finn, it's Marshal Dillon. Listen, I just got a call from Tallaght. There's been another shooting, maybe forty minutes ago. The niece of Jimmy Byrne. I want you guys to go up to O'Shea's room and see if he's there. Don't waste time getting the manager. Knock on the door, pound on it if you have to. If he doesn't answer, one of you go down and get the manager, and the other stay at the door. Let me know what you find. Suel and I are heading out to Tallaght. Call me when you have something," Dillon said and disconnected.

"You're thinking it's O'Shea?" Suel said.

"I'm thinking there's a pretty good chance maybe he got out of the Merrion somehow and, I don't know, could he take a taxi to Tallaght? Or did he have a car parked around the block?"

"Let's get over there. I've got flashing lights in the boot of my car. They'll get us there just that much faster," Suel said and hurried over to his desk.

While Suel drove, Dillon placed another call to Noel Leonard at Dublin Morgue. When he was dumped into voice messaging, he hung up. He phoned Eric Bergman and ended up leaving a message. "Hi Eric, Jack Dillon. We're on our way to the scene of another murder. Would you place a call to passport control and have them be on the lookout for Sean O'Shea? You sent me his passport information yesterday. At this stage, he's a person of interest in four murders, and we don't want him leaving the country. Thanks." Dillon then called passport control and spoke with someone who promised to put Sean O'Shea on the watch list.

By the time he disconnected, Suel was just a couple of minutes away. Most vehicles had been pulling to the side of the road due to the flashing lights. Just now, they were behind an elderly female driver who apparently never checked her rearview mirror. At the moment, Suel was leaning on the horn and not getting any result. Two blocks later, she put on her blinker and turned at the corner, oblivious.

Suel swore and sped up. Alderwood Green appeared a minute later, and he made a left turn. He slowed immediately and pulled to the curb. Four squad cars were parked in front of the corner unit in a series of attached homes. A Dublin Morgue van was backed up in front of the entrance to the front garden area with the rear doors open. Three uniformed officers were out front talking to people, probably local residents. Two men in plain clothes were knocking on the front door three units away.

Suel turned off the engine, clicked off the flashing lights, and they hurried out of the car. Dillon hung his ID with the lanyard around his neck and hurried toward the front door.

The unit was narrow, very narrow. A red Toyota was parked in what would have been the front garden, although the area was now completely covered with gravel. The license plate on the Toyota identified it as a 2016 model.

A uniformed officer stood at the entrance to the drive. "Gentlemen?"

"Special Branch, DI Tiernan phoned us," Dillon replied and held up the ID hanging around his neck.

The officer nodded and said, "I believe he's in the sitting room, but you'll have to enter through the back gate. I'm afraid the body was discovered just inside the front door."

They hurried along a stucco wall seven feet high. There was a gate at the end of the wall, at least twenty feet away. Another uniformed officer stood just outside the gate. They went through the same routine with their IDs before the gate was opened.

They stepped into what, at one time, was probably a grassy area. There was still some grass, although very long and in need of cutting weeks ago. It was slowly but surely being covered by a brownish moss and a particular weed Dillon didn't know the name of.

Tiernan and another man sat at a wooden table on a poured concrete patio. As Dillon and Suel approached, it was obvious the white paint on the table was flaking off. Seated across from Tiernan was a young, dark-haired girl, approximately mid-twenties. Under normal circumstances, she would have been pretty, but just now, her eyes were puffy and swollen from crying. Her nose was red, and a trail of black mascara ran down both her cheeks. A pile of crumpled Kleenex was on the table in front of her.

Tiernan gave Dillon and Suel a nod as they drew near and said, "Maybe wait for us in the kitchen. We're just finishing up here."

The girl coughed, blew her nose, and tossed another Kleenex onto the pile.

THIRTY-FOUR

Dillon and Suel slipped a pair of latex gloves on and headed into the kitchen through the sliding glass door. The kitchen was small. A red Formica topped table with chrome legs and two chairs was against the wall. An empty wine bottle and glass sat on the three-foot-long kitchen counter. Four tea mugs and a couple of plates were piled in the kitchen sink at the end of the counter. A toaster and an open bag of bread were next to the wine bottle. Two pieces of toast were still standing in the toaster slots. A two-burner stove stood at a right angle to the counter. Suel walked over and placed a hand over the toaster. "No heat. They've been here for a while."

Dillon heard a noise from out in the front hall, and he opened the kitchen door. An officer in plain clothes was photographing what was probably blood on the staircase. There was a gurney with a girl's body lying on top of a black body bag. Just now, a man in white scrubs was lifting the end of the body bag over the girl's feet.

"Noel?" Dillon said.

Noel Leonard from Dublin Morgue looked up. "Oh, Dillon, all the way down here in Tallaght. I never would have guessed."

"We've been working some cases with Tallaght Garda. I'm afraid this is one more," Dillon said and then noticed the dark hair with blonde highlights on the victim. He recalled the description by Patrick O'Shea's neighbor, Eoghan Walsh, "spotty hair." His wife, Kiera, had corrected him and said, "dark hair, with blonde highlights." They were describing the young woman who apparently visited O'Shea on a weekly basis. Dillon wondered if maybe O'Shea had been in some sort of relationship with this girl.

"Hello? Dillon?" Leonard said.

"What? Oh, sorry, Noel, just looking at the victim and remembering something on another case."

"I'll leave it to you guys, but from what we can determine, she answered the door, and someone put a gun to her head and pulled the trigger."

Dillon shook his head. "This is Nora Lynch?"

"That's what the woman said. Apparently, they share the place, if you can believe it. Not a lot of room here to share."

"I'll say. We saw the other woman out back talking to Tiernan. You know if she saw anything? The other woman. Anything like a description of the shooter?" Dillon said.

"Not that I'm aware of, but I'd be the last to know."

"She didn't see whoever it was," the man taking pictures said. "You're with Special Branch?"

"Yeah, Jack Dillon."

"Paddy Suel, also with Special Branch," Suel said.

"Mick Malony, I'm out of Tallaght. I work off and on with Ward Tiernan."

"Yeah, we've been working with Ward and DCI O'Brien. Started with the Bell case, the Manhole Pub yesterday, and now with this one, we're up to five murders," Dillon said.

Malony shook his head. "Yeah, I know it's been going crazy. We're almost afraid to pick up the phone."

"You wouldn't be related to Kevin Malony, would you?" Suel asked.

Malony nodded. "Yeah, he's me da."

"Get out. Really? I would have thought you were still about twelve years old."

"That was ten years ago. Of course, my folks still think I'm about twelve."

"You see anything unique taking the photos?" Suel said.

Malony seemed to think for a moment and shook his head. "Seems to be pretty much what the doc said. She opened the door. Someone shoved a gun in her face and pulled the trigger. It probably took me longer to say that than it did to do the deed. What an absolute shame."

There was a sudden noise from the kitchen as Tiernan, another officer, and the woman stepped in from the patio.

"Hold them up a moment, Paddy. Let me help you, Noel," Dillon said and carefully moved the victim's blonde highlighted hair into the body bag. He focused on the bullet hole just below her left eye.

Leonard zipped the body bag up to her knees and then lifted the short, red silky robe she wore off the edge and into the body bag.

Dillon was still staring at the wound just below her left eye. Based on the powder burns and residue on her face, the gun couldn't have been more than two or three inches away. Her hair and the body bag covered the back of her head so he couldn't see an exit wound. He'd get that information by sometime tomorrow.

"All right with you if I take a picture of her face? I think I might be able to link her to Patrick O'Shea," Dillon said.

"O'Shea? The guy who was just cremated out at Mount Jerome?"

"Yeah, that's the guy."

"Be my guest," Leonard said.

Dillon pulled out his phone and took two quick photos of Nora Lynch's face. "Thanks, Noel. Hey, were you working on the autopsies from the shootings at the Manhole Pub?" Dillon asked as Leonard zipped the bag closed.

"I was scheduled to, but then we got this call. It's basically cut and dried, so they let me ride along. Tully's out in the van now writing his report."

"Give him our best," Dillon said.

Suel stuck his head out of the kitchen door. "She'd like to go upstairs."

"Let me just move the gurney out of here," Leonard said.

"I'll give you a hand," Dillon said.

Leonard turned around, facing the open front door, and reached behind with both arms to take hold of the gurney. He stepped out of the house and down the two front steps. Once Dillon made his way out the door and off the steps, Leonard turned around and said, "I got it from here, Dillon. Thanks."

"No problem. Hey, I left a message on your line asking you about the autopsy results on the Manhole victims."

"Anything specific you wanted to know?"

"Just if there was anything unique. Oh, and I wanted to confirm it was the same weapon in all three cases."

"Let me see what they find out, and I'll get back to you. Thanks again," Leonard said. He pulled the gurney around the red Toyota and out toward the van.

Dillon stepped back inside. Suel was standing in the sitting room. He was on his cellphone and shook his head with a disgusted look on his face. The woman who had been talking with Tiernan suddenly stepped out of the kitchen. She looked exhausted, and her arms were crossed over her chest as if she was trying to hold herself together. She looked at Dillon with a deadpan expression as if she saw him, but it didn't really register. She took the first step on the staircase, then stopped, stared at the splatter of blood on the second and third steps, and vomited.

"Oh, shit," she groaned and hurried up the stairs. Dillon heard her coughing and then what was probably the bathroom door being slammed. He headed for the kitchen door, and just as he stepped into the kitchen, he heard the toilet flush overhead.

"Did you learn anything?" he asked Tiernan as he closed the kitchen door behind him.

Tiernan shook his head. "Not much. She knew a guy she dated from time to time. No problems to speak of. They were both home last night watching a movie. The victim went up to bed a little after eleven. Michele Hughes, that's the woman we interviewed, went up to bed shortly after that. She was in the kitchen this morning when the doorbell rang. Apparently, Nora was either just coming down the stairs or in the hallway. She called out she'd answer the door, and Michele heard the gunshot a few seconds later. She looked out the kitchen door, saw the Lynch girl on the floor, ran out the back door, and dialed 999."

Dillon just shook his head. "I might have a link to Sean O'Shea."

"Sean O'Shea, was he the lad shot over in Finglas?"

"No, that was Sean's younger brother, Patrick. One of Patrick's neighbors described a woman with dark hair and blonde highlights paying a visit to him three or four times a month. Let's round it up to weekly. If it was this Nora Lynch, and then Patrick O'Shea is murdered, maybe that ties it in with her uncle, Jimmy Byrne. Maybe her murder this morning, along with the three men at the Manhole, are all payback.”

“Hmm, maybe not as far-fetched as it originally sounded.”

“What did you say your woman’s name was?” Dillon said and raised his eyes toward the ceiling.

“Hughes, Michele Hughes.”

“You mind if I check with her and see if she has any knowledge of Patrick O’Shea?”

“Be my guest. I’ll give you a few minutes, and then we will be going through Nora’s bedroom.”

“Keep me posted if you find anything,” Dillon said and stepped back into the hallway. Suel was still in the sitting room. He was on his phone and looking out the window. Dillon heard him say, “No, that can’t be right.” Dillon side-stepped the fresh vomit from Michele Hughes, the puddles of blood from Nora Lynch, and headed up the stairs.

THIRTY-FIVE

The layout on the second floor was basically the same as the homes of both Patrick O'Shea and Dennis Bell. Neither one had been very large. This place was barely half the size. There were two small bedrooms with the doors next to each other. Dillon knocked on the doors, and when he didn't receive a reply, he opened them. Both rooms were empty. He knocked on the bathroom door.

A woman coughed and then said, "Sorry, occupied."

"Michele, my name is Jack Dillon. I'm with An Garda Síochána, Special Branch. I'd like to ask you a couple of questions."

"I'm really not at my best right now. Can you wait? It's been a hell of a day so far."

"Yeah, believe me, I know, but it's important we get the answers to these questions sooner rather than later. We don't want whoever did this coming back here and looking for you." Dillon waited for a long moment before he said, "Michele? Are you all right? Michele?"

The door suddenly opened, and Michele peeked out. Her hair looked recently brushed, and her face had been washed. Although her eyes were still puffy and red, the tear-driven mascara had been removed from her cheeks.

"You think this person might be looking for me? Detective Tiernan said I couldn't stay here, so I'm going to pack a suitcase. I have a brother picking me up in a half-hour."

"I think that's a very good idea. There are still officers outside, and Detective Tiernan is still here. I wanted to ask you about Nora. Did she ever mention someone by the name of Patrick O'Shea?"

She nodded. "Yes, that creepy uncle of hers told her she had to go out with him. It was an on-again, off-again relationship. She liked him, I guess, but she didn't want to be with him the rest of her life, if you know what I mean. She even tried to get me to go out with him."

"Did you?"

"No, all he wanted was time in bed. I've been through that enough in my life to not want to put up with it anymore."

"Did she know that Patrick O'Shea had been murdered?"

"Yeah, she did. In fact, we saw it on the news the other night. She called him right away. Of course, he didn't answer."

"Would you happen to have his phone number?"

"No, I didn't want to talk to him, but Nora has it on her phone. It's in her room if they haven't taken it already," she said. She opened the bathroom door wider, stepped into the hall, and walked into the bedroom at the top of the stairs. "Yeah, there it is, right on that little table next to her bed." The "little table" was actually an upside-down plastic wastebasket. The phone sat on top of a copy of ***Fliuch***, a soft-porn magazine.

"Okay, let's leave it there. DI Tiernan will be coming up in a few minutes to get it. Did Nora ever talk to you about Patrick's business?"

"Business? That's a pretty strong term. I know he wanted to get in with her uncle, Mr. Byrne, but then something went wrong on that end. Not sure what. In a strange way, the fact that her uncle didn't like Patrick maybe made him more attractive to Nora. It was maybe two months ago when her uncle told her she wasn't allowed to see Patrick anymore."

"And did she stop seeing him?"

"She did for maybe a week and then spent three days with him. They went down to Cork, and she had a really fun time. She came back from Cork all crazy and in love. She told me she was going to get her uncle to change his mind."

"And did she?"

Michele shook her head. "I don't know. If she did, she never told me about it. Now this, God," she said, and the tears began to roll down her cheeks again.

"Okay, I appreciate you telling me this, Michele. If you have any questions or if I can be of any help, don't hesitate to call me," he said and handed her his business card.

She glanced at the card, nodded, and hurried back to the bathroom.

Dillon heard the lock click once she closed the door.

DI Tiernan was just coming up the stairs, carrying a box of evidence bags. Mick Malony followed him. "How'd it go?" Tiernan said.

"Interesting," Dillon said, and they stepped into Nora's bedroom. Dillon filled Tiernan in on his conversation with Michele and finished up with, "So if you can toss that phone in an evidence bag, we can have the Tech Lab review it. If there's a phone number on there for Patrick O'Shea, we can have them try to track the phone and find out where it is. It may just lead us to whoever murdered him."

"Dillon?" Suel called from downstairs.

"Well, there's my better half," Dillon said.

"Why don't you take that phone and bring it to the Tech Lab. It will save us at least a day on getting it there. At this stage, anything will help," Tiernan said.

"Good idea," Dillon said as Tiernan handed him an evidence bag. He stepped over to the upside-down wastebasket and retrieved the phone.

"Dillon, damn it?"

"Coming, Paddy," Dillon shouted.

"Good to see you guys. I'll keep you posted, Ward. Mick, can you email me your picture file when you have a chance, please?"

Malony nodded and said, "Nice to meet you, Dillon. Good luck with your man Suel downstairs." They all laughed.

"I'm coming, Paddy. I'm coming," Dillon said as he hurried down the stairs. He narrowly missed stepping in the blood and vomit and hurried out the front door. Suel was standing a few feet from the front steps. He did not look happy. "What's up?" Dillon said.

"Just off the phone with Dermot Roach."

"Who?"

"DI Dermot Roach, he's supposedly keeping an eye on your man O'Shea."

"Oh, yeah. Did they find him, O'Shea?"

"No, they can't find him."

"What?"

"You heard me. Once we called, they went up to the room and didn't get an answer. Argued with that self-important knacker of a manager, finally got him to let them in the room, and O'Shea was gone. Clothes and suitcase were still in the room, but he was gone. They checked both restaurants, no sign of the bastard. You want me to tell them to head back to Special Branch?"

Dillon thought for a moment and shook his head. "No, let's get over there. I want that manager to show us their security tapes. Tell them to stand fast. We'll be there in twenty minutes."

"We'll be there a lot sooner than twenty minutes," Suel said just as a black Mercedes skidded to a stop next to the squad car parked on the street. A muscular-looking guy with a ponytail jumped out of the passenger seat and opened the rear door. A shorter man hurried out and ran toward the house.

"I'm sorry, sir, but you're not allowed—"

"Get the hell out of my way," he said, pushing the uniformed officer aside and knocking his hat off as he hurried past. The large muscular guy was following, although not too quickly. He stopped to say something to the officer.

"Hold on there a minute. We're conducting an investigation," Dillon said.

"Get the hell out of my way," the man shouted and attempted to push Dillon aside. Dillon automatically grabbed his arm, lowered his shoulder, and flipped the man onto the gravel.

He landed in a sitting position with a loud "Uff" and didn't move.

"You all right, sir?" the muscular guy asked. "Lads, sorry, we just got the news Jimmy's niece has been shot."

"This is Jimmy Byrne?" Dillon asked.

"Oh, Christ on a cross," Suel said and leaned down to help the muscular guy raise Byrne back onto his feet. Byrne was wide-eyed and gasping for air.

"Here, bring him over to the Toyota," Suel said and took hold of Byrne's right arm. The muscular guy grabbed his left arm, and they led him to the trunk of the Toyota, turned him around, and had him lean against the car.

"You just got the wind knocked out of you," Suel said. "Take some deep breaths, and you'll be better. Just relax. We're part of the investigation, sir," Suel said. "I'm sorry to say that Nora Lynch was killed. She was shot in the head and died instantly. They've just taken her to the Dublin Morgue."

"No, no," Byrne said in a scratchy voice.

"Ah, sir, I'm afraid it's the truth," Suel said, looking at the muscular guy as he did so.

"I need to see her," Byrne gasped.

"Let me call and tell them you're on the way," Dillon took out his cellphone.

"Let's get the hell out of here," Byrne croaked, still unable to get his full voice back.

The muscular guy led him back to the car. As they walked past, he gave a nod to the officer Byrne had pushed. He opened the door, and Byrne climbed into the backseat. The muscular guy hurried into the front passenger seat, and the black Mercedes sped down the street.

"Nothing like a first impression," Dillon said. He quickly phoned Dublin Morgue and warned Gráinne, the receptionist, about the approaching visitor.

THIRTY-SIX

uel pulled in front of the Merrion Hotel and parked in a no-parking zone. He placed the An Garda Síochána logo on the dashboard and climbed out of the car.

Dillon was already on his cellphone calling DI Roach. "Yeah, Dermot, we just pulled up in front. Where are you guys?"

"I've been trying to call you. We found him. He was swimming in the spa."

"You're there now?"

"Yes, sir. I've been watching him swim laps in the pool."

"Stay right there. We're on our way," Dillon said.

They hurried in the front door. The doorman in the top hat got a surprised look on his face but never changed his stance with his arms casually folded behind his back.

"Which way to the spa?" Dillon asked.

"Down the hall and out the back. Follow the signs," the doorman said.

"Much appreciated," Suel said as Dillon hurried down the hall.

They followed the signs to the spa, passing the restaurant where they'd met O'Shea earlier. They took a number of turns, and then, suddenly, there it was as they stepped outside and into a leafy garden. The entrance to the spa was on the far side of a long, rectangular pool of water with a fountain. Other than an older couple drinking tea at a table beneath an umbrella, the place was empty. They hurried around the pool of water and into the spa.

There were four tables and a small bar. A server dressed in a gray suit coat and matching slacks was carrying a tray with three wine glasses toward a table. He smiled, gave a nod, and headed toward the three women seated in the corner. Dillon and Suel hurried toward the glass doors on the opposite wall. DI Roach was seated in one of four upholstered chairs in a small area raised three feet above an elegant, blue-tiled pool with three massive pillars on either side. The base of the pillars was illuminated by lights in the floor of the pool.

A man, presumably Sean O'Shea, was just now swimming on his back toward the massive piece of artwork at the far end of the pool. He was wearing goggles, a white swim cap, and blue swim trunks. He was the only person in the pool area. Soft classical music drifted over the pool and added a surreal atmosphere to the elegant surroundings.

"Roach," Dillon said as they stepped into the area.

Roach turned in the chair and looked at them. "He's been swimming laps since we first spotted him," he said in a soft voice. "This is why we couldn't find him. We were watching outside. He left his room and came down here, obviously never leaving the hotel."

"How long have you been here?"

"Thirty or forty minutes at least. Tried to call you a few times, but the call just dropped. I was afraid you were involved in something and didn't want an interruption."

"Not a bad place to work a stakeout," Suel said, looking around.

"You can say that again. They even brought me a tea," Roach said and nodded at the pot and mug resting on the glass top table in front of him. There was an empty plate with a few crumbs, and Dillon wondered what he'd eaten.

"I would guess he's not going anywhere in his swimsuit," Dillon said just as O'Shea swam up to the white-tiled stairs in the corner of the pool and climbed out of the water. He walked over to a white lounge chair, one of four on that side of the pool, and picked up a towel. He removed his goggles and swim cap and placed them in some sort of shopping bag. He patted himself with the towel and pulled on a white, knee-length, terry-cloth robe. He picked up the shopping bag and headed toward Dillon and Suel.

"Gentlemen," he said as he took the three steps up from the pool area. "How nice to see you. Can I interest you in some tea and biscuits? My treat." The terrycloth robe was embroidered with the Merrion Hotel logo.

"Thank you, but no. You seem to be quite adept in the water, Mr. O'Shea," Dillon said and caught sight of a pair of jeans in the shopping bag.

"Oh, please, call me, Sean. I happen to find it relaxing. Nice to have the opportunity to relax. I'll be heading back to the States shortly. As you can imagine, this trip has been a stressful and exhausting experience."

"I'm sure it has been. Were you thinking of swimming in those jeans?" Dillon said, indicating the shopping bag.

"What? Oh, no. I wore them down here. The hotel has a policy about walking the halls in swimming attire. Fortunately, they loaned me this robe in the locker room. You sure I can't interest any of you in a tea?"

"Thank you, but no, we've got places to go and people to see."

"Well, okay. I think there might be a nap in the near future. Didn't get a lot of sleep last night," O'Shea said, smiled once more, and headed for the door.

Once the door closed behind O'Shea, Dillon asked, "Where's your partner."

"He's cooling his heels over in the locker room. There's a door leading outside, and we didn't know if O'Shea would go back to his room or head into the locker room. Looks like I got the better part of the deal," Roach said.

"Keep an eye on him," Dillon said and looked at Suel. "Is someone scheduled to watch O'Shea tonight?"

"Yes, coming in at 7:00. You need anything, Dermot?"

"No, I'm good. Let me get my partner out of the locker room. One of us will set up outside, and the other will be by the staircase just in case O'Shea decides to take a back exit. Either way, he has to come through the lobby," Roach said.

"I'm thinking we head over to Dublin Morgue. It would be nice to have a pleasant chat with Jimmy Byrne," Dillon said.

"I'm not sure that's even possible, but we can try," Suel said.

Dillon and Suel hurried out to the lobby and just caught sight of Sean O'Shea as he reached the top of the stairs and headed down the hallway to his room. "Yeah, I bet he needs some rest after last night's entertainment," Suel said.

"Do you think that whole thing just now might have been staged?" Dillon said.

"Staged? How so? Roach watched him in the pool for the better part of an hour. You think he drove over to Tallaght in a swimsuit, shot Nora Lynch, and then snuck into the pool? You would have seen him leave if he was driving somewhere. Roach was watching the street and the car park once you left. They had the back exit covered."

Dillon nodded and said, "I'm thinking he wore the jeans, maybe a t-shirt, and was out and back before the guys even knew he was gone. I don't know. What do you say to heading over to Dublin Morgue? Let's see if we can learn anything from Jimmy Byrne. We should have questioned him when we had the chance."

"Come on, Dillon. You saw him push the officer. He'd just gotten word his niece had been shot. He was beside himself rushing into the place."

"We could have charged him with assault, pushing your man the way he did."

"Oh, yeah, and that would have lasted for all of five minutes. Forget who he is for a moment. No judge or jury, if it ever came to that, would find him guilty under the circumstances. God, a family member was murdered, and he just wants to fix the problem. It's life, is what it is. All the money in the world, and at the end of the day, it doesn't make a damn bit of difference."

"What better place to chat him up than the Dublin Morgue," Dillon said.

THIRTY-SEVEN

They were there in short order. Suel parked a half-dozen car lengths behind Byrne's Mercedes, currently blocking the left turn lane. The driver was in the car and, at the moment, being given the finger by a couple on a motorcycle. Given the appearance of the couple on the motorcycle, it was probably the wise decision not to respond.

Dillon and Suel entered through the side entrance and stepped into the empty lobby. Gráinne, the receptionist, was seated at her desk behind the bulletproof glass. She smiled as they stepped up to the counter.

"Everything okay with the visitors?" Dillon asked.

She nodded and leaned forward. "It comes with the territory. If you're here, you're not expecting to have a fun time. They've been back in the viewing room for a good twenty minutes, but that's not all that unusual. Everyone has a different way of saying goodbye. Was it your man's daughter?"

"No, his niece," Suel said.

"Oh, but still, just heartbreaking, and so young. God bless."

"We'll give them as much time as they want. See if we can't get a few words with your man Byrne on the way out," Dillon said.

"I wonder if it would be better if I spoke to him," Suel said. "You know, after the introduction you gave him in front of his niece's place."

Dillon thought about that for a moment and decided it wasn't such a bad suggestion. "You'll ask him if he has any idea who's responsible for his niece, the three guys at the Manhole, and Dennis Bell?"

"I'll ask, but you know as well as I do that he'll shake his head and ask what in the hell we're doing with our time and why haven't we made any arrests."

"Yeah, probably, but there's always that slim chance. I'll wait for you out by the car."

"I'll attempt to talk to him outside. Give him a chance to step out of here and maybe take a deep breath."

They heard muffled voices in the hall and hurried out of the lobby. Dillon made his way down the street to Suel's car. He leaned against the hood of the car and was far enough away that he doubted Byrne would see him but still close enough that if Suel was in trouble, he could get there in short order.

He needn't have worried. Byrne and the same muscular guy with the ponytail who had guided him to the back of the Toyota stepped out of the building. Dillon couldn't hear what Suel said, no doubt some innocuous introduction. Byrne shook his head, waved his arms, and steamed toward the waiting Mercedes. The muscular guy looked at Suel, seemed to shrug, and hurried to catch up to Byrne. He opened the rear door of the Mercedes. Byrne slipped in and yelled something out the window at Suel. The muscular guy slid into the front passenger seat, and the Mercedes screeched around the corner.

"So, how'd that go?" Dillon asked.

"About like we expected. You ready to head back to Special Branch?"

"Maybe we check inside just to see if Byrne said anything in there."

"Might as well as long as we're here," Suel said, and they went back inside.

"Forget something?" Gráinne asked as they stepped into the lobby.

"Wondered if you picked up anything from Jimmy Byrne, who just left."

She shook her head. "Only that he was very upset and very unhappy. Who can blame him?"

"Any chance we can talk to whoever dealt with him?"

"I think so. That was Noel Leonard."

Of course it was, thought Dillon. Gráinne paged Leonard, and he opened the door to the lobby a few minutes later. He was dressed in blue scrubs and wore a face mask.

"Hi Noel, sorry to interrupt, just wanted to ask if you picked up anything from Jimmy Byrne. He was the man viewing Nora Lynch, his niece."

"Yeah, he introduced himself. I asked if he'd wait a bit. I thought it would be best to get her cleaned up and out of the body bag, but he wanted to see her right away. In fact, he was adamant about it. God, we'd only been back maybe twenty minutes, half-hour tops."

"You pick up on anything he said?"

"Not really. I mean, the man was upset, really upset, understandably. Asked a couple of questions about her wound. I answered as best I could. He actually thanked me before he left. Can't blame him. It's just an awful thing to have to go through."

"Anything else?"

"Only that I hope you get whoever is doing this stuff. I feel like we're suddenly back in the 1970s during the Troubles."

"We'll see what we can do. You got anything, Paddy?"

Suel shook his head.

"Thanks, Noel. Hang in there," Dillon said, and they headed out to the car.

"God, this day feels like it's already been a week long," Suel said and started the car. Dillon pulled out his cellphone. "Oh, please, don't tell me you want to stop at Byrne's house."

"No, nothing like that. I just want to check with Mick Malony at Tallaght and see if he had a chance to send me those photos he took this morning."

"What do you expect to find?"

"Nothing, to tell you the truth. I just don't want to leave anything to chance. I'll look at the pictures, nothing to see we don't already know, and we'll cross it off our list."

"Just about everything has been crossed off the damn list," Suel said.

"Yeah, you aren't kidding."

Dillon ended up leaving a message for Mick Malony. Suel pulled into the security lot at Special Branch, and they headed up to the office. "I'm going to see if anyone left some cookies or treats in the break room," Suel said. "You want anything?"

"No, thanks, I'm sweet enough."

"I'll be the judge of that," Suel said and hurried into the break room.

The light on Dillon's desk phone was flashing, and he picked it up and pushed a key. "Message from extension one-one-five." click. "Hi Dillon, Rory Phelan, down in Forensics. Got the results back on that red thong. I'll be here until five if you want to stop down."

Dillon thought about getting Suel and decided, since it was almost 5:00, he'd just hurry down to Forensics. He waited maybe ten seconds for the elevator, then hurried down the stairs and almost ran through the hallway. If Rory had a name, it might be someone who was on the scene when Patrick O'Shea was killed. He pressed the intercom button next to the forensics door twice.

"Yeah, how can I help?"

"Rory?"

"Yeah, is that Dillon?"

"Yes."

"Perfect timing. I was just getting ready to leave," he said, and the door suddenly buzzed.

Dillon pulled the door open and stepped up to the counter. A stainless steel call bell rested on the counter, and Dillon hit the top three times.

"Be with you in just a second, Dillon," Phelan called from somewhere in the back of the lab. He appeared a moment later with a plastic tray and a three-page document stapled together. "Thanks for hurrying down. This is what we got," he said, sliding the document across the counter.

Dillon glanced at the first and second pages. Basically, all medical information, blood type, DNA, and so on. Page three listed the individual that the thong was traced to, along with a photo. Dillon stared at the photo for a long moment. Her hair appeared to be a lot shorter and much darker.

"You look like you know her," Phelan said.

Dillon shook his head. "No, at least not personally. She was the victim of a shooting just this morning. Nora Lynch."

"Oh, no. Boyfriend? Estranged husband?"

"We don't know. We think she might be the fifth person in a series of possibly related murders."

"This have anything to do with those three guys shot in that dreadful pub?"

"Yeah, the Manhole Pub. At least we think so, but we're running into a number of brick walls as far as getting any information. So, at least for now, it's all just hypothetical."

"Well, we'll send this evidence over to the property room. You got a case number on the woman's murder?"

"No, I don't. I'm sure there is one. I've been running all day and—"

"Relax, Dillon. I'll get it tomorrow morning. You can hang onto that file. That's your copy I printed off."

"Thanks, Rory, much appreciated."

"Okay, now get out of here so I can go home," he said and laughed.

Dillon went back up to Special Branch. Suel was seated at his desk. Two chocolate brownies rested on a napkin next to his phone. "Where'd you run off to?" Suel asked as he picked up one of the brownies and bit off half.

"I had a call from Rory Phelan down in Forensics. You remember the thong I found between the sheets in Patrick O'Shea's bed?"

"Yeah, you took it to Forensics about a month ago."

"Actually, more like a week ago, but yeah. He ran the tests," Dillon said, waving the three-page test results.

"And?" Suel said as he stuffed the second half of the brownie into his mouth.

"And guess who it turns out left her thong in the bed?"

"I've no idea."

"The thong belongs to Nora Lynch."

"Nora? Jimmy Byrne's niece? The woman who was murdered this morning?"

Dillon nodded. "Yeah, apparently, she was a weekly visitor, at least according to O'Shea's neighbors. I took a picture of her face before Noel zipped up the body bag and was going to show it to the neighbors. Hopefully, see if they could confirm she was the woman they saw over there. I guess that question has been answered by the thong."

"You think her continuing to see him after her uncle told her not to was the reason O'Shea was killed?"

"I suppose it's possible, but if you're suggesting Jimmy Byrne had something to do with it, say he gave the order to kill Patrick O'Shea, wouldn't he make sure his niece wasn't there when the killing took place?"

"Maybe someone made a mistake?"

"God, I can feel another headache coming on," Dillon said.

Suel opened a desk drawer and placed a bottle of aspirin on the desk. "Help yourself. Just save two for me."

THIRTY-EIGHT

It was half-past-seven when Dillon turned onto his lane and drove down to his house. The porch light was on at Tara's, and her car was gone, but Dillon was too tired to care. He pulled into his drive, closed the two gates behind his car, and unlocked the door. Lucifer met him at the door, jumped off the front stoop, and assumed the position right next to the driver's door on the car. Maybe hoping he'd start Dillon's day off on the wrong foot, literally.

Dillon picked up the four envelopes from the floor and glanced at them. All commercial ads, two for car insurance, one for the internet service he'd had for the past three years, and a mailer for Tesco groceries. Actually, being able to toss all the mail into the recycling bag turned out to be the only day brightener he'd had.

He found half a chicken breast in the back of the refrigerator and a dish of curry from earlier in the week. He warmed them up in the microwave and ate, standing at the kitchen counter, wondering about Sean O'Shea.

He watched the ten o'clock news with Lucifer at his feet, and they headed up to bed before 11:00. He slept fitfully and was up at 5:00 the following morning. He let

Lucifer out and coaxed him back in with a biscuit ten minutes later. He filled a travel mug with coffee and drove into the city center and the Merrion hotel.

It was just after 6:00 in the morning, and Dillon parked on the street in front of the hotel. No one was seated on the bench keeping an eye on the parking ramp or the door to the hotel. Dillon went to open the hotel door, but it was locked. He rang the doorbell. A moment later, a doorman, not the same man as yesterday, opened the door.

"Sir?"

Dillon took his ID on the lanyard from his pocket, draped it around his neck, and said, "Good morning, sorry to disturb you so early. I'm looking for two An Garda Síochána officers. They would be in plain clothes. They were here overnight and—"

"Did they have a room, sir?"

"No, they were maintaining a, ahh, security watch for one of your residents. They would, or rather should be, watching the entrance and exits."

"Two gentlemen?"

"Yes."

"I don't know anything about this, sir. Unfortunately, our daytime manager isn't due in for two more hours. Might the night manager be of some assistance?"

"Yes, I suppose. Where is his office?"

"I'm calling her now. If you'll just wait a moment, and—Ma'am, Henry at the entrance. I have an officer here with An Garda Síochána, and he—No, ma'am, not that I'm aware of. He's looking for two officers who were working here over the evening. No, apparently a security issue of some sort. Yes, I'll tell him. Thank you," he said and hung up.

"Find them?"

"Actually, no. She didn't seem to have any knowledge of this, sir. If you'd step over to the reception area," he said, extending his hand to the left. "She'll be there in just a moment."

Dillon walked across the white marble floor to the reception counter. No one was there, and he was about to go back to the doorman when a woman called, "Sir."

Dillon turned and watched as a blonde woman headed toward him. She wore a gray skirt, a white blouse, and was in the process of pulling on a gray blazer.

"May I help you, sir? Pardon me. I was doing paperwork in the office. It's unusual we'd have someone at the counter at this hour. How may I help you?"

Dillon held out the ID around his neck and said, "It was my understanding that there would be two officers from An Garda Síochána preforming a security check on one of your residents. They were supposed to be here until relieved."

"Officers here? I'm not aware of that. Are you sure you have the proper hotel? There are—"

"Yes, in fact, I was on duty here myself yesterday afternoon. Two officers relieved me, and they were to be relieved by two more yesterday evening."

"I was aware officers were here yesterday but, umm, who was the resident you were protecting?"

"An American gentleman by the name of Sean O'Shea."

"Let me just check. That rings a bell, but this is a busy time of year. Tourist season, you know. One moment," she said and stepped behind the reception counter. She turned the computer on and, a moment later, began typing. She suddenly smiled. "Oh yes, here we are. Bridge Street Capital, Mr. O'Shea checked out of the hotel yesterday evening at 5:15." She looked up and smiled at Dillon.

"Does it say where he went?"

"He requested a taxi taking him to Dublin airport, Terminal Two."

"Terminal Two. Do you happen to have an airline listed?"

"I'm afraid not, sir. Just Dublin airport, Terminal Two."

"All right, thank you. Sorry to bother you."

"It's what we're here for, sir. If we can be of any further service, don't hesitate to let us know," she said in a tone that sounded like anything but.

"Many thanks," Dillon said and hurried out to his car. He slid behind the wheel and called Special Branch.

"An Garda Síochána, Special Branch," a voice said after two rings.

"Hi, this is Marshal Jack Dillon, Special Branch. Can you give me the cellphone number for officer Dermot Roach please?"

"What is your warrant card number, sir?"

Shit, Dillon thought. "Just a moment while I pull it out," he said. He put his phone on speaker, set it on the passenger seat, then pulled his warrant card out and read the number.

"Thank you, sir," the man said, and Dillon could hear the keyboard clicking. He grabbed a pen out of the console. "That was Officer Dermot Roach, R-O-A-C-H, in Special Branch?"

"Yes."

"Here's the number, sir." As he read off the phone number, Dillon wrote it on the palm of his hand. "Anything else you need, Marshal Dillon?"

"No, this will do. Thank you." Dillon input the number on his cellphone.

Roach answered on the second ring. "DI Roach."

"Dermot, Jack Dillon. I'm in front of the Merrion Hotel. They told me O'Shea left for the airport last night."

"Yeah, right around a quarter after five. He took a taxi out there, Terminal Two. No one alerted you? We phoned it in."

"Do you know if he actually went to the airport?"

"Yes, sir. We followed him. The taxi dropped him off at Terminal Two. I followed him into the terminal. He checked a bag and got his boarding pass. I followed him up to the second level and watched as he passed through security."

"Did you watch him board the plane?" There was a long pause. "Dermot?"

"No, sir, I didn't. I just watched him go through security."

"What airline did he fly?"

"Delta, Terminal Two."

Dillon disconnected. He thought about heading to the airport but decided it would be quicker to head to Special Branch and call. It was early enough that the rush hour was barely underway, and he pulled into the secured parking lot twelve minutes later. He was still breathing heavily when he got a Delta supervisor on the line and explained what he was looking for.

"And you don't know where Mr. O'Shea was headed, sir?"

"No, unfortunately. I think his final destination might have been the city of Boston in the United States, but I can't be sure."

Dillon waited for what seemed like forever. Finally, the man came back on the line and said, "I have a Sean O'Shea that booked a ticket from Dublin to Amsterdam, actually on Swiss Air, departing at 8:00 and arriving at 10:40 last night. Amsterdam to Boston, again on Swiss Air. That flight departs at 7:00 this morning, arriving in Boston. The local time in Boston will be a 7:40 AM arrival."

"And this is for Sean O'Shea?"

"Yes, sir, a first-class ticket on both flights. The credit card was American Express listed to Bridge Street Capital. Anything else I can help you with, sir?"

"Can you tell me the cost of the flights, please?"

"For both flights, booked one way. The cost is six thousand four hundred and forty eight euros, sir. Anything else I can help you with?"

"No, that should do it."

"All right, thank you, sir. Enjoy your day," the man said and disconnected.

Dillon found it interesting that O'Shea booked a flight last night to Amsterdam. Money didn't seem to be an object for him, booking first class on both flights. Did he spend the night at the airport? Maybe in the Delta lounge. Was he fleeing the country? Or had he just had enough of Ireland after losing his brother?

He decided to phone the US Marshals' district office in Boston. He went on Google for the phone number and had just input the number when his cellphone rang and vibrated, signaling an incoming call. He glanced at the cellphone screen and saw that DI Tiernan in Tallaght was calling. If he was calling, it couldn't be good. He hung up his desk phone just as it started to ring and answered his cell.

"Hi, Ward. Do I want to know why you're calling at this hour of the morning?"

"God save us. We've got another."

"Another? You mean a murder?"

"Afraid so. I think you and Suel talked to him the other day. Right here, as a matter of fact. We're at Tallaght Trainers, the boxing club. Your man's name is Dara Boyle."

THIRTY-NINE

Suel picked Dillon up at Special Branch.

"Sorry to call you so early," Dillon said as he climbed into the passenger seat.

"Not to worry. I'd been up for an hour," Suel said.

Dillon glanced over at him. His shirt was wrinkled, he needed a shave, and there was a touch of red lipstick on his neck. "At least wipe the lipstick off your neck."

Suel ran a hand across the left side of his neck. "Oh, sorry about that. Well, not really, actually. What do you have on this Dara Boyle? Isn't he Jimmy Byrne's enforcer?"

"Yeah, at the Tallaght Trainers boxing club. I called you as soon as I got off the line with Ward Tiernan."

"Are you thinking your man, O'Shea?"

"I was until I learned he flew to Amsterdam last night and is on his way to Boston as we speak." Dillon filled Suel in on his call to Delta Airlines and O'Shea taking an 8:00 flight out of Dublin last night.

"Lucky him that he left, but that leaves us with even less than we had before. If that's even possible," Suel said.

"I couldn't disagree. What about our two Dodder Demon friends?"

Suel shook his head. "Connell and McArdle? A couple of has-beens. The two of them together could barely be able to make themselves lunch, let alone leave the house and shoot someone. They'd have to invite Boyle to their house and get him to sit across from them after he loaded the gun for 'em. No, they're from a different time and place, although they may not realize it yet."

"What about Jimmy Byrne?" Dillon said.

"Byrne? Where'd you come up with that? With everything that's happened, you think Byrne would want to kill the very man he put in charge of keeping him safe?"

"Maybe Byrne was so pissed off about his niece's murder that he went after Boyle for not protecting her."

Suel shook his head. "If we had a list of suspects, I wouldn't even put Jimmy Byrne at the bottom of it."

"Just trying to come up with something, anything."

"Yeah, well, that last one doesn't work worth shit."

Suel pulled into the former industrial area, older warehouses, a plumbing supply shop, a print shop, and a vacant building. The squad cars up ahead marked their destination. Dillon still wore the lanyard around his neck, and as Suel slowed, he lowered the window and held up his ID to one of the officers.

"Best park in the lot here and walk over to the Trainer's club," the officer on Suel's side of the car said.

Suel turned into the parking lot. The building was an empty one-story structure with a For Sale sign out front and another in the large window facing the street. The parking lot had a half-dozen cars already parked in it. Probably more activity than it had seen in the past year. Suel pulled into a parking space and turned off the car.

The Tallaght Trainers club was just next door, maybe fifty feet away. The back of the building had a variety of colored graffiti spray-painted on the wall, but nowhere near as much as the front and the sides of the building.

The parking lot behind the place was cordoned off. Both uniformed and plain-clothes people were milling around. The Dublin Morgue van was there, again with the rear doors open. What looked like a stylish black car was cordoned off with white and blue tape. The car was up over the curb and sidewalk. It had crashed into a tree that was now leaning against the side of the building. The hood was buckled, and the grill on the front of the car and the one headlight Dillon could see were shattered.

Two people, a woman and a man in white boiler suits, appeared to be dusting for fingerprints. A plain-clothes man Dillon recognized as Mick Malony was taking photographs of the car from the passenger side. Dillon could see Dara Boyle's body still behind the steering wheel. The windows were down, and his head was partially out of the open driver's window. Blood was splattered across the inside of the windshield.

"There's Ward Tiernan over by the van," Suel said, and they walked in that direction.

Tiernan nodded as they approached, and the officer he was talking to walked back into the Tallaght Trainers club. "Sorry to start off your day with another one of these, lads."

"Anything so far?" Dillon said.

Tiernan shook his head. "Just like all the others, not a damn thing. Forensics are trying for fingerprints, and I'm keeping my fingers crossed, but if this is like the other scenes, and it seems to be turning out that way, the whole thing is banjaxed."

"When was he found?" Suel asked.

"Not much more than an hour ago. Apparently, he has his own key. Comes in early every morning and works out before anyone else is around. The maintenance man came around the corner and found him just the way you see," Tiernan said and nodded toward Boyle's car slammed up against the tree.

For the first time, Dillon noticed the logo on the car. "Is he driving a Tesla?"

Tiernan nodded. "Yeah, you guessed it. I think it's the first one I've ever seen. One of the lads said they go for ninety thousand euros. If I had something like that, no doubt some knacker would probably rear-end me on the first day."

"Lot of good it did Boyle," Suel said.

"Three rounds were fired. Any one of them could have been the kill shot," Tiernan said and shook his head.

Dillon glanced around but didn't see anything that looked like a camera. "No security cameras?"

Tiernan shook his head. "No, none. Which, of course, accounts for the graffiti all over the building. I think they must have figured, you know, a boxing club, who would dare to spray paint graffiti on the place? You can see how well that worked, and now this. Whoever it was had to know that your man was the first one here in the morning."

"Yeah, and maybe even watched him coming in here. Boyle probably took the same route every morning. You said he had a key and was a regular?" Suel said.

Tiernan nodded. "Yeah, worked out every day, seven days a week. Lot of good it did him. He comes around the corner, and your man fires three rounds. Based on the scene, your man had to be standing in the lot. Apparently, Boyle always parked in one of those reserved spots next to the building there. Your man is probably standing just over there," Tiernan nodded at the corner of the building. "Maybe he was hiding alongside his vehicle. Boyle comes around the corner. Even if he saw the gun, it was too late to get away."

"He was basically trapped. The shooter is suddenly there, maybe five feet away. Boyle has to slow down if there's a car around here, and he's about to pull into the parking space," Dillon said.

Tiernan nodded. "A couple of things come to mind. First off, like I said, whoever did this knew Boyle's routine. Knew it well. The next thing is, three shots were fired. Boyle's in a moving vehicle. Moving fast enough that when he's shot, he plows into that London Plane tree and knocks it into the building. He's hit three times. Each one of the shots could have killed him. Whoever the shooter was, he knew what he was doing. Those three rounds are beyond being simply lucky shots. Whoever pulled the trigger is an experienced stone-cold killer."

"What about your man, this American, O'Shea?" Suel asked.

Dillon shook his head. "The problem with him is that he was on a flight last night to Amsterdam and from there flying to Boston. He's heading to the US. In fact, he's in the air somewhere over the Atlantic now."

"Are you sure?"

Dillon nodded. "Dermot Roach followed him to Terminal Two last night at 5:15. O'Shea checked a bag, and Roach watched him go through security. I phoned Delta Airlines this morning and spoke to a supervisor. O'Shea purchased a one-way ticket going back to Boston. I don't know this, but maybe our conversation yesterday, as brief as it was, put the fear of God in him, and he headed back to Boston."

"You think he may have set someone up to do this?" Tiernan said.

Dillon shrugged. "Anything's possible. But I think between the death of his brother, Suel and I sitting with him at breakfast, even if it was just for a couple of minutes. Then he realizes that we've got someone watching him twenty-four hours a day. I'd say he decided to leave, get the hell out of town, and with any luck, he'll never come back."

"Amen to that," Suel said.

"Which brings us back to who did this?" Dillon said.

"We've got someone checking security cameras on the surrounding buildings. Maybe they'll pick up someone driving in and out. Barely sunrise. It's not like there would have been a lot of traffic," Tiernan said.

FORTY

Dillon and Suel headed in the direction of the Tesla with Dara Boyle's body still in the front seat behind the wheel. Dillon glanced over at the Dublin Morgue van, hoping he might see Noel Leonard, but neither man in the process of pulling the gurney out of the back was Leonard.

Mick Malony was taking photos of the Tesla and the damage to the front of the vehicle and the tree. With the images, Forensics would be able to approximate the vehicle's speed at the time of impact.

"How fast do you think he was going?" Suel asked, looking at the corner of the building, maybe thirty feet away.

"He wasn't speeding, that's for sure," Dillon said. "He had to slow down to make the turn, and then, even if he sped up, he had to slow down to pull into one of those reserved parking places. The shooter pops up and fires at a moving target. Even if the car was moving slowly, firing three shots and not missing, Tiernan's right. Whoever did this knew what the hell they were doing. My sense is, once Boyle was hit, his body had a muscular reaction. He stomped on the accelerator, and the car sped into the tree. Be interesting to see what the autopsy says, but I would think death was immediate, and we're viewing the logical reaction."

"Which brings us back to who did this?"

"Can we agree that there is some connection to Dara Boyle's murder here, Nora Lynch yesterday, Hogan, Ginty and your man with the tire track face at the Manhole Pub, Ding-Dong Bell, and probably Patrick O'Shea?" Dillon said.

"Yes, I think we can. And, can we agree that our logical suspect is currently traveling halfway around the world to Boston and is, therefore no longer a suspect, at least in this particular case?" Dillon seemed to think about that for a long moment. "Dillon?"

"I was going to make a phone call earlier, and Tiernan's call got me sidetracked. Hold on," he said, pulled out his cell, and hit a speed-dial number. A moment later, he said, "Yes, thank you, my name is Marshal Jack Dillon. I'm currently in Dublin, Ireland working a murder investigation. Time here is five hours ahead of you. Would you please connect me to the Boston District office? Yeah, hang on," Dillon said, then gave his Marshals badge number and another number he read off his US Marshals ID. He glanced at Suel and nodded. "That flight with O'Shea on it is landing in Boston early this morning US time. I want to—"

Dillon held up his index finger, signaling to wait, and said, "Hello. Yes, thank you. I'm US Marshal Jack Dillon calling from Dublin, Ireland. I'm attached to An

Garda Síochána, Special Branch. I need someone to check the arrival of a passenger on a flight from Amsterdam to Boston. The flight is Swiss Air, arriving in Boston at 7:40 local time." He went through the same routine again, providing his badge and ID numbers. Once that was completed, he repeated the arrival time of the flight and again mentioned that it was a Swiss Air flight.

"The individual's name is Sean O'Shea. His flight was purchased using an American Express card registered to Bridge Street Capital. I believe he is a Boston resident. He's a person of interest in a series of murders here in Dublin. No, you do not have to take him into custody. In fact, please don't. We simply need to have confirmation that he did, indeed, board the flight departing from Amsterdam. Yes. If someone could contact me as soon as possible at this number. Thank you. Yes. That's correct. Thank you," Dillon said and disconnected.

"Now you're thinking O'Shea didn't go to Boston?"

"I just want to make sure, that's all. He bought the ticket for six grand. But he's a rich guy. I'm getting a nagging feeling again," Dillon said.

Mick Malony walked over to Dillon and Suel. "I'm beginning to feel like I see the two of you every day."

"It seems to be shaping up that way," Dillon said.

"Did you have a chance to view the file of the Nora Lynch images I sent you?" Malony said.

Dillon shook his head. "Unfortunately, not yet. You have any thoughts?"

"Only that it was a most unfortunate situation. This one isn't much better, but at least it's not some innocent who answered a knock on her door."

"Anything stand out to you at this scene?" Suel said.

"Three rounds fired, and all three hit their target. Two in the head, a third in the neck just below the jawline. Whoever did the shooting, they were good. Couldn't have been more than a second or two to get the shots off and at a moving target. That's pretty amazing."

"Yeah, unfortunately for Dara Boyle."

"You going to want this file, too?" Malony asked Dillon.

"Yeah, might as well, if you don't mind," Dillon said.

"I'll send them as soon as I'm back at the station. I should check in with DI Tiernan."

"Good to see you again, Mick," Dillon said.

"Yeah, sorry it's under these circumstances."

"You want to hang here for a while?" Suel asked.

"You're saying that like you have something else in mind."

"I'm thinking we're not going to accomplish anything hanging around here. They'll examine and take the body to Dublin Morgue. Tow the car to impound. Apparently, there's no one we can talk to and ask what they may have seen. Why don't we try to talk to Jimmy Byrne? See what he thinks."

"Not a bad idea," Dillon said.

They touched base with DI Tiernan before they left and then climbed back into Suel's car. "You want me to call in and get Byrne's address?" Dillon said.

Suel shook his head. "Don't bother. I know where the knacker lives. He's down in Rathmines. At no surprise on one of the most expensive streets in all of Dublin."

"You're kidding me?"

"I only wish," Suel said. "You can't tell me crime doesn't pay. I find it interesting that your man Byrne has more money than he can spend, and his niece was splitting the rent in a place that isn't much bigger than a doghouse, and now he's all upset. So f'ing typical of the privileged lot in this country."

Once in Rathmines, Suel turned onto Temple Gardens. A quiet street of unattached, two-story brick homes with slate roofs. All the homes looked to be over a hundred years old. Toward the end of the street, Suel started to turn left and immediately stopped.

Dillon could see Byrne's house through the eight-foot-high wrought iron gates, but a vehicle on the other side of the gate was blocking any entry. As if that wasn't reason enough, the two armed individuals approaching the car served as another reason to stop.

Suel lowered his window, and the man on his side of the car stopped a few feet away. The second man walked over to Dillon's side and stood maybe five feet away, opposite the rear door.

"Mr. Byrne is not receiving visitors this morning," the man said to Suel. He had the look of someone you would not want to mess with. Solid, muscular, with close-cropped hair, and then there was the pistol handle protruding from his belt.

Suel said, "We're with An Garda Síochána, Special Branch. We spoke briefly with Jimmy yesterday. We have some information I suspect he'll be interested in."

"Youse can tell me, and I'll pass it on to Mr. Byrne."

"Afraid I can't do that. If he wants the information, I have to tell him personally."

The man seemed to think about that for a moment and then said, "Let me see some identification." Suel pulled out his warrant card and handed it to him.

The man studied it for a moment and said, "What about your friend?"

Dillon handed his warrant card to Suel, who gave it to the man. He seemed to study Dillon's card for at least twice as long as he did Suel's and eventually handed it back to Suel, who returned it to Dillon.

"Hang on a minute," the man said and pulled out his cellphone. He stepped away from the car and spoke into his phone. After a minute, he nodded at Suel and waved his arm at the gate. The car blocking the entrance suddenly started and backed up to the side. Another muscular guy hopped out of the car and opened the double gates. "Drive in and park in the front. Leave your car unlocked," the man said.

Suel pulled ahead and up the drive toward the front door. "So I'd say Byrne got the message that someone isn't pleased," Dillon said.

"Yeah, interesting. I'm wondering if you should stay in the car."

"I think that might cause more problems. In fact, what do you think about me telling him about Dara Boyle? Hopefully, he'll think I'm trying to smooth things over with him."

"You want to take that chance?" Suel said. He pulled behind the black Mercedes Dillon recognized from yesterday at Byrne's. Suel placed the car in park and turned it off.

"Yeah, I promise I'll be gentle," Dillon said.

"Suit yourself. Just remember you're playing with fire here."

FORTY-ONE

yrne's red-brick house was three stories tall. Based on the size of the windows, the ceilings in the place were probably ten feet high. The front of the house featured a large three-sided, two-story extension on either side of the front door. The door was actually inset six feet in an entrance with a curved top.

A man was seated on a wooden chair at the entrance. An assault rifle rested across his lap. His hands were positioned on the weapon in such a way that he'd be able to raise it and fire before Dillon or Suel could successfully draw their pistols. Dillon recognized the weapon as a Heckler & Koch HK433. He'd fired one a few times. The magazine held thirty rounds. He was going to make a comment but thought better of it.

The man didn't bother with a greeting. Instead, he said, "Place your weapons in the box," and nodded at a cardboard wine box in the corner on the floor.

They placed their pistols in the box and stepped back.

"Let me warn you. You'll be searched when you step inside. If you've got anything strapped to an ankle or hidden in your pants, put it in the box, now. They'll shoot you inside without a second thought."

"I'm clean," Suel said.

"Same here," Dillon said.

"Okay, just don't think you can fool them in there. Everyone is wound pretty damn tight this morning."

"No, we're good," Suel said.

Dillon nodded.

"Okay, in you go," he said and knocked on the door twice, paused, and knocked two more times.

A moment later, the lock clicked, and another guy opened the door. He signaled with a wave of his head that they could enter. As they stepped into the entryway, he said, "Assume the position against the wall, lads. We'll double-check you."

Dillon and Suel leaned against the wall. Someone patted them down and then said, "They're okay."

"Follow me," the guy who opened the door said and led them down a paneled hall. He stopped at an oak door and knocked.

"Yeah," someone shouted from inside. The guy who led them opened the door and stepped inside. Once Dillon and Suel entered, he closed the door on his way out of the room. All four walls were covered with eight-foot-high bookshelves, except for three of the walls where the middle bookshelf was only four feet high. Above the four-foot bookshelf hung an antique oil painting in a gold frame, a landscape in all three cases. The books were all leather bound with gold letters on the spine, and

Dillon was positive Jimmy Byrne had never read any of them.

"Well, if it ain't the Guards. No doubt with good news. Come on over and brighten our day, lads," Byrne said. He was seated in a brown leather recliner. Next to him on a couch was an older gentleman, maybe seventy-five. Byrne held a crystal glass with close to an inch of what looked like whiskey. He took a sip as Dillon and Suel approached.

"Thanks for making the time to see us, Jimmy," Suel said. "You doing okay?"

"I've recovered from the assault the other day if that's what you're referring to," he said and glared at Dillon.

"Sorry about that, sir. Glad you're on the mend. It's just that the scene inside was heartbreaking, and I guess after dealing with it, I lost my cool. I thought you might have been a neighbor or a reporter, and I didn't want you going in there."

"A neighbor or a reporter? That's good, real good. You're a fecking guard, and you don't know who in the hell I am?" Byrne shouted.

"I know who you are."

Byrne took another sip from his glass and said, "So what day brightener did you come to tell me?"

"Unfortunately, it's regarding Dara Boyle. He was shot early this morning at the Tallaght Trainers club. It appears his death was instant," Dillon said.

Byrne appeared to be unaffected by the news. "I'm guessing I'd be wasting my time asking the likes of you if an arrest has been made. I don't suppose you have anyone in mind as the shooter. You've no idea who did this. You're blind as fecking bats, the lot of yas."

"Do you have anyone in mind, sir?" Dillon said.

"Do I have—It could well have been one of your own. Dara's going in early to work out like he does every day. Minding his health. Not hurting so much as a fly. Now you ask me if I have anyone in mind? I'll tell you who I have in mind, you mess of blind gobshites. You ever think your man Sean O'Shea from the US of A might be someone of interest? Jaysus, God, I can't drive from here to the grocery store without one of yas following me, and this plonker arrives and starts shooting me mates, murders me niece, and the pair of yas are here asking the likes of me, who did it? Go on, the both of yas. Get the hell out of me sight," Byrne shouted and drained his whiskey glass.

"As soon as we learn something, we'll be in touch, sir," Suel said and gave a tug to Dillon's sleeve.

"You take care, sir," Dillon said and followed Suel to the door.

Suel stepped out, and as Dillon took hold of the doorknob, Byrne called out, "How much is he paying the likes of yas? Huh? How bleedin' much?"

"Let's get the hell out of here," Suel said, just as the guy who patted them down stepped into the hall.

"This way," he said and watched as they approached.

They collected their pistols from the box outside the front door. Once in the car, Dillon checked his magazine to make sure it hadn't been tinkered with. Suel turned on the car, backed up, and drove around Byrne's black Mercedes.

"Good thing we left. I was tempted to pull one of those bookcases over on that privileged prick. Who was the old guy in there?" Dillon said.

"I might be mistaken, but I think it was Byrne's uncle, Rooney Byrne."

"Is he the patriarch or something?"

"He took over when Byrne's father was killed. That was back in 1980 or '81. Byrne never really knew his old man, and Rooney stepped in, basically raised him, and brought him up through the ranks. The mother drank herself to death two or three years after the father was killed. Rooney is the man who made Byrne who he is today."

"He's a privileged twit is who he is," Dillon said. "A god-awful privileged twit."

"No argument from me," Suel said. "How come you didn't mention that O'Shea was headed back to the States?"

Dillon shook his head. "I didn't think it would make any difference. Byrne would have just gone after us for letting him leave the country. Pretty tough talk from the head of one of the larger crime organizations in Dublin."

"Yeah, I know what you're saying. Look, based on the security he has around him, whoever is out there doing this definitely has the man's attention. As far as I'm concerned, that just keeps him out of our hair, and that's fine with me."

"Good point. Are we headed back to Special Branch?" Dillon said.

"Yeah, unless you have somewhere else we can waste our time."

"No, Let's get back there. I'll have those two image files from Mick Malony to go through."

"Yeah, and I want to give Shannon a call," Suel said.

Dillon shot him a look.

"Relax, just kidding."

FORTY-TWO

Dillon's desk phone was blinking when he got back to Special Branch. He had two messages. "Hey, Dillon, Chris Becker returning your call. Great to hear you're still vacationing over in Ireland. Sorry it took so long to get back to you. I was at a conference down in Dallas, and then the wife and I took a couple days and visited her sister out on Padre Island.

"I did some searching on Sean O'Shea. You were correct about his three tours in Afghanistan. He was in a special forces unit. Information is a little murky on what exactly they did, so my guess would be some pretty top-secret stuff. He got out of the service with the rank of Captain, awarded a Bronze Star, Silver Star, and Distinguished Service Cross, along with the usual. So, whatever he was involved in had to be heavy duty. I'm thinking behind the lines action.

"From there, he went into civilian life, started an investment group, Bridge Street Capital, and apparently became quite successful. He's been investigated numerous times by the Boston police and at least two state agencies but never charged. In one instance, he sued the Massachusetts Department of Revenue, and they settled out of court for an undisclosed amount. Last known address was in Boston, but he hasn't been there for three years. Bottom line, he's smart, probably connected, and not the guy you'd want to mess with. Sorry, I don't have more info, but that's all I could find. We need to get together sometime. It's been too many years. Later, Dude."

Dillon hung up and thought for a moment. Sean O'Shea had combat experience. Given the medals awarded, he'd seen some serious action. Did that make him even more dangerous, or did it have the effect that he'd do almost anything to avoid conflict? If he didn't live in Boston, why did he book a flight there?

He listened to the second message, Noel Leonard, at Dublin Morgue. "Hi Dillon, meant to call yesterday, but we've been jammed. We completed the autopsy on Nora Lynch. One round to the head as you know. No trace of alcohol or drugs, and she was two months pregnant. Any questions, give me a call."

It just doesn't end, Dillon thought. He recalled the comment Michele Hughes, Nora Lynch's flatmate, had made. How Lynch and Patrick O'Shea got back together after a week apart and went down to Cork two months ago.

"Dillon, you're looking deep in thought. I'm heading out to one of the food trucks for some lunch. You want to come with, or can I bring you something?"

"I'll go with you," he said and followed Suel out the door. Over soft shell tacos and tea, Dillon told Suel about the phone messages.

"Okay," Suel said, taking a large bite of his taco. "So your man was in the army and had combat experience. That's not unusual in the States. And as for not having a mailing address, I would guess a quick search on you might end up the same way."

"But not for a government agency like the US Marshals," Dillon said.

"Sounds like the guy made a chunk of money and decided to move out of the big city. Who can blame him? Is he married?"

"I don't know."

"Maybe he's got a wife and kids, and it's something as simple as leaving the city and moving to a better school district. If he was that successful, maybe the house is listed under his company name, you know, like his hotel room was at the Merrion. What was the name of the company?"

"Bridge Street Capital, in fact, that was the name on the title for Patrick O'Shea's house."

"Yeah, so there you go, nothing to worry about. Eat up. I'm thinking I might need one of those ice cream tacos to give me enough strength until dinner. You up for it?"

Dillon shook his head and said, "No, you go ahead."

Back at his desk, Dillon was going through the crime scene photo files Mick Malony, at Tallaght, had sent over. There wasn't much to see in either the Nora Lynch or the Dara Boyle images. They were basically short and sweet.

Nora Lynch had been shot at very close range. She was probably dead before she hit the floor. Same thing with Dara Boyle. He was shot three times, two in the head and one in the neck. Dillon looked at the close-up shots of Boyle. He found it interesting that the neck shot had hit Boyle's skull and snake tattoo. He was still thinking of that when his cellphone rang.

He pulled it out of his pocket and didn't recognize the number, although the call was coming from the United States. "Jack Dillon."

"Is this US Marshal Jack Dillon?"

"Yes, it is. Who's calling, please?"

"My name is Daunte Fredrick. I'm with the US Marshals Service in Boston, and—"

"Is this regarding the Swiss Air flight and passenger Sean O'Shea?"

"It is, sir, and unfortunately, Sean O'Shea was not on the flight."

"Suel," Dillon called and signaled Suel to come over. "Are you sure? He purchased a one-way ticket for over six thousand euros flying from Dublin to Amsterdam and Amsterdam to Boston. One of our officers watched him purchase the ticket, check his bag, and clear security."

"Interesting you say that, because his luggage did arrive. It's still at Boston airport being held for us. We've filed for a warrant to take possession of the suitcase. We're just waiting for that to be issued."

"But O'Shea wasn't on the flight?"

"No, he was not. A further check with the airlines found that he did not board the Dublin to Amsterdam flight. It would appear he never left Dublin, and he is out six grand. I have the airline email stating he was a no-show on the Dublin Amsterdam flight. Their policy at that point is they cancel the rest of the itinerary, but he's still charged for the flights."

"If you would send me that email, please, Daunte," Dillon said and gave him his email address.

"Coming your way in just a moment. Say, you mind if I ask you a personal question?"

"No, how can I help?"

"How'd you score gettin' posted over in Dublin? You taking it easy there?"

"Long story how I got here, and I've never worked harder."

"Hmm, I'm clicking the send button now. You on a cellphone?"

Yes."

"Okay, you got my number there. Call me if you have any questions."

"I will and thank you."

"My pleasure, sir," he said and disconnected.

"What's up?" Suel was staring at the close-up image of Dara Boyle with his arm partially hanging out the open driver's window.

"That was a US Marshal out of Boston by the name of Daunte Frederick. Turns out Sean O'Shea is going to be charged six thousand euros for flights he never took."

"What?"

"Yeah. Apparently, he never left Dublin, let alone flew to the States. The bastard has been here all the time."

"But you called the fecking airline, and they said he took the flight."

"I called shortly after it took off. Now that I think about it, all the guy confirmed was that O'Shea had a ticket. He never confirmed he actually boarded the flight."

"Damn it. That brings us back to Dara Boyle this morning and puts your man, O'Shea, back at the top of everyone's list."

"I need to call DI Tiernan and DCI O'Brien. You want to go in and let McCabe know? We need to get an arrest warrant issued and fast."

"We need to find this bollocks first," Suel said just as Dillon's computer signaled an email coming through.

Dillon brought up his email account. There it was, an email from the US Marshals' Boston District. He clicked on the link and opened the attached file from Delta Airlines, listing Sean O'Shea as a no-show, canceling the itinerary, and stating that the charges remained.

"Oh, Christ. Let me print this off for you. Give a copy to DCI McCabe. I'm going to forward this to Tiernan and O'Brien along with the passport image and information on O'Shea."

"Good idea," Suel said. "Have Tallaght apply for the arrest warrant. They'll get it faster."

Dillon nodded as he typed. "Copies of this are printing now," he said.

Suel hurried over to the copy machine.

Dillon put together a quick email with Sean O'Shea's passport photo, information, and the Delta Airline attachment from Daunte Frederick. He emailed them to DI Tiernan and DCI O'Brien. He picked up the phone and called DI Tiernan at Tallaght station.

Tiernan answered on the second ring. "What's up, Dillon?"

"Ward, are you at your desk? I just sent you and DCI O'Brien an email a moment ago. I just got a call from the US Marshals' District in Boston. It turns out Sean O'Shea never flew out of Dublin to Amsterdam and never flew from Amsterdam to Boston, although his luggage did arrive in Boston."

"I thought you told me he bought a ticket for six thousand euros. Didn't someone from Special Branch watch him at the airport?"

"He did buy a ticket for six grand, and he's being charged that. The DI who followed him at the airport watched him go through security but didn't follow him to the gate."

"Oh, for the love of—Oh, just got your email. Hang on for a second." Dillon waited. Tiernan came back on the line a minute later. "Yeah, I'm looking at your email now."

"I'm thinking you guys should get the arrest warrant out on O'Shea. I want to call the embassy, have them alert passport control. He's bound to still be in the country. I'd say there's about a ninety-five percent chance he's responsible for Dara Boyle this morning, and I think you might want to give Jimmy Byrne a call and let him know as well."

"I suppose we had better. Any idea where O'Shea is?" Tiernan said.

"No, we'll be checking on credit card use and freezing the card."

"I'd better get moving on this. Anything happens, let me know."

"I'm calling DCI O'Brien in just a minute," Dillon said.

"Good luck," Tiernan said and disconnected.

FORTY-THREE

Dillon didn't arrive home until almost 9:00 that night. It had been an awfully long, lousy day. Amazingly, Lucifer hadn't left a mess to clean. He pulled a frozen shepherd's pie from the freezer and placed it in the microwave. He and Lucifer settled in front of the TV and watched Graham Norton. Dillon even shared a bit of the shepherd's pie with Lucifer. He dozed off in his chair and woke to the sound of his cell phone ringing.

"Dillon," he answered.

"It's Tiernan, Dillon. I'm in Rathmines. Someone slammed into Jimmy Byrne's Mercedes and killed him."

"What?" Dillon said and shook his head, hoping to wake up.

"We're at Milltown Road and Richmond Avenue South. Two-car crash. Four dead. One of them's Jimmy Byrne. He was shot."

Dillon was now fully awake. "Give me that intersection again." He wrote it down as Tiernan repeated it, then thanked him and said he was on his way.

He phoned Suel. "Aw, Jaysus, I'm not giving the likes of you a ride home, wherever you are. What's up?"

"I just got a call from Tiernan. Jimmy Byrne's been shot. He's dead. A car crash."

"Slow down. You're not making any sense."

"Apparently, a car rammed Byrne's Mercedes. Byrne was shot. Tiernan said four people are dead. I don't know if one of them is O'Shea. I'm heading there in just a minute."

"I'd better join you. That's Rathmines jurisdiction. Tiernan's going to be on the sidelines. You know where this is?"

Dillon looked at his note. "He said the intersection of Milltown Road and Richmond Avenue South."

"I know the area. It's along the Dodder River. Close to the Churchtown Road bridge over the Dodder. I'll meet you there," Suel said and disconnected.

Dillon wondered for a moment if Suel had been with Shannon. He rose from his chair and picked up the ceramic dish off the floor that the shepherd's pie had been in. Lucifer had licked it clean. He set the dish in the kitchen sink, drank a glass of water, and hurried out the door.

He started his car and backed out of the drive. He glanced at the clock. It was almost 1:00 in the morning. He headed across town to Rathmines. He wasn't exactly sure where the Richmond Avenue intersection was, but he knew how to get to the Dodder River, and Milltown Road ran along the river. Just a few minutes later, he saw the flashing lights ahead.

Two officers were directing traffic back the way they'd come, not that there was much traffic at this hour. Fortunately, Dillon's ID and warrant card were still in his pocket. He showed them to the officers and continued ahead, parking behind a squad car.

The crash scene was illuminated by a series of battery-operated lights on metal stands positioned around the scene. Dillon ducked beneath the crime scene tape. The Dublin Morgue van and two EMT vehicles were on the scene. He picked up on the fact that no one was hurrying around, which suggested there wasn't anyone in need of urgent care.

Byrne's Mercedes was now more of a U-shaped pile of metal. A silver BMW had broadsided the Mercedes just at the driver's door and pushed it off the road and into the side of a steep weed-covered hill. The rear door on the passenger side of the Mercedes was open, and at the moment, a woman was dusting it for fingerprints. Twenty feet up the hill was an apartment building lit up like a Christmas tree. People were peering out the windows, looking through the trees to the crash scene below.

Dillon spotted Ward Tiernan on the far side of the crash site talking to two men and headed over. Tiernan caught sight of him as he approached.

"This is him, here. Dillon, thanks for coming," Tiernan said. "This is DI Tommy Carroll and DI Rayland Purcell, both with Rathmines Garda."

Dillon nodded, smiled, and shook hands. "Marshal Jack Dillon, Special Branch. What the hell happened?"

Carroll said, "The Mercedes was hit by that Silver BMW, a Hertz rental, by the way. We got someone attempting to find who rented the vehicle."

Dillon glanced at Tiernan, who nodded. "My money's on Sean O'Shea."

"That's the name we're hearing," Carroll said.

"Whoever is checking on that rental with Hertz, if it's not under O'Shea's name, it may be under Bridge Street Capital. That's apparently the man's company, and he's been using an American Express card with that name. No sign of O'Shea?" Dillon asked.

"No. Whoever was driving the BMW was injured. There's blood on the driver's seat. The driver made his way into the back seat and out the rear door on the passenger side, and there's blood there as well. Could be serious, or maybe it's just a split lip. The driver of the Mercedes and an elderly man were killed in the crash. Two individuals on the passenger side of the Mercedes were shot. One of them, Byrne, was shot four times. The man in the front passenger seat was armed but never drew his weapon."

"Can I take a look at the victims?"

Carroll glanced over. The medical examiners were still on site, examining the victims. "Maybe wait until the MEs are finished."

Suel showed up a few minutes later. He introduced himself to Carroll and Purcell. Everyone chatted and then waited for the medical examiners to finish up. Once they got the go-ahead to move in closer to the scene, they slipped on latex gloves. The first thing Dillon noticed was that Byrne had been shot four times in the face. Based on the wounds, he guessed a small-caliber weapon. The armed man in the front passenger seat was the same thug with the ponytail who had accompanied Byrne when he'd attempted to push his way past Dillon at Nora Lynch's home. He had one bullet hole in his forehead. The older man Carroll had referred to was Byrne's uncle, Rooney Byrne. He hadn't been shot, but he and the driver had probably been killed instantly in the crash.

Dillon, Suel, and Tiernan stayed around for another four hours, basically twiddling their thumbs. Not that there was anything they could do. Dillon climbed into bed a little before 6:00. Lucifer woke him at 8:00. Dillon let him out into the front garden and went back to bed. He woke just before 11:00.

He let Lucifer back in the house, grabbed a shower, and headed to Special Branch. He had three phone conversations with DI Tiernan and one with DCI O'Brien. He and Suel met with DCI McCabe and brought him up to date. Passport control had been alerted to the situation, as had the airlines along with the ferries heading to the UK and the EU.

Time passed without a sign of Sean O'Shea. His fingerprints were found on the BMW. The DNA from the blood in the driver's seat and on the rear passenger door was a match to O'Shea's military records, which had been acquired with the help of the US Marshals' office in Boston.

Dillon and Suel turned their attention to Ukrainian arrivals and a scheme to take advantage of that particular situation. Time passed, and Sean O'Shea was replaced by other more current concerns. Dillon drove past Nora Lynch's home in Tallaght and saw a For Sale sign out front. A painter's van was parked in the driveway.

He stopped for a moment and looked at the place, remembered how small it was inside, and shook his head. Not only her murder but the deaths of nine other people, and no conclusion. It was tough to take, and for Dillon, that was the downside.

FORTY-FOUR

The stack of files was still on Dillon's desk. He called Eric Bergman, passport control, and anyone else he could think of, but everything they could do had already been done. He wondered if maybe O'Shea had headed north, up to Belfast. He could have paid a fisherman, out of Torr or someplace, to take him across to Southend in Scotland. From there, someone like O'Shea could disappear forever. The Mideast, South America, Africa, hell, he could be back in Boston for all Dillon knew, and he'd be none the wiser.

Another day and no further ahead, he'd have to let go soon or risk losing what was left of his sanity. He turned onto his lane and drove past Tara's house. She was just getting out of her car, and she gave him a friendly wave and a smile. A month ago, he would have grabbed a bottle of wine and headed over. Tonight, he did what he'd done for the past couple of weeks. He let Lucifer out, rummaged some leftovers for dinner, and settled in front of the TV.

He'd almost drifted off to sleep when his cell rang. He pulled it from his pocket, didn't recognize the number, and was about to delete the call, but something stopped him. "Marshal Dillon," he answered.

"Oh, hi, Marshal. Eoghan Walsh here. Don't know if you recall our conversation a couple of months ago. Keira and I live just a few doors from the former home of the O'Shea lad who was murdered."

"Yes, oh yes, I remember, Eoghan. What can I do for you?"

"Well, I'm not sure. I was up in the middle of the night last night. Couldn't sleep, and I'm looking out the window. A taxi pulls up at the opposite end. Now, this is 3:00 in the morning. A man gets out, walks toward the O'Shea house, and disappears. It's been bothering me all day. I walked past the place three different times today and didn't notice anything amiss. I walked past maybe an hour ago, and I swear I saw a light go off on the first floor. Not a room light. It was more like light from a candle or a flashlight. The place is supposed to be empty. Kiera told me to give you a call."

Dillon was already at the front door, slipping on his shoes. "I appreciate the call, Eoghan. I'll have someone check it out. Just to be safe. Do not go down there. Stay in your house and make sure your doors are locked."

"You think something is amiss?"

"I think we should check just to make sure nothing is amiss. Thank you for the call," Dillon said.

He hurried out the door and into his car. He called Suel, put the cellphone on speaker, and backed onto the lane.

Suel answered, "It's late, Dillon."

"Hey, I just got a call from Eoghan Walsh. He lives about four doors from Patrick O'Shea's place. He thinks he saw a light on inside, a flashlight or maybe a candle."

"O'Shea's place? You don't think?"

"Not sure what to think, but I don't want to ignore it."

"I'll meet you there. You want to put in a call?'

"For backup? We don't need one more false alarm or calling out six men on double overtime to find out it's a couple of kids from across the way."

"Okay, I'll meet you there. Park on the next street over," Suel said.

"I'm only about ten minutes away," Dillon said.

He lied. It was more like five minutes when he pulled to the curb on the next street over. Suel pulled in less than ten minutes later. Dillon already had his bullet-proof vest on. The word GARDA was in yellow letters on the front and back. As Suel pulled in behind him, Dillon hurried over.

"You really think he's in there?"

"There's only one way to find out," Dillon said.

Suel opened his rear door, pulled out his vest, and slipped it on. He released the magazine in his pistol, checked it, then reinserted it. "Let's go."

They hurried around the corner. The O'Shea place looked quiet. Everything was dark. There was a For Sale sign out front. The Garda tape crisscrossing the front door had been removed. A lockbox that no doubt held a key for the realtor was attached to the brass door knocker. Wooden panels covered the lower half of the first-floor windows.

"You really think O'Shea is in there? The place is for sale," Suel said.

"Well, no one is looking at it this late. We've come this far. Let me climb the wall, and I'll open the back gate for you."

"If the place is for sale, they've probably replaced the glass door in back."

"We can check, just to be sure," Dillon said. He walked over to the side gate and pushed it, expecting it to be locked. Instead, it opened a good six inches.

"What the hell?" Suel whispered.

Dillon pushed the gate all the way open, pulled out his pistol, and they quietly walked around to the back of the house. The glass door leading to the patio was still covered by two wood panels, and Patrick O'Shea's bloodstains remained on the steps. It appeared no one had made an effort to remove them.

Dillon pointed at the wood panels covering the door and raised his index finger to his mouth, signaling quiet. He glanced at the windows. Everything seemed quiet. He stepped up to the bottom panel and carefully pulled it away from the doorframe, revealing the door and no glass. He signaled Suel with a wave of his hand to follow him inside.

Dillon stepped into the kitchen and knelt down next to the dining room table. Suel settled in next to him. The door leading to the front hallway was open, which struck him as strange. He pulled out his flashlight, just over five inches long, and set it to the lowest setting before he turned it on. He aimed the dim light at the open doorway and spotted what he was looking for. A string maybe ten inches from the floor was stretched across the doorway.

He turned off the flashlight and whispered into Suel's ear. "There's a string across the doorway. That means he's in here somewhere. Follow me. I'm going to remove it but mind yourself. We're going to take our time."

Suel nodded and followed Dillon as they tiptoed toward the door. Dillon stopped at the doorway, turned on his flashlight, and peeked around to the far side of the doorway. The string was tied around an empty wine bottle on either side of the door. Dillon studied the bottles for a moment. They were empty, and that was it, no device attached. He carefully took hold of the bottle on the righthand side and moved it next to the bottle on the opposite side of the door.

As he turned and nodded at Suel, they heard what sounded like a chair being moved in the sitting room. They both froze. There the sound was again, and a few later, once more.

Suel tapped Dillon on the shoulder. He closed his eyes and opened his mouth, mimicking someone snoring. Dillon nodded and slowly moved ahead. The snoring continued.

They slowly moved down the hallway to the entrance of the sitting room. Dillon waited a moment, then peeked into the room as the snoring continued. There he was, Sean O'Shea, asleep on the couch opposite the fireplace, snoring. A wine bottle and an empty glass were on the floor in front of the couch. Dillon checked the doorway, no string.

He signaled with his hand that he would move toward the couch, and Suel should step just inside the room. With his pistol aimed at O'Shea, Dillon slowly approached. Suel took up a position at the end of the couch and aimed his pistol at O'Shea.

Dillon moved around the coffee table to the far end of the couch as O'Shea continued to snore. He shoved his pistol into his belt and signaled his next movement to Suel.

Suel nodded.

Dillon crossed his arms, right arm over the left, and slowly reached down. He suddenly grabbed hold of O'Shea's shoulders and rolled him onto the floor between the coffee table and the couch.

As soon as he hit the floor, Suel landed with a knee on O'Shea's back and his pistol pressed against the back of his head.

"Uff," O'Shea groaned and coughed as Suel dropped on top of him.

"Don't even think of trying anything, you bloody wanker," Suel shouted as Dillon slapped a handcuff onto O'Shea's wrist and pulled his arm up behind his back.

"Ahh, for Christ's sake, you're going to break my damn arm," O'Shea groaned.

Dillon grabbed the other arm and slapped the handcuff on the wrist. He nodded to Suel, and they reached down. Each one grabbed an arm and raised O'Shea back onto the couch. Suel stepped over to an end table and turned on a lamp. O'Shea's nose was swollen, red, and now had a distinctive curve in the middle. Dillon recalled the blood on the driver's seat and the rear door of the silver BMW that broadsided Byrne's Mercedes. He must have broken his nose in the crash.

"Hold on, you two. Just hold on for a minute. Let's maybe think about working something out here."

Suel shook his head and gave the standard required caution, "You are not obliged to say anything unless you wish to do so, but whatever you say will be taken down in writing and may be given in evidence."

"I want my attorney," O'Shea said and then remained quiet.

Dillon called Special Branch and requested a squad car. Once he disconnected, he smiled at O'Shea and said, "You're a hard man to stay in touch with, Sean. Thought you should know, Nora Lynch, Jimmy Byrne's niece, was two months pregnant with your brother Pat's baby. That would have been your niece or nephew."

"What? That can't be. He, he would have told me."

"Happy to show you the medical records. She was in bed with him the night he was killed."

"You're lying. He told me they broke up."

"Well, apparently, they got back together."

EPILOGUE

It took eight months, but Sean O'Shea eventually went to court surrounded by four solicitors. Charges were dropped in the murders of Dennis "Ding-Dong" Bell, Brennan Hogan, Connor Ginty, Adam Dyer, the man with the tire track tattoo, Nora Lynch, and Dara Boyle. He was convicted of vehicular homicide in the deaths of Rooney Byrne and the driver of Byrne's Mercedes, Michael Logan. He was given fifteen-year sentences to be served consecutively. In the murders of Jimmy Boyle and Seamus Hanlan, the man with the ponytail, O'Shea was found guilty and sentenced to life without the possibility of parole. In other words, he would spend the rest of his days behind bars.

Dillon celebrated by taking Eoghan and Kiera Walsh out to dinner, where they discussed everything except Sean O'Shea. He was home just after 9:00 that evening and felt as if a weight had been lifted from his shoulders. He let Lucifer out and then coaxed him back in with a biscuit and was about to settle in front of the TV when his cellphone rang.

"Dillon," he answered and prayed it was something that could wait until tomorrow.

"Hi, Dillon," Tara said. "I just saw the news report on that American murderer you arrested. He's just been sent to prison, and I wondered if you wanted to celebrate and come over for a glass of wine. I've got two bottles of a very nice Sauvignon Blanc I think you might like."

Duty calls…

THE END

Thank you for taking the time to read **Payback Brother.** If you enjoyed the read please consider leaving a review. It really helps.

Don't miss the sample of **The Heist**, the next book in the Jack Dillon Dublin Tales series on the following page.

THE HEIST
PROLOGUE

2001 - New Orleans

The Patrick Kincannon Abstract Art Museum was constructed in 1974 under the guidance of art collector Patrick Kincannon to house his personal art collection for the public to view. Kincannon died in 1987, leaving his substantial estate to the museum.

In the early hours of March 18th, 2001, two individuals, Martin Lane and Eddie McDonnell, dressed as police officers, parked at the side entrance to the museum.

They'd been sitting in the car for over two hours. It was almost 1:00 in the morning.

"Come on, Eddie, either we're going to do it tonight, or I'm going home. It was St. Paddy's Day, and I've missed the entire night of women too drunk to remember their own name. We've been sitting here twiddling our thumbs, and I've had it. So, either we go, or I'm driving you home, and I might still catch a pint at Cooper's and hopefully find some little dream who is too drunk to care."

"Jesus, will you ever calm down, Martin? I said we'd do it, and we will."

"Okay, fish or cut bait, man. I'm going. You with me?" Lane said as he opened the driver's door and stepped out of the car. He glanced at McDonnell, still looking unsure about what to do, and slammed the driver's door.

McDonnell shook his head and climbed out of the car. "You follow me," he said as he stormed past Lane. He headed toward the side door, the security entrance, pulling his police officer's hat on as he went. He gave three long rings to the security doorbell.

It took a couple of minutes before the light flicked on, and a man looked out the window. Seeing the two dressed as police officers, he gave a quick wave and opened the door. "Hi, guys. What's up?"

"We had a report of a silent alarm going off. Just want to check and make sure everything is okay," Lane said.

"Silent alarm? I don't even think we have one."

"Oh, yeah, you do. It alerted us about twelve minutes ago."

"It's not showing up on our screen."

"Yeah. It's designed not to do that. Mind if we just take a quick look?"

"No, no, that's not a problem. Come on in."

"Just procedure, but we need to check your ID as well, you know, just in case."

"Yeah, sure," the man said, pulling out his wallet and handing his driver's license to Lane.

"Thomas Fischer," Lane read. "And how long have you been working here?"

"This is my third year. I work the night shift. Live downstairs in the basement apartment."

"Anyone else on staff with you tonight, Thomas?"

"No, just me. Terry, he's the morning shift, comes in around 7:00. I sleep till noon and head over to Orleans U for classes in the afternoon."

"Let's take a look at your security system," Lane said as he handed the driver's license back to Fischer.

"Just back this way," Fischer said and headed down the hall to a U-shaped desk behind a floor-to-ceiling glass wall. Three computer screens were arranged on the desk. As they stepped into the office, McDonnell pulled out the roll of duct tape.

Lane pulled out his pistol and waved it at Fischer. "I think it would be a good idea if you got down on your knees."

"What the—Hey, wait a minute. I told you I'm the security guy. I work here. I—"

"On your knees, now."

"But I—"

"Now, damn it!"

As soon as Fischer knelt down, McDonnell pulled Fischer's arms behind his back and duct taped his wrists together. He lowered Fischer onto the floor, wrapped the tape over his eyes and his mouth, and then taped his ankles together.

"Check out these screens. Can you turn off the alarm systems?"

"I think so, give me a moment," McDonnell said. There was a Rolodex next to one of the computer screens, and he thumbed through it until he came to a card labeled Security Central. There were three passwords just below the 800 phone number. "Okay, here we go," he said and began typing on the keyboard. Two minutes later, the alarms had been disconnected. "We'll head up to the Abstract Expression room once we get the phone call."

It wasn't long before the phone rang. McDonnell lifted the receiver and said, "Kincannon Abstract Art Museum. Yes, not a problem. Something set off our alarm. Probably a mouse, but the police are here going through every room. Yes, just a moment," he said and pulled the Rolodex closer. "Our code is one-seven-seven-three-J-M-five-zero. Yes, thank you for checking. We should be back to normal within the next hour or so. Yes, sir. Thank you," he said and hung up.

"Let's go," Lane said as he wrapped duct tape around the leg of the U-shaped desk and then wrapped the tape around Fischer's ankles. Once that was completed, they headed into the front lobby and up the stairs to the second floor using their flashlights.

They both pulled out a box cutter armed with a razor blade. It took just seventeen minutes to cut eight Mark

Rothko canvas paintings from their frames and roll them up. They placed four rubber bands around each rolled canvas and hurried back down the stairs. After checking on Fischer, still taped to the leg of the desk, they hurried out the door, into their car, and drove off.

ONE

Dillon heard the toilet flush and rolled over on his side. He opened his eyes and blinked a few times. The digital clock on the dresser read 5:55 AM. A moment later, he heard what sounded like the shower come on, and a few seconds after that, the shower door closed. He sat up and positioned his pillow against the powder blue upholstered headboard.

Nessa's bedroom, like the rest of her house, with the exception of Dillon's clothes on the floor, was neat and tidy. He debated getting dressed and leaving but decided that would cause an immediate end to the beginning relationship, so he waited patiently while reviewing the previous evening.

They'd had dinner at the Bald Eagle in Phibsboro with his partner Paddy Suel and a woman named Kira whom Dillon had never met. Try as he may, he couldn't recall Kira's last name. Not that it really mattered. Suel seemed to go through partners even faster than Dillon, and that was saying something. Although, given their jobs in Dublin's An Garda Síochána, Special Branch, it wasn't at all unusual. Still, Kira seemed like a nice enough woman, and Suel obviously fancied her, at least for the moment.

He thought about Nessa. They'd been an item for almost ninety days, which for Dillon was heading toward almost a record with an Irish woman. Of course, there was always Tara, his neighbor. He'd been in an on-again, off-again, physical relationship with her for a number of years, usually enhanced with a bottle or two of wine. She clearly had no interest in a long-term solo relationship with him, nor he with her. It was more a matter of convenience for both of them, and that was just fine.

"Your turn," Nessa said, stepping out of the steamy bathroom. A powder-blue towel was wrapped around her lovely figure, and a smaller white towel was wrapped around her hair. "Did you hear what I just said?"

"I think you said you wanted to crawl back into bed with me and—"

"Don't get your hopes up. Besides, we both have to get to work, and before you go, you've got to deal with your special friend Lucifer. Lord only knows what havoc he caused with you here for the night."

"I told you we could have gone to my place last night."

"And have him chew up another one of my thongs? I don't think so."

"How do you know that wasn't me?"

She glanced over and said, "Good point. Come on now, into the shower. I'll put the coffee on. Will you stay for breakfast?"

He shook his head. "No, you don't need to be cooking for me first thing in the morning. I'll grab a quick shower and get out of your way," he said as he climbed out of bed.

"Perfect. I'll have coffee ready for you when you come down," she said and gave him a peck on the cheek as he headed into the bathroom.

When he entered the kitchen, she was standing at the marble-topped kitchen counter, running the hairdryer over her shoulder-length blonde hair. She had traded the powder-blue bathroom towel for her powder-blue bathrobe. A mug of steaming coffee was on the opposite side of the kitchen counter, and a steaming mug of tea with about three drops of milk sat in front of Nessa.

Dillon knew it would be instant coffee, something he hated and an item that Irish tea drinkers were unable to comprehend. He took a quick sip, tried not to grimace, and said, "Busy day ahead?"

"We have a wretched zoom meeting at 10:00, a complete waste of thirty minutes, but better than sitting in the conference room for twice that amount of time. I'll never understand. They want everyone working, and then they insist we waste our time listening to nonsense on a zoom call. God save us."

Dillon took two more sips of instant coffee and said, "I'll leave you to it. With any luck, they'll cancel the meeting, and you can work through the morning."

"If only," she said and lifted her chin as he stepped around the counter to give her a kiss.

"Thanks again for last night. I don't like sharing you with other people, but it was a fun evening."

"Oh, the two of them, one crazier than the next. It was a fun night. Give me a call tomorrow, and we'll chat."

He gave her another kiss, and she pointed the hair-dryer at him. "I'll call you tomorrow. Thanks again," he said as he stepped into the front entryway and out the front door. He closed the door behind him and checked to make sure it was locked. He climbed into his car and drove home. He let Lucifer out into the front garden and went upstairs to change.

TWO

Forty minutes later, he was in the Special Branch break room, sipping from a mug of coffee, when DI Paddy Suel walked in. "Well, nice to see you survived the evening, Dillon. Things are still going well with Nessa?"

"Yeah, so far. You look happy, which suggests Kira hasn't come to her senses yet."

"Lovely evening, nice dinner, and then some romance before I had to head home."

"Who knows, Paddy, it might be the two of us have finally lucked out and found the perfect women?"

"We'll see about that. I was just thinking that—"

"Dillon and Suel, if you wouldn't mind joining us in my office, please," DCI McCabe called from his office door.

"Oh, for the love of—Now what have you done, Dillon?"

"Don't look at me, Paddy. I'm sure this is about something you've managed to screw up." Dillon set his coffee mug on the counter and followed Suel into DCI McCabe's office.

"Gentlemen, if you wouldn't mind closing the door behind you," McCabe said as they entered. Two formal-looking men, one on the couch, the other in the wingback chair, studied Dillon and Suel.

It was the odd time that McCabe would be seated on the black leather couch instead of behind his desk, but that was where he was now. Next to him on the couch was a man Dillon guessed might be in his mid to late fifties. Neatly trimmed gray hair, with a sharp part on the left side. He wore a dark blue suit, a starched white shirt, and a red, white, and blue striped tie.

The man in the wingback chair looked to be twenty years younger. Black hair shaved on the sides and a crew cut on the top. Dillon's first thought was ex-military. He had a square jawline and wore dark gray trousers, a black sport coat, and a starched white shirt. His tie was black with some squiggly purple design.

McCabe stood and said, "US Marshal Jack Dillon, Detective Inspector Paddy Suel. This is US Senator Noel Brussard." McCabe nodded toward the gray-haired man who extended his hand but didn't bother to stand.

"Nice to meet you," Dillon said as he shook hands. Brussard had a strong grip. He gave Dillon's hand two shakes, released his grip, and gave Suel's hand two shakes.

"The senator's chief of staff, Wendell McCarthy," McCabe said as McCarthy stood and shook hands with Dillon and then Suel. "Have a seat, gentlemen," McCabe said.

Suel quickly slid into the other wingback chair, and Dillon pulled over one of the client chairs from in front of McCabe's desk, setting it between Suel and McCarthy.

Dillon immediately had the feeling something was about to be dumped on Suel and him. They'd both been through it too many times to count. Politicians who'd want a tour of, well, name it, Mountjoy Prison, the Docks area, or even the Irish Dance studios. No doubt they were in Dublin on a taxpayer-funded tour. They'd fly over in first class, stay in separate suites in a five-star hotel, have a chauffeur supplied by the American Embassy, eat at the best restaurants, and basically take a week-long vacation at taxpayer expense. Once back in DC, someone on the lower rungs of the ladder would be forced to write a lengthy report no one would ever read." To what do we owe the pleasure?" Dillon said.

McCarthy cleared his throat and said, "We're over here on a personal matter. The senator's daughter, Melanie, is attending Trinity University—"

"An art major," Brussard interjected.

McCarthy nodded and said, "There seems to be a bit of a problem. She was assaulted by—"

"Attempted assault," Brussard interjected

"By two individuals in Dublin's Temple Bar section."

"Could you be a little more specific as to the assault?" Dillon said.

"Sexually suggestive comments from two men. One of them grabbed her. Tried to force her into a car. She was able to break away, and the men fled," McCarthy said.

"Are you aware that we investigate murders and terrorist situations?" Suel growled, not hiding his anger.

"Which is exactly why I thought the two of you would be perfect for this situation. It's just a small step from what we might call a failed attempt to create an international incident. I'd like to nip any potential problem in the bud, and I'm sure you would as well," McCabe said in a tone that suggested *'You two are going to be dealing with this. So let's get on with it.'*

"Couldn't agree more, sir. Happy to look into this. Would there be a file available with the school or the local Garda station?" Suel said.

"Yes, we've given DCI McCabe a copy of our file, such as it is. As I'm sure you can understand, Melanie was hesitant about reporting this to the staff at Trinity. She was afraid they would confine her to campus or information on the incident would somehow end up in the newspapers."

"Is the school investigating?" Dillon asked.

"Actually, they've not been informed," Brussard said, "in the interest of keeping this private. The last thing we need is reporters and the media standing outside her dormitory or classroom. Good lord, it's one of the reasons we sent her over here for college, just so she could get away from the media, and now this."

"When did this happen?" Dillon asked.

"Just a few days after she arrived in August. Let me be honest. She is loving the fact that she is pretty much anonymous on campus. No one seems to know that her father is in congress. If news of this comes out, we may well have to find another school before the spring," Brussard said.

Suel cleared his throat and asked, "The incident is in your file?"

Both men nodded.

"Very well, we'll begin immediately," McCabe said and stood. "How long will you be in Dublin?"

"Three more days," McCarthy said. "I want to stress that Melanie is unaware of our being here, and we'd like to keep it that way."

"You're not going to be meeting with her?" Dillon said.

"No, it would only make her that much more upset," Brussard said.

"All right, hopefully, we can bring this to a close and quickly," McCabe said, shooting a glance at Dillon and Suel. Everyone shook hands, and McCabe led Brussard and McCarthy out of his office, through the Special Branch office, and into the hallway, directing them to the elevator down the hall.

"Lord love a duck," McCabe said, stepping back into the office and almost, but not quite, slamming the door closed. "And I thought dealing with our politicians was bad. God help the States if this is what they have running the country. All right, here's the *so-called file*," he said, emphasizing the last three words as he handed a thin file to Suel. "Check things out, keep it low-key, and get back to me. I haven't looked at this. Let me know what you think. Hopefully, all we're dealing with is a young woman who was acting stupid. Questions?"

"No, we'll be on this right away, sir. Thank you," Suel said.

"Happy to help, sir," Dillon lied.

McCabe saw them to the door, and once they stepped out, he said, "DI O'Toole and Kelly, a moment of your time, please."

THREE

Dillon groaned and said, "I need some a coffee." "I could use something a lot stronger than coffee," Suel said as they headed into the break room.

They were seated with the file, such as it was, scattered across the table, seven sheets of paper, two with photographs Dillon figured were from a high school yearbook. Against his better judgment, Dillon had finished his coffee and couldn't bear to deal with a second cup. "Anything stand out to you, Paddy? This seems to me like a lot more than a young woman having too much to drink. There's always something crazy happening down in Temple Bar, oftentimes alcohol-fueled, but still."

Suel shook his head. "I don't think we're going to learn anything until we actually talk to her. Even if she had too much to drink, trying to force her into a car? For Christ's sake."

"We'd better check the records. Logic tells me this has happened more than once. If these idiots were unsuccessful, what's to stop them from driving around the corner and abducting someone else?" Dillon seemed to think for a long moment. "I don't know. I get that they want to keep this quiet, but do you know anyone at Trinity, Paddy? I think we need to make them aware of this. We don't have to mention the girl's name. Just tell them we're investigating an incident near the school."

"Yeah, I think you're right. Meanwhile, O'Toole and Kelly just got called in to work that murder investigation down in Phibsboro, and we're going to be poking around Trinity College making sure—"

"Come on, man. Whoever it was apparently tried to force her into a car. Things go downhill from there awfully fast, and murder and or rape is one of the results."

"Yeah, I know. Where are they from anyway? They never mentioned it."

"Brussard? Louisiana, New Orleans, to be exact. I've caught him once or twice on the news. He's one of those politicians who seems to keep his head down. Votes whatever way the party tells him to vote."

"Yeah, and now those two are over here essentially on the sly, probably to the cost of about ten grand."

"I think you're probably on the low side. Politicians, you gotta wonder," Dillon said, shaking his head.

They went through the file twice, in just twenty-five minutes, and nothing seemed out of order, but then there was minimal information. There was a copy of an email from a boy, a student, saying Melanie had a nice figure and she must work out. Nothing really out of line. In fact, Dillon recalled himself at the same age making a similar, although more descriptive comment, which led to a meeting with a young lady's two older brothers.

Suel arranged the papers in front of him, handed them to Dillon, and said, "I'm afraid to ask what our next step is going to be."

"You know as well as I do. We need to head over to Trinity and talk to the girl. Then seek out the boy who sent the email, this Kevin Walsh from Cobh down in County Cork. The kid didn't do anything wrong. As a matter of fact, given some of the comments you and I have made to women, Paddy, I'd say the kid was down-right polite."

"Be nice if we could help move him toward some-one else, for his own damn good. Can you imagine, as a kid, let alone an adult, having a date with a woman, and suddenly you've got someone like one of us coming after you? I pity the lad and feel especially sorry for the girl. She's going to have a 'No go' sign hanging around her neck if she doesn't already. Might as well get it over with. I'll drive," Suel said.

It only took fifteen minutes, and they were headed over the O'Connell Street bridge just two blocks from Trinity College. Suel drove up Westmoreland Street, past the Edmund Burke Statute and the Irish Whiskey Museum. He pulled into a parking area labeled 'Staff Parking' and parked next to a white Audi A1.

Dillon opened the file and said, "According to her class schedule, she's in an art history class in the Creative Arts Building that gets out in fifteen minutes. Do you know where that building is?"

Suel nodded. "It's on the far side of the campus, about a ten-minute walk. Does it give a room number?"

Dillon read the number from the sheet in the file. "One-seventeen."

"Let's go. It can't be more than ten minutes from here," Suel said as he climbed out of the car.

Dillon had been on the campus countless times, attending concerts, interviewing staff, and working on different cases over the past few years. The campus was just as lovely as he remembered. There were at least as many tourists as students on the sidewalks. Of course, the Book of Kells, a major tourist attraction, was housed here in the Trinity College library. The library itself was a popular attraction.

Suel led them across campus to the Creative Arts Building with six minutes to spare. As they entered, an information office was located just to the right. They walked past and headed down the hall, took a left turn, and stopped outside of room 117. There was a window in the door, and Suel glanced in, looked for a long moment, and stepped back.

"She's in there. Not hard on the eyes. I'm amazed there's only one lad sending her email. She's a sight. We'll be able to talk to her as she steps out."

"Remember, we're not to mention the meeting with her father," Dillon said.

"So how are we going to explain our file and the fact that we've read copies of the emails sent to her?"

Dillon seemed to think for a moment and said, "Leave that to me. I've got an idea."

A moment later, a bell rang, various doors up and down the hall opened, and students stepped out. Dillon felt transported back to his college days for a second or two when suddenly Suel brought him back to the here and now by saying, "Excuse me, Miss Brussard? Melanie Brussard?"

Suel had been right. She wasn't hard on the eyes. In fact, she was downright gorgeous. Blonde, with an extremely nice figure. No wonder the boy from Cork sent her an email.

"Excuse me. Miss Brussard?" Suel repeated.

Her blue eyes seemed to flash for a second before she smiled and said, "Yes?"

"My name is Patrick Suel, and this is my partner, Jack Dillon. We're with An Garda Síochána, Ireland's National Police Force." Suel glanced over at Dillon, looking for help.

"We're actually with An Garda's Special Branch. As part of our service, we check in with American students and make sure everything is going okay. We'd like to give you our cards in the event you ever need any assistance, and we'd like to see if there's any way we might be of help."

"Oh, how nice of you," she said and smiled. "I'm just headed down to the art studio. Would you mind if we talked along the way?"

"That would be just fine. You'll have to lead the way," Dillon said.

They chatted for no more than ten minutes and were suddenly in the building's basement in front of a door labeled studio. Melanie Brussard never mentioned anything regarding an email or the assault incident in the Temple Bar area back in August. She led them into the art studio. There was the slight scent of turpentine and at least a dozen different easels lined up against the wall, all holding paintings in various stages. Landscapes, two portraits, a bowl of fruit, what appeared to be four people in a pub, and then down at the far end, a large canvas, four feet by five feet. The background was purple, and there were three rectangles, one on top of the other. The top one was a rust red color, and the bottom two were black.

Dillon was about to comment but bit his tongue just to play it safe. Good thing, Melanie Brousard strolled past the lovely works in progress and stopped in front of the three rectangles on the purple background.

"What do you think?" she said, then, fortunately, added, "I'm copying Mark Rothko's *Rust, Blacks on Plum*. He painted it back in 1962."

"An absolute work of genius," Suel said. "I recognized it but couldn't recall the artist's name, Mark Rocco."

"Rothko," Melanie corrected.

"Yeah, what did I say?"

"You said Rocco. Rothko was born in Latvia and moved to the US, Portland, actually, before moving to New York City where he painted."

"Latvia? Oh, I thought it was Russia, my mistake, I guess," Suel said.

"Oh, well, actually, you're right. He was born in 1903, and at that time, Latvia was part of Russia," she said.

"Marvelous work, absolutely marvelous. I'm trying to recall when he passed away."

"1970, took his own life, unfortunately."

"If I recall, his paintings increased in value following his death," Suel said.

"Yes, as so often is the case. They've gone for as much as sixty-three million, at least that's the highest I recall, but there certainly could be ones selling for more."

"Most interesting and very well done, I might add. Things are going well for you here? You're enjoying school, meeting new friends?" Dillon said, in an effort to get a word in edgewise.

"Oh, yeah, things are going very well. I've been quite busy copying the Rothko works. This will be my fourth Rothko work. I've four more to do after this one."

"Well, that will certainly keep you busy," Dillon said. "Want to thank you for your time. It's been wonderful to meet you." He handed her his business card, and Suel did the same, pulling his pen out and scribbling something on the back of his card. "I should mention that there have been two or three issues over in the Temple Bar area. Do you know the area?"

"I've been there once or twice," she said, suddenly avoiding eye contact.

"Best to be on guard. A couple of attempted abductions. Two thugs trying to force a woman into their car. Have you heard about them?"

"No, no, I'm not aware of anything like that."

"If you or a friend should see something like that, please give us a call. Of course, you know not to travel alone. Even if it's a short distance, it's best to have someone with you. My cell number is on the card, just in case you need some help. Very nice to meet you, Melanie. Should you need anything, feel free to call."

"Thank you, very nice to meet you both. Please stay in touch."

"Oh, we will. You do the same," Dillon said.

Suel gave a wave as they headed out the door and called, "See you later."

FOUR

Neither one spoke until they were out of the building. "Nice looking young woman," Suel said.

"I can't say I disagree. What the hell is going on? And that painting. Is that for real? She's supposed to be getting an Arts degree, and she painted that? The thing looks more like graffiti from a restroom in an abandoned building."

"I think her looks got her into that class. Odds are ten to one that the teacher is some horny old coot."

"I don't get that art style. Let's head back. I'm thinking I'll do some research and see if there were any other abduction incidents reported. Did you notice she avoided eye contact when I mentioned Temple Bar?"

"Yeah, makes me think she might be avoiding any mention of the incident altogether. You think we should bounce this off McCabe?" Suel asked.

"Let's hold off until we check and see if there have been other abduction attempts. If there have, it might be it's a couple of rookies, and they're in the learning stage. It'd be nice to nail their worthless asses before they're successful."

"God, I'd give anything to be investigating that murder in Phibsboro."

"That makes two of us. You're preaching to the choir on that note, Paddy."

They'd been back in the Special Branch office for fifteen minutes when Suel stepped over to Dillon's desk. "You find anything on other incidents?"

"Not yet. I wanted to check out the senator for a moment," Dillon said and turned his laptop toward Suel. There was an image of Senator Noel Brussard on the screen.

"I checked out that artist, Rothko. That painting of hers, those rectangles on the purple background, that's one of his paintings. It's called *Rust, Blacks on Plum*. It went for millions back in the nineties and was stolen from some museum in New Orleans."

"Stolen?"

"Yeah, pretty famous robbery, according to the stuff I read. A bunch of paintings were stolen. Thieves were dressed as cops and got into the museum in the middle of the night. Tied up your man supposedly running security. Made off with eight of the paintings, none of which have ever been recovered."

"And the senator's daughter is making a copy of one of them?"

"Apparently. They had a picture online of the thing. It looked just like the painting she was working on. Come on over to my desk. I've got it up on my computer."

Dillon stepped over to Suel's desk. The image took up most of the computer screen, and Suel was correct. It looked just like the painting Melanie Brussard was doing.

"What am I missing here? She didn't mention anything about the abduction attempt. She's making a copy of a painting that was stolen twenty years ago from a New Orleans museum. We're not supposed to mention that her father is in town. Does any of this make any sense?"

"Think we should talk to McCabe?" Suel said.

Dillon shook his head. "I got a better idea. I know we weren't supposed to mention the boy to her."

"Kevin Walsh from County Cork?" Suel said.

"Yeah. I'm thinking of looking him up and seeing what he has to say."

"Based on the email he sent, he seems like a nice kid. Oh, and by the way, that email was dated almost five weeks ago. Apparently, he hasn't sent anything since."

Dillon nodded. "He's probably lined up hot and heavy with some other girl. It would be nice to touch base with him all the same."

"We both don't need to go, do we?"

"No, I'll do it. In fact, if I head back over there now, I think his schedule said he had a class in the middle of the afternoon."

"Good luck," Suel said.

Dillon drove back to Trinity College and parked in the same spot Suel had parked in earlier. Kevin Walsh's class schedule listed a statistics class that ended at 3:00. Dillon was back on campus a good half-hour before the class ended. He took his time walking across the campus to the Hamilton Building. Walsh's classroom was on the second floor, in room 207.

Dillon glanced in through the glass panel next to the door. He counted sixteen students, each one looking more bored than the next. The class schedule for Kevin Walsh had his student ID image in the upper left corner. Dillon spotted him immediately, apparently fighting to keep his eyes open.

Ten minutes later, the bell rang. The professor, a rotund man who looked close to sixty, spoke for another minute or two and then dismissed the class. Everyone hurried out the door.

"Kevin, Kevin Walsh," Dillon called as sixteen young men hurried from the classroom.

Walsh gave a questioning look as he stepped over to Dillon. "I'm Kevin Walsh," he said.

"Hi, Kevin. I'm hoping to get a minute of your time. I'm Marshal Jack Dillon, assigned to An Garda Síochána, Special Branch."

"You're American?"

"Yes, I am. Just checking into a couple of things. You'd emailed Melanie Brussard a few weeks ago, and—"

"Yeah, and she told me not to contact her again, and I haven't. Is there some kind of problem? Is she okay?"

"Oh yeah, as far as we know, she's just fine. Her father is a United States Senator, and because he's in politics in the States, we just have to check things out. Standard security procedure is all."

"I can't even remember what the email said. Something like nice to see you or meet you or something. Haven't seen her or sent her an email since. I didn't want to date her if that's what you're thinking. I got a girlfriend back home."

"Melanie seemed all right?" Dillon asked.

"No, to tell you the truth, she seemed like a right pain in the arse. Told me not to contact her again, and I haven't. Life's too short to put up with that attitude. Pretty sure I haven't seen her since. Is she even still here at Trinity?"

Dillon nodded. "Yeah, still here. How long have you had the girlfriend?"

"How long? What is this? Did I do something wrong? Did someone report me for something?"

"No, it's one of the many things we do. Just checking to make sure everything is working out for you. Is there anything we can do to help you?"

"Yeah, you can stop with the questions and let me get to the library. I've got an exam tomorrow."

"Oh, well, don't let me hold you up. Good luck on that exam."

"Yeah, thanks," Walsh said, then headed down the hall. He looked back at Dillon twice. After the second time, he shook his head, walked down the hall a little faster, and disappeared behind a door marked 'Staircase.' Dillon waited a few more minutes to give Walsh plenty of time to disappear.

"How'd it go?" Suel asked when Dillon got back to the office.

Dillon shook his head. "The kid isn't stupid. He thought my questions were idiotic, and he's right. We chatted for all of thirty seconds, and he walked away shaking his head. Told me he thought the Brussard girl was a pain in the arse, and he hasn't contacted her since. Has a girlfriend back home and basically doesn't need the hassle. You check on any assaults in Temple Bar?"

Suel said, "No, haven't gotten to that point yet."

"I'll start in on it. You want to contact Trinity and ask if they've had any students assaulted? Obviously, they don't know about Melanie Brussard. It would be interesting if they're aware of any other incidents."

"Yeah, I'll give them a call."

"I'll get in touch with Pearce Street Garda Station and see what they have on Temple Bar assaults," Dillon said.

TO BE CONTINUED . . .

Thank you for taking the time to check out the sample of <u>The Heist</u>, the next book in the Jack Dillon Dublin Tales series. Assaults aren't the only thing that are about to happen. Better grab a copy . . .

Don't miss the list of books by Mike Faricy on the next page.

Books by Mike Faricy
Crime Fiction Firsts

A boxset of the first four books in four crime fiction series:

Russian Roulette; Dev Haskell series
Welcome; Jack Dillon Dublin Tales series
Corridor Man; Corridor Man series
Reduced Ransom! Hot Shot series

The following titles comprise the Dev Haskell series:
Russian Roulette: Case 1
Mr. Swirlee: Case 2
Bite Me: Case 3
Bombshell: Case 4
Tutti Frutti: Case 5
Last Shot: Case 6
Ting-A-Ling: Case 7
Crickett: Case 8
Bulldog: Case 9
Double Trouble: Case 10
Yellow Ribbon: Case 11
Dog Gone: Case 12
Scam Man: Case 13
Foiled: Case 14
What Happens in Vegas… Case 15
Art Hound: Case 16

The Office: Case 17
Star Struck: Case 18
International Incident: Case 19
Guest From Hell: Case 20
Art Attack: Case 21
Mystery Man: Case 22
Bow-Wow Rescue: Case 23
Cold Case: Case 24
Cash Up Front: Case 25
Dream House: Case 26
Alley Katz: Case 27
The Big Gamble: Case 28
Bad to the Bone: Case 29
Silencio!: Case 30
Surprise, Surprise: Case 31
Hit & Run: Case 32
Suspect Santa: Case 33
P.I. Apprentice: Case 34
Rebel Without a Clue: Case 35
Puppy Love: Case 36

The following titles are Dev Haskell novellas:
Dollhouse
The Dance
Pixie
Fore!
Twinkle Toes
(*a Dev Haskell short story*)

The following are Dev Haskell Boxsets:
Dev Haskell Boxset 1-3
Dev Haskell Boxset 4-6
Dev Haskell Boxset 7-9
Dev Haskell Boxset 10-12
Dev Haskell Boxset 13-15
Dev Haskell Boxset 16-18
Dev Haskell Boxset 19-21
Dev Haskell Boxset 22-24
Dev Haskell Boxset 25-27
Dev Haskell Boxset 28-30
Dev Haskell Boxset 1-7
Dev Haskell Boxset 8-14
Dev Haskell Boxset 15-19
Dev Haskell Boxset 20-24
Dev Haskell Boxset 25-29

The following titles comprise the Jack Dillon Dublin Tales series:
Welcome
Jack Dillon Dublin Tale 1
Sweet Dreams
Jack Dillon Dublin Tale 2
Mirror Mirror
Jack Dillon Dublin Tale 3
Silver Bullet
Jack Dillon Dublin Tale 4

Fair City Blues
Jack Dillon Dublin Tale 5
Spade Work
Jack Dillon Dublin Tale 6
Madeline Missing
Jack Dillon Dublin Tale 7
Mistaken Identity
Jack Dillon Dublin Tale 8
Picture Perfect
Jack Dillon Dublin Tale 9
Dublin Moon
Jack Dillon Dublin Tale 10
Mystery Woman
Jack Dillon Dublin Tale 11
Second Chance
Jack Dillon Dublin Tale 12
Payback Brother
Jack Dillon Dublin Tale 13
The Heist
Jack Dillon Dublin Tale 14
Jewels To Kill For
Jack Dillon Dublin Tale 15
Retirement Scheme
Jack Dillon Dublin Tale 16
The Collector
Jack Dillon Dublin Tale 17

Jack Dillon Dublin Tales Boxsets:
Jack Dillon Dublin Tales 1-3

Jack Dillon Dublin Tales 4-6
Jack Dillon Dublin Tales 1-5
Jack Dillon Dublin Tales 1-7
Jack Dillon Dublin Tales 6-10

The following titles comprise the Hotshot series;
Reduced Ransom! Second Edition
Finders Keepers! Second Edition
Bankers Hours Second Edition
Chow Down Second Edition
Moonlight Dance Academy Second Edition
Irish Dukes (Fight Card Series)
written under the pseudonym Jack Tunney

The following titles comprise the Corridor Man series:
Corridor Man
Corridor Man 2: Opportunity knocks
Corridor Man 3: The Dungeon
Corridor Man 4: Dead End
Corridor Man 5: Finger
Corridor Man 6: Exit Strategy
Corridor Man 7: Trunk Music
Corridor Man 8: Birthday Boy
Corridor Man 9: Boss Man
Corridor Man 10: Bye Bye Bobby

Corridor Man novellas:
Corridor Man: Valentine

Corridor Man: Auditor
Corridor Man: Howling
Corridor Man: Spa Day

The following are Corridor Man Boxsets:
Corridor Man Boxset 1-3
Corridor Man Boxset 1-5
Corridor Man Boxset 6-9

THANK YOU!

Contact the author:
- Email: mikefaricyauthor@gmail.com
- Twitter: @Mikefaricybooks
- Facebook: Mike Faricy Author
- Website: http://www.mikefaricybooks.com

Published by

MJF Publishing